CW00518398

Born in Liverpool of
convent educated. He
at Liverpool College of Art at the time of and
Lennon, followed by a period in Nottingham
studying Architectural Ceramics, and eventually
culminated with a degree in Furniture Design at
Leeds.

She worked for twenty years in the Scenic Design
Department at Yorkshire Television, retiring as
Head of the Design Group, to Spain, in the year
2000.

Agnes is married to a retired General Medical
Practitioner and has two children and two
grandchildren.

The Canvas Bag is her first novel.

To the Fletcher family
in memory of your
holiday in Alcalali.
With very best wishes
Agnes Hall.

The Canvas Bag

Agnes Hall

Libros
INTERNATIONAL

ISBN 1-905988-10-9 978-1-905988-10-5

Cover design by Mischa Fulljames *www.mischart.com*

Published by Libros International

www.librosinternational.com

To my beautiful grandchildren, Gabriel and Eliza

My daughters, Jayne and Sarah

*And last but not least to my husband Geoff
(with thanks for not reading The Canvas Bag
until it was finished)*

Part One

MIKEY

Chapter One

They had worked steadily since dawn, cutting row after row of turf, with the sharp bladed *sleans,* tossing the cut blocks up onto the bank beside them.

The rain had started in the early afternoon, at first merely a light drizzle, which had changed to an insistent downpour as the afternoon had worn on. It had caused the black earth to stick to their boots, so that they felt that they were dragging lead weights with each step that they took. Despite their protests and regardless of their sodden clothes, which clung to their bodies and chilled them to the bone, JJ had insisted that they finish the job.

The silence was occasionally broken by a grunt or a groan from Mikey or Anthony, his brother, or an occasional muffled oath from JJ, their father, all too tired and wet for conversation, all three of them concentrating on finishing the job.

Mikey paused and rested for a moment. In an attempt to stop the rain from trickling down his neck, he turned up his collar against the driving rain, wondering as he did so why he was bothering.

*(*slean – sharp bladed 'L' shaped tool used for cutting turf)*

'Amn't I soaked already,' he muttered to himself, shaking his head but continuing to cut the blocks of turf, feeling more and more resentful as he did so.

'I hate this bloody place. I hate this bloody life.' He avoided JJ's eye as he spat the words out.

'Watch your mouth,' JJ replied, glaring at him.

Mikey wished that he had the courage to throw the *slean* down and walk away from the wet and the dirt and the poverty that was all part of the farm but he knew that he had no choice but to continue. There was nowhere for him to go, although the thought of spending the rest of his life living like this horrified him.

At last, JJ pushed the brim of his cap up away from his eyes and said, 'Right! That's enough cut!' But the relief that Mikey and Anthony felt was short-lived with the words that followed. 'We can start the stacking.'

The boys glanced wearily at each other.

'C'mon. What are you waiting for? The job's not finished yet!' JJ growled.

'I don't know why we're laying out the turves, now, Da,' Mikey challenged his father. 'Why can't they be left' til the rain's stopped? They're not going to dry in this weather and aren't we all soaked to the skin! We'll be after catching pneumonia, so we will!'

'You'll not get any wetter than you are now and it's a job that has to be done, whether it's today, tomorrow, or next week. We're here and we'll finish what we've started.' JJ's reply was curt.

Mikey groaned but knew that his father was unlikely to change his mind and, by arguing, he was only prolonging the agony. He began quickly to pass the blocks of turf to Anthony, who in turn passed them to JJ, who stacked them carefully and methodically in rows, allowing room for air to circulate around them to help the drying process when the better weather came.

'Slow down, will ya!' Anthony protested as the speed with

which Mikey was passing the turves caused him to drop them. 'I've only one pair of hands.'

'Is it all night you want to be here then?' Mikey glared at his brother.

He intercepted a look from JJ and knew that he was courting trouble but he couldn't help himself.

'If it's slow that you're wanting…...' Very slowly and deliberately, he passed each turf to Anthony. '…..it's slow that you'll have.'

The work continued, the misery that the rain was causing now taking second place to the antagonism that flowed between Mikey and Anthony.

JJ had witnessed the exchange of words but didn't interfere. As far as he was concerned, the job was to be completed no matter how long it took.

'Slow enough for you now, is it?' Mikey goaded Anthony, who muttered under his breath.

Mikey caught the word 'Idjit!' and grinned.

As the last of the turf was put in place JJ said, 'That lot will tide us over for a while. If the two of you hadn't been at each other's throats it would have been done a lot quicker and we would have been at home, warm and dry, long ago!'

Mikey looked at his father and knew that he was right but he had been unable to resist provoking Anthony. He looked at his blistered hands, flexed his shoulders to ease the stiffness, and wearily throwing his *slean* on the back of the cart, climbed up onto the seat at the front where he was joined by Anthony and his father. He drew his knees up in front of him and wrapped his arms around them, as though by making himself as compact as possible it would help to keep the cold and wet at bay.

The cart headed towards the farm, crossing the ford which, although an easy passage today, was often impassable when the heavy rains came. Mikey's head began to nod and despite the cold and wet he dozed, lulled into sleep by the swaying movement of the cart, only to be woken as the cart finished its journey and shuddered to a stop.

On the far side of the yard, through the haze of rain, he could see two of his younger brothers, Declan and Kieran, pushing the old barrow with the wobbly wheel, piled high with dry turf from the barn. Despite the rain the two boys weaved a giggling, crooked path between the barn and the thatch-roofed farmhouse, where a column of smoke drifted from the chimney, struggling and twisting its way towards the sky. His two sisters, Lily and Annie, stood in the open doorway, silhouetted by the flickering light from inside, dancing about in an effort to keep warm whilst waiting to help unload the turf from the barrow.

'Is it all night you're going to sit there or are you going to give us a hand?'

JJ's sharp voice startled Mikey into action and muttering complaints under his breath, he climbed down and began to unload the tools from the back of the cart whilst JJ and Anthony untethered the horse and led it into the barn before rubbing it down and leading it to the bucket of food which awaited it.

Finally, work finished for the day, they jostled for position on the old wooden bench that sat in the porch next to the tin bath. They each removed their boots and Mikey stuck his finger through a large hole in the sole of one of his, knowing that he would have to wait for Anthony's cast-offs before there was any chance of dry feet. He massaged his toes to ease the numbness knowing that he was luckier than many, including all the younger members of the family who had no shoes at all.

In turn, the three of them banged their boots against the wall to release the clinging blackness from the soles, and then they left them lined up against the porch wall in readiness for the following morning.

JJ went through to the house, stripping off his wet clothes as he did so.

'I've got to get out of this place,' Mikey muttered to Anthony, as he followed his father. 'I'll go mad if I don't.'

He kicked impatiently at one of the old hens, which was scavenging for food around the floor and began to wriggle out of his clothes, pulling off his wet jacket and shirt and throwing them onto a chair. Hopping about, he balanced on each leg in turn as he pulled off his trousers.

His mother, Bridie, stood at the sink, with Brendon, the youngest of his brothers. Brendon sat with his shoulders hunched, his arms across his chest, his feet in the water-filled stone sink as Bridie finished washing him. When Bridie lifted Brendon down from the sink, JJ took her place and began to wash himself in the water left behind.

'There's more hot water in the bucket on the fire, if you need it,' Bridie told JJ.

'Sure this'll do me fine,' JJ replied. 'Let the two lads have it.'

There was a silence whilst JJ continued washing himself until Mikey said, 'I'm not staying in this place forever, you know.'

JJ stopped what he was doing. 'Oh yeah! And where might you be off to then?' he asked. When there was no reply he turned his head to look at Mikey. 'Did the cat get your tongue or what?'

Mikey responded sullenly, 'I dunno. England mebee. All I know is that I'm going to leave this place as soon as I can. There's nothing here for me.'

He sat down on a wooden stool, his arms wrapped around his body and, shivering with the cold, shuffled the stool so that he could rest his back against the wall as he waited for his turn to wash. The only warm part of the house was near the fire at the opposite end of the room next door and there was a constant battle amongst the children to get next to the source of heat, but before he could enjoy that privilege, Mikey had to get washed and changed.

A lamp flickered on a shelf, casting dancing shadows about the room. Strange disembodied shapes, sometimes friends and sometimes fiends. Condensation from the washing, drying on a creel, caused rivulets of water to run down the glass of the small and only window. Black mould gathered in the corners, constantly scoured away by Bridie but always returning. The damp had seeped through the whitewashed walls and surfaced as powdery patches: white, dusty flakes that rubbed off onto clothes and fell like snow onto the stone-slabbed floor. A makeshift wooden worktop with a length of sagging string nailed across the front supported a faded curtain, an attempt by Bridie to hide the soot-blackened pans on the shelf below.

'They say that there are plenty of jobs in England,' said Mikey.

'Not for young lads of fourteen there aren't,' Bridie interrupted sharply as she returned after hanging the wet clothes to dry in front of the fire.

'They say that you can earn good money there,' Mikey persisted.

'They, they, they,' said Bridie irritably, tucking strands of her once bright red hair, now dulled with a lacing of grey, back into the coil at the nape of her neck from which they had escaped. 'Who are "they", for heaven's sake? Will ya stop this foolish nonsense and hurry up and get washed so that we can all get a bite to eat.'

She gathered her long skirt around her and with a toss of her head summoned the children to the table, before lifting the big pot of potatoes from the fire, her hands protected from the heat with an old piece of cloth.

Mikey washed hurriedly, dried himself and put on the threadbare but dry clothes that Bridie had left in readiness and joined the others at the table, where JJ sat with bowed head. As Mikey sat down JJ raised his head and said, 'Dear Lord, thank you for the food on this table today!' He then looked pointedly at Mikey. 'And, dear Lord, make some of us a bit more grateful for what we have instead of whining and griping all the time.'

Mikey glared at his father.

'What have I to be grateful for? No matter what it's like in

England it can't be any worse than it is here. I'll be out of here as soon as I can.'

JJ's face reddened as he bellowed at Mikey. 'That's enough now! You've said more than enough! Any more from you and you can get to your bed.'

Mikey stood defiantly, knocking his chair backwards as he did so. He grabbed a hot potato from the pot and began to walk away from the table, tossing it from hand to hand, wincing from the heat as he did so.

JJ had also stood and went to follow Mikey, but Bridie quickly moved to his side and held his arm.

'Sit down will you and eat, otherwise I'll take the pot away and you'll get no more 'til the morning.'

She looked around the table at the other children who had all fallen silent as they had watched the confrontation between Mikey and JJ.

'Did you not hear me? C'mon eat up before I take the pot away.' Then she turned to JJ. 'I don't know what gets into the two of you. Like father. Like son. The two of you are as bad as each other.'

Mikey had reached the doorway and turned and yelled back at them in frustration, 'But I'm not like him. I'm getting out of here. I'm not going to live the rest of my life the way he does.'

He slammed the door behind him and ran out into the yard.

Chapter Two

Mikey knew that he had been lucky to escape a thrashing from his father the previous evening. He had spent a cold and miserable hour in the barn with only the horse to keep him company, until he thought that his father's temper was likely to have cooled down. When he had returned to the house, he had been relieved to find that his father was already asleep and had crept quietly onto the straw mattress that he shared with Anthony, where he now lay, the covers wrapped tightly around him.

It was still not fully light but Mikey had already heard Bridie moving about, raking out the fire and had felt the draught as JJ had opened the door and gone out into the yard to draw some water from the well.

He heard Bridie's voice calling to them, telling them to get up and felt Anthony beginning to move beside him, slowly stretching, then climbing out of bed and beginning to pull on his shirt.

'You'd best be getting up unless you want to land yourself in more trouble,' Anthony said, nudging Mikey. 'C'mon! C'mon!' He thumped Mikey in the back, wanting to irritate him and even the score after Mikey's actions the previous day.

'Oh! Give over, will ya,' Mikey said, wrapping the

bedclothes more tightly around him. 'I'll get up when I'm bloody ready.'

'Watch your mouth now, boyo,' Anthony replied, imitating his father before he left the room and went to collect his trousers from in front of the fire where they had been left to dry the previous night.

It was always an effort for Mikey to get out of bed in the morning and he lay as long as he could, dreading the cold chill that would descend once the covers were thrown back, but he knew that Bridie's wrath would descend upon him the longer he lay, so he eventually jumped out of bed, pulling on his shirt and stumbled, shivering, to join his father and Anthony. He ladled some buttermilk out of the big jug and began to drink it eagerly, then helped himself to a couple of cold potatoes out of the dish, which Bridie had left ready on the table.

JJ, frowning, glanced at his son and Mikey waited, expecting some remonstration for his behaviour the previous evening and when it did not come, Mikey breathed a sigh of relief, because he knew that he had deserved it.

It was market day and Annie and Lily were left in charge of the four younger boys once a month whilst Bridie joined the menfolk on the trip to town. It was the only time, apart from mass on Sunday, when she had a chance to meet and chat to any of the other wives in the area and to catch up on some of the local happenings.

JJ and Anthony finished their breakfast and went into the barn to put the horse in harness while Bridie gave the girls last minute instructions before they set off. The cart was loaded up with a basket of eggs, large slabs of butter fresh from the churn, wrapped in muslin, and sacks of potatoes collected from the potato pit, where they had been stored after harvesting. That done, they set off.

When they reached the town, JJ tethered the horse to the wooden fencing at the side of Hickey's general store. He had an arrangement with Jerome Hickey, the owner, to supply him with whatever provisions he was able to spare. The potatoes were no problem to JJ, he was usually able to have his fill of those but sometimes JJ would have loved to have had a couple of eggs as part of his meal, but that was possible only on very rare occasions. They were usually sold, either to Jerome Hickey, or at one of the markets and the money used to buy whatever was needed in the way of clothing, or tools for the farm, or added to the savings that went towards the rent.

As they began to unload the produce from the cart, Anthony glanced up and with a grin on his face said to his mother, 'I see that the county news is about to arrive, so it is.'

Maggie Gowan, who lived with her husband, Big Jim Gowan, at one of the neighbouring farms was hurrying down the street towards them.

Bridie groaned but knew that there was no escape. Maggie was the first to know all the latest gossip and felt that it was her prime duty to pass on whatever she knew, to as many people as she could, as quickly as she could, before anyone else had the opportunity to do so. She arrived panting.

'Have you heard that Joseph Flynn is back home, on holiday? My God, you should see the clothes on him! And the shoes! They must have cost a fortune! He's over there with his mammy and daddy. They say that he sends them money home every month.'

'Sure, money isn't everything. Wouldn't I rather have my family around me than a pot full of money,' Bridie replied and, glancing around, saw that Mikey, overhearing Maggie's tale, had deposited his armful of goods in Hickey's store and was running off down the road in Joseph's direction.

'I wish you hadn't said anything about Joseph in front of Mikey.' Bridie said stiffly. 'His head's full of leaving as it is without any encouragement from anyone else.'

'Where's the harm in it,' Maggie sniffed. 'If he didn't hear it from me, he'd hear it from someone else and if he wants to go, he'll go when he's good and ready anyway.'

'It's easily told that you have no children of your own, Maggie, otherwise you wouldn't be saying such things,'

Bridie said as she turned away and followed her son, tossing a comment over her shoulder as she did so. 'There's too many families already have lost their children across the water.'

Mikey was listening intently to what Joseph was saying when Bridie joined them.

'Ah! Liverpool's a grand big city and there's plenty of work as long as you're prepared to work hard. You can earn a good wage there, far better than here, where there's not enough work for a man and half the people haven't two coins to rub together. I've found myself a decent place to live and I'm never short of food in my belly. I have meat twice a week and sometimes fish as well and I still have enough to send money home to mammy and daddy. '

'Have you no thoughts of coming back home? Surely you must miss your Mammy and Daddy and your brothers and sisters?' Bridie asked Joseph.

'Sure it was no life for me here. Of course I miss my mammy and daddy, but I can take better care of them working in Liverpool and sending a bit of money home to them than I could if I was here with no job and me just an extra mouth to feed. And I manage to get back to see them once a year or so.'

In the cart on the way home Mikey sat deep in thought, dwelling on what Joseph had said. Eventually, knowing in advance the response that he was likely to receive, he said, 'Joseph Flynn says that there's plenty of work in England.'

'There may well be,' Bridie said, 'but not for the likes of you. What sort of work do you think that you could do? Nobody there will take on a young boy when there are more than enough grown men willing to work.'

'And where do you think that you'd find the money for your fare? We've scarcely enough to get by without giving you handouts,' his father spoke sharply. 'Hasn't the Englishman, Edwards, put the rent up again!'

Mikey decided that there was no point in continuing the conversation any longer. He knew that he was unlikely to get any support from his parents in his wish to move away and would just have to think of a way to get the money for his fare without involving them but how he would manage to accomplish that, he had no idea.

Weeks passed and the stacked turves dried out and JJ decided it was time to collect them and bring them back to be stored in the barn.

It was dusk as they completed their last load and the sky began to darken. Within a few minutes a light rain had started. The rain continued as they drove back to the farm with the cart loaded high with turf and it continued throughout the night.

JJ and Bridie lay in bed listening to the rain battering outside and, when they left their bed the following morning, the rain was so heavy that they could scarcely see across to the other side of the farmyard.

'Wasn't I stupid not taking the opportunity to cut the hay when I had it!' JJ said to Bridie in exasperation. 'I could kick myself. I could have sworn that it wasn't going to rain yet. Let's hope it doesn't go on too long or the hay will be ruined.'

Hay had replaced potatoes as the main crop for JJ. Fear of another blight, like the one of fifty years earlier, had generated the decision that he would never rely solely on potatoes as his main source of income, although potatoes were still the main source of food for the family. He also had a cow, a pig and a few hens and was better off than many.

Three days later, it was still raining.

'Sure, we'll be alright. It can't go on raining for ever,' JJ said, looking at the worried expression on Bridie's face as they went about the farm doing whatever tasks the weather would allow and doing what they could to prevent the water seeping into the already cold and damp house.

But the rain still continued.

'Thank God we got the turf in when we did,' JJ said, as they huddled around the fire.

'It's no good having turf to keep us warm if we've no money

to pay the rent and we're thrown out of the house,' Bridie was quick to respond.

The land that JJ farmed was owned by an Englishman, whose name was Thomas Edwards. He was the largest landowner in the area, with an estate of over 40,000 acres.

JJ and Bridie had never met Edwards, who scarcely ever travelled to Ireland to view the workings of his estate, which had been divided up into smaller pieces of land that were rented out to tenant farmers, of which JJ was one.

The estate was administered by John Mitchell, also an Englishman, who collected the quarterly rent from the tenants. Most of the other farm administrators in the area demanded no actual money from the tenants, but made them work the land and then took the produce. In return they were provided with a roof over their heads and little else, but John Mitchell, on the instruction of Thomas Edwards, demanded money in payment as rent. If it was a good year this worked to the advantage of the farmer who worked the land, but if it was a bad year it caused major problems and, as JJ well knew, there weren't many good years. To add to the problem, John Mitchell was not the most sympathetic of administrators and was quick to turn families out of their homes if the rent wasn't paid, so Bridie and JJ were constantly under pressure to ensure that it was paid promptly, even if they had no food in their bellies. It was a constant source of complaint from JJ.

'The English have it made. They own the land and do nothing with it and it increases in value. We farm it and the rent goes up and up and all the time the money ends up in their pockets. They win whichever way you look at it.' JJ shook his head.

Mikey had, on many occasions, heard his father bewailing the fact that a substantial amount of Irish land had been 'stolen by the English.'

The possession of Irish land by Englishmen was not new. It had begun many centuries earlier when the Normans, arriving from England and Wales, had landed in Wexford and conquered the Irish. They had changed the existing law, where property and land was owned by the extended family or clan, to a Common Law based upon personal ownership and the beginning of the rot was started with many of them settling and claiming Irish land.

Nearly four centuries later, when Henry VIII founded the Church of England and broke away from the Catholic Church of Rome, the loyalties of the inhabitants of Ireland were divided, with the Irish remaining Catholics and the English becoming Protestants. After the Battle of Kinsale in 1601, when the Irish and their Spanish allies were defeated by the English, Ireland became governed by an English central administration, based in Dublin.

Later, to further subdue the Irish, large groups of Scottish Presbyterians and English Protestants were deliberately encouraged to settle in some of the northern counties and the Irish were driven off 500,000 acres of some of the best farming land in the country.

Regular uprisings by the Irish in protest at what was happening occurred, but in 1649, when Oliver Cromwell landed in Dublin to quell an uprising of the Irish against the English, a mass slaughter took place and a further large-scale confiscation of land followed. As the years passed, more and more rights were taken away from Irish Catholics. They were forbidden, amongst other things, to receive an education, enter a profession or vote or purchase land.

And so the Irish Catholics had ended up very much second-class citizens in their own country and JJ and Bridie and thousands of other Irish Catholic families who had inherited these circumstances now had to scrape a living, often with the products of their labours lining the pockets of absentee landlords.

The following morning, with the rain still falling, JJ and Bridie rode out in the cart to survey the sodden fields and the flattened crops. The damage was worse than they had expected.

As they drove back to the farm they were both silent until eventually, JJ said glumly, 'I don't think that we've any choice but to sell the pig. That should just about make up the rent money.'

The pig was the last remaining of the litter and it had been intended that it would be killed and cured and part of it sold, but JJ and Bridie had hoped that a small amount of it could have been kept to provide them with a few precious meals of meat spun out throughout the winter months. But the animal was worth more as a stud and the decision was taken to sell it as soon as they could.

When they returned to the farm, the horse was left in harness and JJ went inside with Bridie.

'Shift yourselves!' he said to Mikey and Anthony. 'We're going into town to try and sell the pig. We should just about make it there and back before dark. We need to get off straight away, the water's rising fast and we'll soon not be able to get across the ford.'

Anthony and Mikey glanced at each other. They knew that it was bad news if the pig had to be sold. They too had looked forward to having the rare experience of a little meat to eat and a break from the monotony of their diet of buttermilk and potatoes, which was now obviously not going to alter.

Whilst the men were away, Bridie, with the help of Annie and Lily, collected the sodden cloths which had been placed at the windows to stop the rainwater seeping in and wrung them out and replaced them. The buckets, which had been placed around the house to collect the water that was leaking in through the roof, were also emptied. The roof was badly in need of re-thatching but it was a job of low priority, particularly when the rent was due.

Bridie was washing the dishes at the sink when she heard the cart trundle into the yard and, wiping her hands on her apron, she went through to the porch, her shawl wrapped tightly around her shoulders. She was unable to hide her disappointment when she saw that the pig was still in the cart.

'You had no luck, then?'

'Wasn't every man and his dog there,' JJ told her. 'All in the same sorry state as us, all worrying about finding the money for the next payment of rent. But at least we got back across the ford. There'll be no more trips into town before the rain stops.'

He put his arm around Bridie's shoulders as they walked into the kitchen.

'Sure, haven't we been here before. We'll get by.'

As they ate their dinner that evening Bridie said, 'I've been thinking. There's two weeks 'til the fair in Crossmolina. Maybe we could take the pig there?'

That night, as every other night, the family gathered together on their knees around the fire to say the Rosary and amongst the requests for blessings for friends and family was a prayer for the rain to stop and for a buyer for the pig.

By the time that the Crossmolina fair arrived, the rain had stopped and a watery sun lit the sky. JJ, Anthony, Mikey and the pig set off once again.

When they reached Crossmolina, they joined an area where farm animals were being sold. The pig was left tied on the back of the cart with the tailgate down, but although a few of the farmers came and looked at the pig, there was little interest shown in buying it and JJ began to give up any hope that he had of selling it, thinking that he would have to return unsuccessfully to Bridie once again. But Mikey had other ideas. He jumped onto the back of the cart.

'C'mon! We're not giving up that easily. If nobody is after coming to look at the pig, we'd better take the pig to them.'

He grabbed the coil of rope that was looped around the pig's neck, pulled it squealing from the back of the cart and set off leading the protesting animal around the field followed by Anthony and a reluctant JJ.

'Isn't it a grand pig we have here,' he stopped and called in a loud voice. 'He's truly a handsome fella. Sure, wouldn't he make many an auld sow happy, so he would. And when he's no longer fit to do that, wouldn't he provide a feast for your table.'

'Will you stop making an idjit of yourself,' JJ said to Mikey, his face pink with embarrassment, whilst Anthony stood holding his sides with laughter as he watched his brother's performance.

But Mikey continued around the field repeating the same refrain until one of a group of farmers leaning on a fence at the side of the field, amused by Mikey's presentation, asked how much he wanted for the animal.

'How much will you give?' Mikey asked.

'How much do you want?' the man asked again.

JJ took the opportunity to intervene and take control of the situation. Some haggling took place and eventually a price was agreed and Mikey handed over the rope to the farmer with a sweeping bow.

'I suppose beggars can't be choosers.' JJ said with a sigh, as he pocketed the cash, which was less than he had hoped for. 'But at least it'll make up the money to pay the rent.'

When they arrived home, Anthony paraded around the kitchen, dragging a piece of rope after himself and mimicking Mikey's performance.

'Now then, Mr McCann! Would you like a nice bridegroom for that beautiful sow that you have there and when he's done his duty, you can roast him in the oven and invite your neighbours around for a feast.'

'Oh my God!' Bridie asked laughing. 'Did you really do that, Mikey? What will people think?'

Mikey grinned. 'Well, we managed to sell the pig, didn't we?'

The trip to the fair, however, had been even more successful for Mikey than managing to sell the pig. He had discovered a way in which he could make some money.

The following morning, when Mikey joined JJ and Anthony

in the kitchen, he found that JJ had already decided that the day was to be spent clearing the ground of sodden crops, salvaging what they could.

He ate his breakfast speedily.

'I'll go on ahead,' he said and, before the astonished JJ could utter a word, he was gone. He set off, jogging his way along the track to where they were to start work. He was almost at his destination when the cart overtook him and, as it passed, JJ shouted over his shoulder, 'What's up with you? You'd think the devil himself was after you.'

What Mikey had no intention of telling JJ was that the fair at Crossmolina had reminded him that most fairs hosted sporting events, with prizes to be won. At school he had performed well at sport, often winning races in his age group and it had occurred to him that if he trained hard he might be able to win some of the races at the fairs.

The remainder of the day progressed as normal but subsequent days followed a new pattern with something previously unheard of happening. Mikey was up and out of his bed before Anthony and, if they were working in the fields, he would set off first, running to wherever they were going to be working.

Bridie and JJ were amazed at the change in their son and, despite being unable to fathom out what had caused the change and what the running was in aid of, they were both relieved that there was no further talk about leaving home.

Chapter Three

It was on Easter Sunday, two months later, that Mikey was able to put his training to the test. They had all had the ritual weekly bath the previous night, when the tin bath was brought in from the porch and placed in front of the fire. Steaming pans of water were poured into it and the wooden maiden, draped in washing, was placed around it to preserve modesty. Priority was given to JJ, followed by Anthony and Mikey and then each of the remaining children took their turn. Bridie had her bath when all the children were in bed.

'We might not have much money, but there's no excuse for dirt,' Bridie said often, as she scrubbed away at the children.

As usual on a Sunday, JJ drove them all to Mass in the cart. It was unheard of for any of them to miss Mass unless they were seriously ill, but Mikey often wondered to himself as his younger brothers sat alongside their parents in the wooden pews, pinching each other to see who would squeal first and incur the wrath of Bridie, what benefit they got from listening to the chanting in Latin when none of them could understand a word. But he equally knew that it would be an unwise person who would suggest any such thing to Bridie or JJ.

It was difficult enough for Mikey to maintain attention at Mass under normal circumstances and this Sunday it was especially so, but at last Mass was over and Mikey breathed a sigh of relief. He knew that the established ritual still had to take place, with the adults assembling outside the church, catching up on local gossip, before they could head for home.

As soon as Bridie indicated that it was time to go, Mikey was quick to help, lifting the younger ones up onto the back of the cart and climbing up quickly behind them. Once they were all settled, JJ jerked the reins and the horse set off at a gentle pace towards the farm.

Mikey had a problem. He had not told his mother that he wanted to go to the fair at Ballina, but he knew that time was running out and he had to broach the subject very soon. He swallowed hard and took a deep breath. 'I'm off to the fair in Ballina, Ma. Can you put my dinner to one side for me, and I'll get it when I get back?'

Bridie responded without even turning her head. 'I most certainly cannot, Mikey. And who gave you permission to go off to the fair, I'd like to ask?'

'Amn't I asking for permission now, Ma?'

'Well the answer's no. You'll stay and have your dinner with the rest of us,' Bridie replied.

The answer was pretty much as Mikey had expected but he thought that it had been worth a try. He had already decided what he was going to do if he met any opposition from his parents and was willing to accept the consequences of his actions, so did not bother to take the conversation any further.

When they arrived home, Mikey helped JJ remove the harness from the horse and led it into the barn. He then hurried around to the back of the barn, which shielded him from sight and, as quickly as he could, skirted around the edge of the field before running down the track and onto the road in the direction of Ballina.

He was still wearing the suit that he had worn to church, a "hand-me-down" from Anthony, which despite Bridie's efforts showed the marks where she had unpicked the hems. The sleeves fell short of his wrists and the legs of his trousers fell short of his ankles but it was the only suit that Mikey had and he knew that Bridie would be furious if he damaged it. It was not just his suit; in turn it would have to be passed on to his other brothers as they grew older but he had no choice other than to run in it. He set off for the fair thinking to himself as he ran down the track, 'One day, I'll buy me a suit as good as Joseph Flynn's. In fact I'll buy me a cupboard full of suits. One for every day of the week and I'll wear them back home to show everyone how well I've done for myself.'

Mikey arrived hot and sweating at the fair, which was one of the biggest fairs in the area and drew crowds from miles around. He had part-walked and part-run the five miles so that he would arrive in good time.

As he approached the field he heard the sound of music and saw that there was a small stage set up at one end of the field where men with fiddles were playing reels and jigs, their feet tapping in time to the music. Children with flushed faces and shining eyes danced on the grass around the stage. Sounds of sheep, cows and pigs, hens, ducks and geese, objecting to confinement in their pens or cages, competed with the music from the fiddles. There was shouting and laughter and good-natured banter as men called to each other extolling the qualities of their animals. Stalls were scattered about the field. Fruit, vegetables and jams were displayed alongside brooms and tools, lotions and potions. Women in fine dresses paraded about and contrasted with some of the stallholders in their ragged and tattered garb. But everyone was enjoying themselves.

Mikey heard shouting and cheering and wandered across to where a crowd had gathered, to see what the excitement was all about. He saw two men wrestling, stripped to the waist, bodies gleaming with perspiration. He recognised one of them as Big Jim Gowan, Maggie's husband, a burly man with a cauliflower ear, who prided himself on his physique.

'C'mon, Big Jim, you've got the beating of him!'

Mikey shouted words of encouragement, then, remembering that he didn't want to attract too much attention to himself, moved on hurriedly towards an area in the middle of the field where there was a boundary marked out with coloured pennants hung between stakes hammered into the ground. This was the area where the sporting activities were obviously going to take place. There was a running track. A rectangular pit filled with sand was the long jump and further along a horizontal pole, resting across pegs on two vertical poles which were hammered into the ground, was the high jump.

Mikey grabbed the arm of a youth with curly, dark hair and of a similar age to himself, who was walking past.

'How d'ya enter for the racing?' he asked.

The lad pointed to a table at the other side of the field. 'At the table over there. They'll tell you what you have to do.'

Mikey wandered across and saw that there was a board where a list of races was chalked up. He decided that he would enter as many as he could, so, painstakingly, he added his name to three separate entry sheets, one each for the one, two and four hundred yard races.

'You'd better shift yourself sharpish, boyo, if you want to run in the one hundred yards!' one of the officials told him. 'It's about to start.'

Mikey was nervous. He had never raced anywhere other than at the village school, where his fellow competitors were his schoolfriends, and he had no idea what the competition would be like at an event such as this. When he reached the running track, he quickly took off his jacket and left it to one side of the start line and joined the other competitors, watching and copying them, anxious not to make a fool of himself.

The race was over almost as soon as it had begun with Mikey finishing in a disappointing fifth place. He felt a little angry with himself, knowing that he could have done better and, realising that his slow start was the problem, was determined that he would be quicker off the mark next time.

The two hundred yard race was called and, once again, he joined the other competitors at the starting line. This time, in his eagerness to get away fast, he started ahead of the gun. He was recalled to the start line along with the other competitors, his face reddening with embarrassment and the race was restarted. His second attempt proved better and at the end of the race he collected a piece of paper from the official at the finishing line which said '*200 yards. 3rd Place*' and put it into his trouser pocket.

There was some time before the last of his races, so he wandered over to the stage for a short time and, sitting cross-legged on the grass, watched the fiddlers and dancers, his jacket slung across his shoulders. He couldn't concentrate on the activities because he was worried that he might miss the start of the race and eventually decided to return to the starting line.

As he was scrambling to his feet he heard a voice behind him. 'You did well there. That last race...... the two hundred.'

The youth who had helped him earlier was standing, smiling at him. 'The name's Barney, ...Barney Gallagher. I've not seen you racing before.'

'Mikey Whelan.' Mikey grinned back at Barney. 'Sure it's the first time I've entered anything like this!' He paused. 'I've entered the four hundred yards as well.'

'I'm entered for the four hundred too,' said Barney, 'but that's a bit of a mix of distances you're doing. Weren't you in the one hundred as well?'

Mikey nodded. 'I've a bit of saving to do. I need any bit of money that I can get.' He took from his pocket the piece of paper which had been given to him by the race official and showed it to Barney. 'What do I do with this?'

'You need to take it over to the table beside the stage. That's where they hand out the prizes but you don't have to collect it now. You can leave that 'til after the four hundred. Are you heading back there now?' Barney jerked his head in the direction of the start. 'If you are I'll walk back with you.'

As they set off towards the start line, Barney chatted. 'I wouldn't want to put any kind of damper on you, Mikey, but

Hughie Murphy'll win the four hundred yards. He goes away to boarding school and every school holidays he's home and entering the races. His folks get private coaching for him. Don't they get private coaching in every bloody thing for him. He's the apple of his mother's eye and a little shite into the bargain.'

'Isn't it well he speaks of you, too,' said Mikey laughing.

'That's Hughie over there,' Barney said, nudging Mikey as they approached the starting line. 'Him with the outfit. You'd think he was going to the dancing, not a race. All dressed up like a dog's dinner!'

Mikey glanced across to where Hughie stood and, at the same time, Hughie glanced around, his eyes resting on Mikey. He muttered something to his friends who turned in Mikey's direction and began to laugh.

For the second time that day Mikey could feel his face turning red. He turned his back, aware that his clothing was the source of the amusement.

'Take no notice,' Barney said, noticing Mikey's embarrassment. 'Sure, he does that to everyone. He thinks he's the bee's knees so he does.'

As the competitors for the four hundred yards were called to the starting line, Barney took Mikey's arm. 'Pace yourself. Save a bit for the finish. But you'll have a hard job to beat Hughie. It kills me to say it, but he's good.'

They were soon under starter's orders. Mikey started off steadily, attempting to keep level with Hughie but soon Hughie drew ahead of the field and Mikey realised that running on his own was no training for running in competition, as he had no yardstick with which to measure his performance.

Mikey worked hard and managed to reduce the distance between Hughie and himself, but despite all his efforts, it was Hughie who crossed the line first, quite a few yards in front of Mikey.

'Well done!' said Barney as he arrived at the finishing line in third place, puffing and panting. 'You've come closer to Hughie than anyone for a long time.'

Mikey heard a voice beside him and turned.

'Would you look at the state of him! He needs to get back to the bog where he belongs.'

He clenched his fist as he realised that it was Hughie and started towards him, but Barney grabbed his arm.

'Ah, stop now, will ya! Take no notice of him. He's not worth getting upset about. I told you he was a little shite.' He raised his voice ensuring that he was heard. 'Haven't you put the fear of God into him, Mikey!'

Then he turned aside and muttered, 'Besides there are more of them than us and I don't fancy taking a pasting! C'mon, let's go and collect our winnings.'

They headed towards the stage and, after collecting their prize money, left the field and went out onto the road together, where they said their goodbyes.

'If you're doing some saving, maybe I'll be seeing you around again entering more of the races,' Barney said.

'I'll be entering as many as I'm able,' Mikey replied as he set off over the stile and across the fields back to the farm, thinking that he now had to face JJ and Bridie and their wrath, but there was no way that he was going to tell them that he had been racing, nor about his winnings. This was the beginning of his "Liverpool" money.

As he approached the farm, his pace slowed and he braced himself. He saw that Lily and Annie were in the yard. Annie ran towards him as soon as she saw him.

'You're in for a thrashing,' she said. 'Daddy was hopping mad at you going off when you'd been told that you weren't to go. He's got the belt ready for you.'

Mikey shrugged his shoulders and went inside. Bridie looked up from her chair by the fire and JJ stood and picked up the leather belt from the table.

'So you've come home, have you,' he said, coiling the belt once around his hand and leaving a tail of it loose. 'Maybe this will make you think twice before you disobey your mother again.'

He lashed out at Mikey with the belt, which struck him with force across his back. Mikey turned to face his father as he drew the belt back again. He gritted his teeth as the belt made contact once again, but continued to face his father and outstare him. JJ was now red in the face with anger at Mikey's defiant stance. Four more whips of the belt landed on Mikey until Bridie said, 'I think that's punishment enough,' and JJ lowered his arm.

Mikey turned slowly and left the house. Once outside, he felt the tears come to his eyes and walked hurriedly to the barn. As he walked, he felt a hand slide into his.

'Don't cry, Mikey,' Annie said.

Mikey blinked the tears away and said gruffly, 'Sure I'm alright. Anyway! He won't be beating me for much longer.'

The money that Mikey had won was secreted away, under the straw mattress that Mikey shared with Anthony but Mikey knew that he had to find a safer hiding place for his winnings. It would be too easy for Anthony to discover it, or even for his mother to find it when she was sweeping the room. He found a rusty biscuit tin, all that was left of a present brought by a well-off cousin visiting from Dublin, as the biscuits were long gone, and he put the money in the tin which he hid in the barn, managing to remove some stones from the wall and create a hiding place.

An uneasy truce now began between JJ and Mikey.

JJ had realised that his son was getting bigger, stronger and more defiant and that the belt would soon no longer be a useful tool of punishment. JJ's own father had used the belt on him and he had been taught that he had to accept whatever was meted out to him in punishment as being justified. He could neither understand nor condone Mikey's defiance. He had been taught the Ten Commandments by his parents as a child and he and Bridie had taught their children to follow those same rules, one of which was to "honour thy father and thy mother", and Mikey, by his defiance, was not following the rules leaving JJ unsure of how to handle the situation.

Mikey continued to go about his work and do what was expected of him and, in exchange, neither Bridie nor JJ opposed his attendance at the fairs, as long as it did not interfere with his chores.

Chapter Four

A strong friendship developed between Barney and Mikey, their mutual dislike of Hughie creating an even stronger bond between them. They were regularly to be seen together on fair days and would often meet up, sometimes after Mass, halfway between their two villages, the dark curly hair and brown eyes of Barney contrasting with the fiery red hair and grey eyes of Mikey who had inherited Bridie's colouring. Sundays and fair days were the only days where it was possible for them to meet up as they lived too far away from each other to have any possibility of meeting up at the end of the working day.

When Hughie was home from school he competed at the fairs and the animosity that Mikey had felt towards him at their first meeting increased, inflamed by Hughie's derogatory comments which were a great source of amusement to Hughie's friends, but which made Mikey determined that at some point in the future he would have his revenge.

Against all his basic instincts, which were to attack Hughie physically when his temper was roused, Mikey restrained himself and waited.

Mikey had realised that his best distance was the four hundred yards. It was the distance at which he felt most comfortable but, added to that, the fact that it was Hughie's main event made Mikey more determined to excel at it.

He bought himself a stopwatch with some of his winnings, from a catalogue that Mike Cauley had in his shop in Ballina, and waited eagerly for it to arrive. When it did, he then started serious training, sometimes joined by Barney on a Sunday afternoon. The track over the ford between the fields of flax became his running track and gradually his speed increased.

But Hughie was also training hard. He had recognised that Mikey was becoming a threat to his domination of the four hundred yards and that when he was away at school, Mikey had become the main contestant in the event so he was determined that he was not going to be beaten by "the bog trotter" as he called Mikey.

Often, Mikey was so tired after his day's work and his running that, after he had eaten in the evening and joined the family in prayer, he would go straight to bed and fall into a deep dreamless sleep, only awakening when Bridie's voice pierced his consciousness the following morning.

Occasionally, he wondered if what he was doing was worth the constant feelings of tiredness but he had only to look around him at the poverty of his existence: the lack of food and warm clothing and the sight of his parents, tired and ageing, to be reassured that to get away was the best thing for him to do.

The "Liverpool" money slowly built up. If the prize was cash it would usually be put straight into the biscuit tin. Sometimes instead of cash there were other prizes or medals. He sold the goods that he received as prizes and whatever cash he received for them was added to that in the biscuit tin. He gave the medals to Annie, whom he had sworn to secrecy, and asked her to look after them for him.

But the secrecy soon became unnecessary when one Sunday, after church, Maggie Gowan said to Bridie, 'Big Jim tells me that Mikey's doing well at the racing. He must have won a fair bit by now, so he must. '

Bridie struggled to maintain her composure. 'Yes! Well, he

was always able to hold his own at the races at the school, so he was.'

She was annoyed that Maggie had information about her own son of which she had no knowledge. She sat silently in the cart on the way home until JJ, after repeated worried glances at her, asked, 'What's up with you then?'

'It appears that we have a young lad with secrets amongst us.'

Mikey groaned in anticipation of what was to come.

'How's that then?' JJ was puzzled.

'Maggie Gowan was able to tell me about Mikey's prowess at the racing, over the last months, when Mikey wasn't able to tell us about it himself. That's what his interest in the fairs is. He's been racing and winning money. She said that he must have made a fair bit of money over the months. What I'd like to know is what he's done with the money when we've been struggling to put food in our mouths and pay the rent?' she asked bitterly.

'Well, have you an answer for your mother?' JJ spoke sharply.

Mikey took a deep breath. 'Maggie Gowan could do with learning how to keep her big trap shut. What I do is no business of hers. It's my money. I've won it and I'm keeping it. It's the money that's going to get me to England.'

'So it's true then.' JJ shook his head. 'Is that all the thanks you have for all your mother and I have done for you.'

'Ah! Leave him be,' Bridie said, shrugging her shoulders and looking with anger at her son. 'Don't waste your energy on him.'

Mikey had known that it was only a matter of time before his parents found out about his racing. He felt lucky that they hadn't found out earlier but he knew that now the moment was fast approaching when he would have no choice but to leave the farm. He had hoped that he could have managed to add a little more to his savings but there was still one opportunity for him to do so, an opportunity that he had no intention of relinquishing. There was just one more fair, one more race that Mikey wanted to compete in, and if he could resist the pressure from his parents until after that, he would be able to go on his way.

Two weeks passed and the tensions within the household increased. Bridie could barely bring herself to speak to her son without a sarcastic comment. She was hurt at his deceit and knew that any sort of control that she had over him was fast dwindling. She was sad because she also knew that he would soon leave home and she could do nothing to stop it. He was the one, of all her children, that she felt the most affinity with. It was not only that he looked like her, both with the same grey eyes and red hair, but they both had the same fiery temperament.

'The Donehue hair and the Donehue temper,' JJ often teased Bridie.

JJ knew all about the Donehue temper. It had been necessary for him to fight each one of the three Donehue brothers for Bridie's hand before he had been able to marry their only sister and change her name from Donehue to Whelan.

But the memory of his determination to win Bridie, regardless of anything else, was not foremost in his mind when he thought about his son. He could not see that the single-mindedness of his own pursuit of Bridie was comparable to Mikey's single-mindedness in his determination to escape life on the farm. He could scarcely contain his anger at Mikey's deceit and pushed more and more work onto Mikey's shoulders. Mikey accepted it uncomplainingly because he knew that the time was fast approaching when there would be an end to it all.

Shortly before dawn on the day of the last fair that Mikey was to attend, Mikey secreted his suit out of the house and placed it, neatly folded, into a worn canvas bag that he had found tucked away in a cupboard. A couple of raw potatoes and a hunk of bread stolen from the kitchen was all that he could manage in the way of food without arousing suspicion. He put it all in the bag with his tin of money and hid it under a hawthorn hedge which bordered one of the fields. He then returned to the house and crept back into bed beside Anthony.

'God! You're freezing,' Anthony muttered half awake. 'Where've you been?'

Mikey didn't reply, but closed his eyes and tried to sleep for a while longer. He had worked late the previous night, sticking to the unspoken agreement with his parents to complete the tasks that he should have been doing if he hadn't been going to the fair, and had gone to bed exhausted, but he knew that he had to carry on as usual to avoid drawing attention to himself.

He arose and dressed as usual to Bridie's call and walked through the steamy and damp kitchen where she stood at the sink in her faded apron, with her sleeves rolled up and wisps of damp hair framing her face, rubbing and grating the clothes up and down against the washboard.

'I see you're off again, are you? To win yourself some more money, no doubt!' She looked at him with disappointment. 'Ah! Mikey, Mikey. What's got into you?'

'Ma!...' he began to speak, but Bridie was not to be placated and turned her back on him saying, 'Go on! Get on with you. Get out of my sight! Get off to the fair!'

His father was in the yard. He glanced at Mikey but then turned his back on him.

Mikey hesitated and sighed, then shrugged his shoulders and left, walking down the track and over the ford without a backward glance, collecting the canvas bag from under the hedge as he went to meet Barney.

'You managed it then, without your ma and da suspecting anything, did you?' Barney asked when they met up.

'I did…. And I tell you, I'm glad to be out of there. They've neither a good word nor thought for me at the moment!' Mikey replied. He was glad to be leaving but in his heart, he wished that his parents could have wished him well and that it hadn't been necessary for him to leave under these circumstances.

'Well! If it isn't the yokel again! Wouldn't you think that he'd get fed up with being beaten!' Hughie greeted them as they arrived to enter for the race.

'You'd do better to save your energy for running instead of mouthing it off! You're going to need all the energy you can muster,' Mikey said as he turned his back on Hughie.

'Would you just listen to the bog-trotter! Who does he think he is? He's away with the fairies. Maybe he thinks that today his luck's going to change and he's going to beat me! Fat chance of that.'

Mikey turned towards him. 'Would ya like a little bet on it if you're so sure of yourself?'

'You've a long way to go before you'll get the better of me, ya yokel,' said Hughie. 'Come on, lads. Let's see the bogman's money. We can't lose. He's not beaten me yet and he's not going to start now. C'mon! Let's see your money!'

To Hughie's surprise, Mikey produced his tin of money from the canvas bag and tipped it out onto the ground. Before long a small crowd had gathered. He had to borrow a stub of pencil and a piece of paper from John Connor, one of the local farmers, and began to keep a note of the bets. Barney became increasingly alarmed when he saw the amount at stake. A great deal of the money that Mikey had won over the months was at risk. He tugged at Mikey's arm.

'I hope you know what you're doing,' he said quietly. 'That's a big sum of money there. It's not too late to back out. If you lose the race, you'll have to start your saving all over again.'

'There's no problem,' said Mikey confidently. 'Don't you be worrying yourself. Despite what you might think, I know what I'm doing.'

The money was collected together and given to John Connor for safe keeping. John pushed his hat to the back of his head and clicked his tongue at the amount of money left in his care.

'It's a good job your ma and da aren't here to see this carry-on' he told Mikey. 'They'd be hopping mad at you, so they would!'

'You wouldn't be telling on me, would ya?' Mikey asked. He grinned, knowing that it wouldn't make any difference whether he did or not. He would be long gone before any word of the day's events would reach his parents and even then, there was nothing that they could do. He held out the canvas bag to John and asked, 'Will you take care of this for me as well, 'til after the race?'

When they reached the start line Eddie Rooney, one of Hughie's friends, positioned himself on Mikey's right side. Barney stood to his left.

'Watch Eddie,' Barney muttered to Mikey. 'He's up to something.'

As the race started, Mikey allowed Hughie to ease slightly ahead and ran a few paces behind his left shoulder. He realised that Eddie was running parallel with him and was slowly forcing him to the edge of the track. He had to reduce his pace to prevent himself colliding with him.

'Pick your pace up,' Barney called to him. 'I'll take care of this one,' and as soon as Mikey had managed to achieve a little space between himself and Eddie, Barney stumbled and fell, grabbing Eddie as he did so and bringing him down with him.

Mikey slowly regained the ground that he had lost, gradually drawing level with Hughie, then slowly easing ahead until, for the very first time, he crossed the line ahead of Hughie.

Barney joined a breathless Mikey at the finishing line.

'Well done! Well done!' he said, jumping up and down. Then, draping his arm around Mikey's shoulder, he said, 'You certainly outfoxed him but you had me worried there for a while.'

'Let's get out of here,' Mikey said, 'while that lot are still licking their wounds.'

The canvas bag was collected from John Connor, the

proceeds from the bets were placed in it and, after collecting the prize money from the race, the two of them set off in the direction of Ballina.

Barney had bought Mikey's ticket at the office in Ballina so that there would be no chance of any rumour reaching Bridie and JJ of Mikey's imminent departure and he handed it over to Mikey now.

'Keep a tight hand on your bag,' he advised Mikey. 'I wouldn't put it past that little shite and his cronies to try and relieve you of your money.'

When they reached the crossroads where their ways were to part, Mikey opened the canvas bag.

'Here, take this,' he said and, despite Barney's protests, shoved a handful of coins into his hand. 'Haven't you been a grand friend to me all these months,' he grinned, 'and if you hadn't had your little snuggle with Eddie, I might not have won the race. No doubt you'll be asking him to marry you next!'

He shouldered his bag again and shook Barney's hand.

'It's time that I was on my way. Watch your back with Hughie now. Don't take any chances. I'd steer clear of him for a bit if I were you.'

'I will,' said Barney. 'Good luck to you, now. I hope everything works out for you.'

They went their separate ways with Mikey's promise that, as soon as he had an address in England, he would contact Barney.

Chapter Five

After leaving Barney, Mikey managed to reach the docks by hitching lifts from passing carts. He had only been to the docks once before when, as a small boy, he had accompanied his Uncle Thomas, his father's brother, who had taken him and Anthony to see some of the big passenger ships. But now he was not just another onlooker, he was actually going to climb on board one of these "great beasts" as his uncle Thomas had called them.

The quayside was a seething mass of activity. Cargoes were being loaded and unloaded. Great cranes were swinging enormous packages above heads. There was shouting, laughter and tears as families said their farewells to relatives, some of whom were on the first stage of their journey to parts far more distant than Mikey's destination: to America, Canada and Australia, and many of those left behind wondering if they would ever see their sons, daughters, sisters or brothers again.

But Mikey was so fascinated by everything about him that he felt neither loneliness nor sadness, just an overwhelming feeling of relief to be leaving and great expectations of what he felt sure was going to be a good life ahead of him.

Soon he was in the queue, climbing the gangplank, his heart pounding. People were hanging over the sides of the ship, shouting and calling to relatives left on the quayside below as they waited for the ship to leave the dock and Mikey wondered if he would be the only one travelling with nobody to wave him off. He settled himself, leaning over the rails fascinated by all the hustle and bustle on the quayside.

There was a sudden, deep blast of noise and the gangplank was drawn away. People began to cheer and the ship slowly eased its way out of the harbour, the slick of black water between the quay and the ship slowly increasing as the ship moved further and further away from land.

Mikey stayed watching until the land disappeared from view and he thought to himself that, not only was it 1900 and the start of a new century, it was also for him the start of a new life.

When he eventually looked around him he realised that most of those on board had already found places to settle for the journey. Some had managed to secure places to sit on the wooden benches around the deck. Others were propped up wherever they could find a resting place, bodies propped up against bodies, crammed against each other. Mikey eventually managed to find a spot where he could rest and survey everything about him, his bag providing a useful cushion for his back.

Before boarding the ship he had taken all his money and stuffed it in the inside pocket of his jacket, tied in an old piece of shirt. He had heard stories of people being cheated and robbed on board ship and he was determined that his hard-won money was not going to disappear like that.

After he had made himself as comfortable as was possible he glanced around him and saw children, tired and fractious with many hours already spent travelling, and weary mothers trying to keep them amused and out of trouble. He had heard tales about the crowding on board some of these ships and not knowing quite what to expect, hadn't realised that it would be quite as bad as it was.

'Leave off, will you!' one man said angrily as two children tussled with each other, jostling him as they did so, and Mikey thought that it did not bode well when impatience and anger were already surfacing so early in the journey.

A group of men were settled on the deck nearby playing cards and it wasn't long before Mikey was edging closer to see how the game was going. He soon decided that he knew the way the game was played and determined to try and join the group. He decided to take only a small amount of money from his pocket to play with and when that was gone he would play no more. He didn't want to expose his money to anyone else so he wandered the deck until he could find somewhere where he could remove it from his pocket, without anyone else seeing what he was doing.

Stepping over bodies, he found an area that was being used as a lavatory and, as he pushed open the door, the stench that met him was overpowering. Even at this early stage of the journey there was evidence all about of stomachs that couldn't cope with the movement of the ship. He was quick to sort his money and return to the group of card players who were sitting cross-legged on the worn wooden boards, a pool of money in the centre.

'It's a good game to watch but a foolish one to play,' said a voice at the side of him. 'Sean Kelly's the name. I can see that you're tempted but don't get involved; you're a young lad and this lot know what they're doing. You'll only lose your money.'

'I appreciate your advice but I'm no fool,' said Mikey. 'I'll mebbe give it a go a bit later, when I've watched a bit more and know the way the game goes.'

'Well, don't say Sean Kelly didn't warn you. Do ya mind if I sit here beside you?'

Without waiting for a reply, Sean sat down beside Mikey and they both watched the game for a while in silence until Mikey leaned forward and asked the group of men,

'Would you let me in on the game?....... I've got money.'

'Sure ya have, but will yer mammy let ya play?' was the first response, amidst laughter.

Mikey fumbled about in his trouser pocket, then opened his fist to display his money.

'I'm not a child. Amn't I already sixteen,' Mikey protested. 'That's all I've got but I'm willing to play with it if there's anyone of you who's man enough.'

'You're a cocky one an' all,' said the man.

'Ah! Let him play,' said another. 'He'll lose it soon enough and then maybe he'll leave us in peace.'

Sean Kelly shook his head at Mikey and said, 'Don't say I didn't warn you.'

The men shuffled about complaining about the disruption but made space for Mikey to sit down amongst them. He lost the first few hands but soon began to get the feel of the game. His eye was good and his brain was fast and it wasn't very long before his money was increasing, so much so that soon his fellow players called a halt to the game.

'You're a sneaky one, laddo! How long have you been playing?' one of them asked.

'Sure, I've hardly played before in my life,' Mikey told them.

They didn't believe him and nor did Sean Kelly who patted him on the back, chuckling.

'Well, aren't you the smart one then. You certainly fooled them.'

Mikey was happy that the game had been halted. The extra money that he had accumulated would be useful but he wasn't going to take any more chances and despite attempts to persuade him to play again a few hours later, he refused, much to the annoyance of one or two who wanted an opportunity to win their money back.

As darkness fell, Mikey stretched out on the hard wooden boards and attempted to sleep. To protect his few possessions, he kept his arm looped through the handles of the bag that supported his head whilst he slept. He suddenly felt very weary, the events of the day were finally catching up with him and he fell into a disturbed sleep.

The muted sounds of babies crying and angry, argumentative voices eventually interrupted Mikey's slumbers and he woke, stiff and aching, as the dark of the night was slowly broken.

He wandered about the ship, discovering that many of the men he spoke to were doing the same as he was, leaving Ireland to try to find work and a better way of life in England. He spoke to some who had already established themselves in work in England and were now bringing their families out to join them and others for whom Liverpool was merely a breaking point in their journey en route to America. He heard tales of how some of the ships had been called "coffin ships" because of the number of people herded together in unsanitary conditions, many of whom did not live to reach their final destination, and was glad that he was going no further than Liverpool.

He met up again with Sean Kelly and they sat and chatted.

'Sure there's plenty of work for everyone, if you're not too proud,' Sean Kelly said, 'but the first thing you need is a place to sleep. There's a room in the house where I lodge...at least there was before I went back home. If you want I'll take you there when we dock. The woman who has the house is a good woman and the room's clean and a fair price.'

Mikey, who had half expected to be sleeping in a barn or a field on his first night, was only too pleased to accept Sean Kelly's offer of help.

The remaining hours of the journey passed with little to break the monotony of the grey sky and the even greyer water. Mikey alternated between sleeping and, despite the cramped and crowded conditions, walking around the ship as often as he could to ease his stiffening joints until there was a general movement of anticipation aboard the ship. He realised by the activity of the passengers that land might not be too far away. Hands sheltered screwed-up eyes, trying to focus on the horizon, as everyone tried to be the first to catch a glimpse of Liverpool.

He heard the shout 'Land!' and joined the others who were

clamouring to the sides to see. Bags, trunks and suitcases were dragged close to the sides as people fought for positions to watch as the coastline grew closer. The subdued and tired atmosphere changed and the air was filled with the lively chatter of people, desperate to put their feet once again on solid ground, their weary faces taking on looks of eagerness and excitement at the thought of arrival.

The entry into the port of Liverpool was a difficult one and the ship was a long time docking. There was a lull in activity as the anchor was dropped and Sean Kelly explained to Mikey that the ship had to wait for the tide to turn to allow access to the port. There were sighs of frustration at the delay but when the anchor was eventually hauled up there was a great cheer as the ship started to move.

'Jesus, Mary and Joseph! How on earth is this great brute of a ship going to squeeze itself in there?' one woman said, looking at the access to the dock.

But the big lumbering ship moved slowly into position, passing ships already docked until it reached its final berth. The anchor was once again dropped. Great, heavy ropes were thrown to the dockside and were tied off, the gangplank was placed in position, the barriers pulled away and the hordes started to descend, pushing and shoving, anxious to make their exit.

Mikey stood to one side whilst Sean Kelly collected his bags.

'So you're sure it's alright if I come along with you then, and see if yer lady has a room?' said Mikey.

'Sure it is. Wasn't it me who suggested it to you?' Sean said. 'It's a tram ride away but the tram stops just around the corner from Mrs Hennessy's door.'

They set off down the gangplank, Mikey following his new-found friend with the handles of his canvas bag looped over his shoulder. His eyes darted left and right, his brain absorbing all the new sounds and sensations. He frowned, puzzled as he looked at the parallel metal rails on the ground between the cobbles. Then he realized that there were cables up above his head and suddenly jumped in surprise, startled by the thundering approach of a tram. He laughed as he realised that the trams ran on the tracks and were connected to the cables above their heads.

'God! Isn't it marvellous,' he said. 'Would ya ever imagine that anyone could think up such a thing.'

He had heard that there were trams in Dublin but, because he had never been there, he had never seen them.

'Well if you think the trams are something, wait until you see the railway,' Sean said. 'It runs up above your head and it goes for miles and miles along the docks. It runs from Seaforth to Dingle and they say there are seventeen stations, not that I've visited many of them, mind. They call it the "Docker's Umbrella" because when its raining heavy the men working on the docks can go and stand under it for shelter.'

Sean stopped and put his bag on the ground. 'Anyway, this is where we get our tram.'

'God! They won't believe all this when I tell them about it back home,' Mikey said, shaking his head in amazement. When there was no response he glanced at Sean who was standing silently, deep in thought.

'I'm not causing you a problem, am I?' he asked anxiously.

'Ah! Tis nothing for you to worry your head about, lad. I've a few problems of my own. I've a wife and three children back there in Ireland but I could find no work, so I keep having to come back to England to work. I miss them and they miss me. I send them as much as I can spare out of my wages but I have to try and save some as well. Soon I'm hoping that I'll have enough money to bring them here but until then it's a bad time for me and for them.'

'I'm sorry for your problems,' said Mikey. 'It must be a hard thing for you and your family to bear.'

Sean shrugged his shoulders and said, 'Thanks for your sympathy, lad, but don't mind me. I'm always hit by the melancholy after leaving them but I'll soon snap out of it.'

As he spoke a green tram arrived and they climbed aboard and settled themselves. Mikey peered out of the window, anxious not to miss anything. It was a silent journey; Mikey absorbing all around him and Sean Kelly with his own thoughts.

'Get up now, will ya,' Sean said eventually. 'This is where we have to get off.'

The tram shuddered to a halt and Sean and Mikey took their bags and climbed down into the street.

Sean headed towards another street opposite the tram stop. They walked for about five minutes until Sean stopped in front of one of the terraced houses. It was larger than many of the others with a window on either side of the front door.

'The lady is called Mrs Hennessy. Her husband was killed last year in an accident on the docks. It was a sad business; they'd only been wed a short time. She's only a young slip of a girl and her husband was a fair bit older than her, but at least he had bought the house, so she's able to make a living.' He produced a key from his pocket and unlocked the front door, saying as they entered the hall, 'She's English but her man was from Cork, so she looks kindly on the Irish, unlike some around here.'

A handwritten sign on the first door on the right said "PRIVATE" and Sean knocked loudly. When the door opened, Mikey's jaw dropped. Mrs Hennessy was far younger than he had expected. She was wearing widow's clothes: a long black skirt and a black jacket. Her hair was dark and her skin, pale and clear, and Mikey thought to himself that there'd been nice enough looking young girls back home but he couldn't think of one that could compare with Mrs Hennessy.

'Hallo there, Mrs Hennessy,' said Sean, shaking her hand, 'It's grand to see you. I've a friend here who needs a room. Have you still the one going spare?'

'I have,' she said smiling, 'but your friend looks a little

young to be away from home on his own. Has he the money to pay?'

'I have,' said Mikey, hurriedly reaching inside his jacket for his cotton parcel. He undid it and showed it to her, coins spilling out onto the tiled floor. He scrabbled about on the floor, chasing the coins that had rolled away and thinking to himself what an idiot he must look in front of this gorgeous woman.

Mrs Hennessy waited patiently, smiling while Mikey gathered up all the fallen coins.

'You'll want to have a look at the room,' she said and began to ascend the stairs. Mikey followed, unable to turn his eyes away from her. Sean nudged him, winked and grinned.

'I'm sure that Mikey will think that the room will be satisfactory, Mrs Hennessy. Isn't that right, Mikey?'

Mikey frowned at Sean, embarrassed that he had made his fascination with Mrs Hennessy so obvious.

'It's a small room, Mikey, but I think that you'll find it adequate,' Mrs Hennessy said as she unlocked the door.

'Sure, I haven't that much to put in it,' Mikey pointed to his bag. 'This is all I've brought with me.'

'I'll leave you to it and give you a knock in a little while when you've had time to sort yourself out,' Sean said and walked off down the corridor to his own room.

The room was small but clean and simple. A single bed with an oak board at the head and foot was placed centrally against one wall, a patchwork quilt spread over it. A chair stood to one side of the bed and a small oak chest of drawers to the other. A matching oak wardrobe stood opposite the foot of the bed. There was a fireplace with a vase of dried flowers on the hearth and a rag rug in front. Another rag rug sat at the side of the bed, on top of the wooden floorboards, which had been stained a dark brown.

'It's a grand room, so it is,' Mikey said as he glanced around him, suddenly overawed and concerned at what the room was likely to cost. He had never seen anything like it in his life. He shuffled his feet in embarrassment, thinking that it was all going to be very humiliating when he had to tell Mrs Hennessy that there was no way that he could afford anything as luxurious as this.

'I may as well show you the kitchen now while I'm at it,' Mrs Hennessy said before he had a chance to say anything. 'You all share it between you.'

He followed her downstairs. The kitchen was a cosy and comfortable room. At one end there was a large, wooden, oblong table with a potted plant in the centre. Eight chairs were placed around the table, three down each side and one at each end of the table. Two easy chairs faced a black-leaded fireplace, where a fire was laid ready in the hearth. A shabby, although comfortable-looking sofa completed the seating. A couple of pictures of flowers hung on long cords from brass hooks, which curved over a picture rail. Above a sink, white lace curtains hung at the window which looked out onto a whitewashed yard. Mikey was deep in thought as he remembered the room where his whole family had lived and eaten, competing for warmth from the fire. This was a totally different world but his concern was how he could tell Mrs Hennessy that he could not afford the room.

When Mrs Hennessy told him the cost of the room, he swallowed hard.

'Is it too much for you? It is one of the smaller rooms because it's a single one. It would be cheaper for you if you shared with someone else but this is the only room that's free at the moment,' Mrs Hennessy said. 'The evening meal is included in the rent of the room. It's nothing special, just plain simple food.'

The food being included in the cost of the room meant little to Mikey. It was still a lot of money and would make a substantial hole in his savings. Mikey stood and thought for a moment whilst Mrs Hennessy stood patiently waiting. Because Sean Kelly had already said that the room was a fair price and Mikey had no idea of the cost of things in England, he decided to take the room, thinking that he could always move on if he found that he couldn't afford it but he knew that he would have to find work as soon as possible.

He gave Mrs Hennessy enough money to cover two weeks' rent in advance and went back upstairs where he took his few belongings out of the canvas bag. He transferred the small amount of money that he had left from his cloth parcel back into the biscuit tin which he had brought with him and put the tin back in the bag, which he then put on top of the wardrobe. He shook his suit and hung it on a hook in the wardrobe, then placed his boots side by side under the chair.

He tested the bed, bouncing up and down. He had never slept in a bed before. There was only one bed back home, and that was the one that JJ and Bridie occupied. The remainder of the family slept on straw mattresses on the floor, the straw periodically changed by Bridie.

'This'll do me just fine,' he thought as he stretched out on the bed, his hands tucked behind his head. 'What more can a man want than a room of his own and a bed that he doesn't have to share with a soul.'

There was a knock on the door.

'Come in,' said Mikey, jumping up from the bed and smoothing his hair, hoping that it was Mrs Hennessy returning, but it was Sean.

'It's a good enough place, is it not?' Sean said. 'Mrs Hennessy will have told you the cost. You might think that it's a lot of money, but you'll get no better value around here and there are some places that won't accept the Irish. They think that we all live like pigs and it's true some do because they have no choice. There are families here that are living in conditions just as bad as back home, if not worse, crowded together sleeping eight or nine to a room. That's the way I started here, sharing with a few others but I decided that I may as well provide a bit of comfort for myself seeing that I don't have my family for comfort and I work extra hours to pay for it. There's a lot that have taken to the drink and spend all their time fighting and causing trouble, God help them. It's partly because they're trying to drown their misery, so they are, but it gives the Irish a bad reputation. Anyway, enough of that, I think that as soon as I've eaten I'll be away to my bed. My eyes feel as if they've a life of their own. Closing and opening without me telling them to.'

'You're right, it is a good place,' Mikey agreed. 'In fact it's the best place I've ever known in my life. It's a palace, so it is, but the rent is going to take its toll on my savings so I'll have to start looking for work as soon as I can; otherwise I'll have no money left. If you can tell me the best places to look for work, I'd be in your debt.'

'Well, you won't be able to do anything 'til Monday anyway, so we'll talk about it later. Now then, do you fancy a cup of tea? I'm parched and I could certainly do with a drop to whet the auld whistle.'

Sean led the way down to the kitchen, where Mrs Hennessy had lit the fire and he put the kettle on to boil.

The brew made and their thirst eased they sat, one on either side of the fire in two of the armchairs and soon both had fallen asleep, exhausted after their long journey.

Mrs Hennessy woke them some time later.

'Now then you two, there's some food ready whenever you want it.'

She brought a big pot of soup and left it at the side of the hearth to keep it hot before ladling some of it into two bowls. It smelt good and Mikey's mouth began to water. He'd forgotten just how long it was since he had last eaten. It was a good thick broth, steam rising from the bowl and on a separate plate, thick slices of buttered bread. Both men ate heartily and then sat back in their chairs satisfied, the warmth of the fire bringing a glow to their cheeks.

They were still sitting silently, each with their own thoughts when the front door slammed and there were heavy footsteps down the hall. Two men entered the room dressed in work clothes and Sean introduced them as Ted and Frank O'Malley, brothers from Wexford, who worked shifts at one of the tobacco factories down near the docks.

'I met Mikey on the boat over. He's taken McArthur's old room,' said Sean, as way of introduction. 'He's looking for work. Are there likely to be any vacancies at your place?'

'Sure I couldn't tell you,' said Frank, scratching his head, 'but there's no harm in asking. Nothing ventured, nothing gained, I say. But myself, I think you're more likely to find work portering down at the docks. The pay is low but you can make it up on tips and there are always people moving on. You could try there Monday morning.'

'Ay, you're right,' Sean said, then yawned. 'I'll take you there before I start work and show you where to go. You'll have to queue and take your chances with everyone else. Anyway I'm off to my bed now. I'll be seeing you all in the morning.'

Despite his tiredness, Mikey stayed chatting with the brothers as they ate their evening meal. Eventually, he too went to bed where he fell asleep almost immediately.

Chapter Six

Mikey woke the following morning and looked around him not recognising his surroundings. Slowly he began to remember his journey and his arrival at Mrs Hennessy's.

The house was silent and he had no idea of the time. He remembered that he had seen a clock on the wall in the hall the previous evening, so pulled on his trousers and shirt and went downstairs. The clock, in its polished mahogany case, its brass pendulum swinging from side to side, registered five o'clock. Because he was used to being awoken early at home, he knew that he would have difficulty getting back to sleep so he went into the kitchen where he added some coals to the embers in the grate and after filling the kettle placed it to boil on the hearth. He made a pot of tea, copying what Sean Kelly had done the night before which had been his first experience of drinking tea and he had enjoyed the taste of it. He took a cup back upstairs with him, where he propped the pillows up against the bedhead and sat, his legs stretched out before him, his cup in his hand, drinking his tea slowly, savouring it. This was luxury, something he had never done in his life before, sitting in bed in the morning, drinking tea. He sighed with contentment. It felt almost sinful to be doing this when he thought about Bridie and JJ and the hard life back home.

After a while he decided that he had better have a wash. He

had been so tired the previous night that he couldn't be bothered to clean himself after the journey but he remembered that Mrs Hennessy, the previous evening, had left a jug full of water and a bowl on the chest of drawers and he poured some water from the jug into the bowl and quickly swilled his hands and face.

It was a bright, clear morning and Mikey decided to set off in the direction of the church, following the directions given to him by the O'Malley brothers the previous night. He nervously found his way back to the main road where he and Sean had alighted from the tram the previous day, carefully checking that he could remember the way back to Mrs Hennessy's. By the time that he had found the church, the clock on the slate-roofed church tower, was registering almost seven o'clock, so he went in and, selecting a pew near the back, he knelt, elbows bent, his head resting on his closed hands and prayed.

Mass began and the Latin, which in Ireland had felt like a nonsense, now provided a familiarity which he welcomed. His mind began to wander. He stood and knelt almost automatically, following the actions of the remainder of the congregation but he was so wrapped up in his own thoughts that Mass was over before he realised and people were standing in readiness to leave the church.

He nodded to the priest who stood outside the church attending to his parishioners, the thought of food foremost in his mind, and walked quickly back to Mrs Hennessy's where the O'Malley brothers were in the kitchen and the smell of frying filled the air.

'Sit down,' Ted said. 'Sure you won't have had a chance to get anything for yourself to eat yet and we wouldn't allow you to starve for the want of a bit of ham. Take a couple of rashers from under the plate on the shelf in the larder and there's some bread there on the board. You can replace it when you're able.'

Mikey helped himself thinking about the diet of potatoes and buttermilk which was often all that Bridie could provide.

The ham sizzled and spat in the pan while he cut the bread and spread butter over the surface. His mouth watered as the layer of hot, thickly sliced ham was placed on the bread melting the golden butter. He sat down munching on his sandwich, so engrossed in his food that he was scarcely able to summon politeness to chat with the brothers whilst they finished their breakfast. He had never eaten so well in his life.

The brothers were going to ten o'clock Mass and it wasn't long before Mikey was left alone again, sitting and drinking his tea. He couldn't believe his luck in landing in a place like this and silently thanked Sean Kelly who, almost as though prompted, appeared in the doorway.

'By God, I was in need of that sleep, so I was,' he said, rubbing his eyes.

'Are you off to Mass as well, then,' said Mikey.

'Ah, I gave the Mass up a while ago now. Back in Ireland, I prayed and prayed for work and I got no answer to my prayers so I thought to myself, what's the use. Why am I wasting my time praying; it's getting me nowhere, so I stopped. The Lord's not going to help me, so I'll just have to take care of myself.'

Mikey was silent at Sean's comments. He thought about his own family and the way they knelt down every night to say the Rosary whether they had food in their stomachs or not and always thanked God for whatever they had, no matter how little. Mikey wondered if perhaps they might have been even worse off if they hadn't said their prayers. He wondered about God and the justice of it all, why some people were rich and lived in big houses and others had to scrimp and scrape just in order to survive and he decided that he probably agreed with Sean in the end. If God didn't provide, then you had to provide for yourself, for after all, it hadn't been God who had provided his fare to Liverpool.

On Monday Mikey went to the docks with Sean and managed to find work as a porter. As Frank O'Malley had said, the pay was low and Mikey realised that if he wanted to stay at Mrs Hennesy's he would definitely have to rely on tips from the customers to make up his pay, so it was in his interest to work as quickly as he could, rushing from one passenger to another.

He was younger than many of the other men working as porters and his youth and speed worked to his advantage. The tips gradually mounted up and it was with a feeling of great satisfaction that he queued up to collect his first pay packet, the tips increasing his wage by almost half as much again. He took his wages back to his lodgings, the first proper wage that he had ever earned.

Each subsequent week when Mikey received his pay he took it back to Mrs Hennessy's where, after paying his rent, he would go upstairs to his room and remove what he needed for himself for the week and put it in the top drawer of his chest of drawers. The remainder was put in the old biscuit tin, which was always put back in the canvas bag on the top of the wardrobe and there his savings slowly grew.

Because ships sailed in and out of the docks every day of the week, Mikey had the opportunity to work seven days a week if he wished and he sometimes did. Occasionally however, he would take Sunday off but always attended an early Mass if he did so. Sometimes instead he would take Saturday off and take a trip into the centre of Liverpool on the tram.

One particular Saturday, when Mikey had been at Mrs Hennessy's for about ten months, he had taken a trip into Liverpool on the tram where he had seen a large group of people gathered outside the offices of The Liverpool Daily Post and Echo and had stopped, curious to know what was happening.

'What's going on then?' he asked.

'The Queen is ill,' he was told. 'They say that she's at death's door. We're just waiting to hear what news there is of her today.'

'Well she's a grand old age, so she is,' Mikey had replied and had shrugged his shoulders and gone on his way. But when he arrived back at Mrs Hennessy's, the conversation there also revolved around the Queen's illness.

There was a heated discussion taking place between Ted and Mrs Hennessy.

'She might have been a good queen for the English,' Ted O'Malley said, 'but she'll be no great loss to Ireland. She might have been better thought of over there if she had tried to stop some of the terrible things that have happened back home.'

'Like what?' Mrs Hennessy asked.

'Well! What did she ever try and do about the famine?'

Ted was referring to the potato famine, which had occurred over fifty years earlier. He and Frank had been taken, as children, by their parents to see the mass graves of people who had died of starvation whilst little had been done by the supposed "Mother Country", England, to alleviate the situation.

'She didn't create the potato famine,' Mrs Hennessy said. 'It was caused by a blight on the potatoes and she did visit Ireland later to try and give her help and support and wasn't she even there last year. She was a good age to be making that sort of an effort.'

'Too little, too late,' Ted said dryly. 'And what about the English who owned farms in Ireland and exported their cattle and grain to England when there were Irish dying by the hundreds who could have done with a bit of meat or a bit of corn. There was nothing done to stop that happening.'

'And what about Gladstone? She supported him in trying to give the Catholics more power and more control over their own lives,' Mrs Hennessy countered. The words bounced backwards and forwards between them.

But despite what Mrs Hennessy said, she knew that her own husband had felt bitter about the treatment of the Irish by the English at the time of the potato famine. A bitterness handed down from his father and grandfather. There had not been many families who had not been touched, either directly or indirectly by the famine and whole generations of many families had been totally wiped out. Some people had long memories and could never forgive the English for what had happened.

But in Liverpool, Mrs Hennessy knew that there was still scant sympathy from the English for the Irish, some of whom lived in total ignorance of what had occurred in Ireland at the time of the famine. Many had no love for the Irish who had arrived in droves in Liverpool and many other cities, often outnumbering the English population and putting a strain on housing and other resources in the process.

Mrs Hennessy, influenced by her husband's opinions, viewed the situation differently from some of her neighbours and felt sympathy for those who were trying to create a better existence for themselves by escaping from the poverty of their homeland.

As the health of the Queen worsened, the numbers outside the newspaper offices in Liverpool increased and on the twenty-first of January 1901, when it was announced that the Queen had died at the age of eighty-one and after ruling for sixty-three years, a period of mourning began.

The Queen's body lay in state for ten days at Osborne House on the Isle of Wight, where she had spent the last days of her life. Then it was taken to the mainland by the Royal Yacht, Alberta and from there by train to London. An eighty-one gun salute was sounded to commemorate each year of her life and a simple service was read before a small congregation.

Queen Victoria's death was of no great importance to Mikey. He couldn't understand what all the fuss was about. He too had heard anti-English discussions amongst his own family as he had grown up and had no particular love of the English, having seen his parents worried and careworn, particularly when the rent became due. Rent that was paid to the absentee English landlord, Edwards.

'I've got better things to worry about,' he told Ted and Frank,' than an old woman who has had no influence on my life.' He laughed. 'And now certainly never will have.'

'You need to learn more about the history of your own country before you decide who has had an influence on your life and who hasn't,' Ted said angrily. 'Why are you here in Liverpool? You've been driven out because there's no work. Foreigners have taken our land away and we have to come here to survive. Do you think that we'd be here if we could have found work at home?'

He shook his head in dismay at Mikey's ignorance and apathy.

'There's no point in looking backwards,' Mikey replied. 'What good does that do? I'm interested in today not yesterday.'

In the time that he had lived at Mrs Hennessy's, Mikey had not been back to visit his parents, although he had sent them letters from time to time, revealing little of his new life but enclosing a small amount of money each time. He had received no acknowledgement from them. Neither his mother nor his father had ever learnt to write but he knew that if they had wished to, they could have asked Anthony or one of the girls to write to him on their behalf.

From the occasional letter he received from Annie he knew that there was still a lot of ill feeling towards him. He had not been forgiven by his parents for the way that he had deceived them nor for keeping the money that he had won at the fairs.

By the time that Mikey was approaching the age of eighteen, he had been living at Mrs Hennessy's house for almost two years and was still working as a porter. It was a job which he found neither physically taxing nor mentally stimulating but it suited him for the moment. He viewed it as a stepping stone. He had grown tall with shoulders and arms well-muscled and was mature far beyond his eighteen years and received more than one interested glance from young ladies passing him in the street. But as far as Mikey was concerned, the only person in whom he was interested was Mrs Hennessy. The problem was that Mrs Hennessy still treated him as a young boy.

Sean Kelly was also still living at Mrs Hennessy's. He had made little progress in his efforts to bring his wife and family to Liverpool and was becoming more and more depressed at the situation. He began to take more and more days off work and, when he was off work, a bottle of whiskey was never far away. Mikey was worried about him and tried to help. He had appreciated the help and friendship that Sean had shown him when he had first arrived in Liverpool and was anxious to repay the debt.

A week passed with Sean not working at all and each night, when Mikey arrived back at Mrs Hennessy's, he found Sean sitting in the kitchen, slumped in a chair in front of the fire.

'Sure it's a bit of the auld melancholy,' Sean had said the first night. 'I've had a letter from the wife and the youngest one is not well at all.' He showed Mikey the crumpled letter that he withdrew from his pocket. 'She's had the scarlet fever and it's left her weak, so it has. My wife is worried sick and finding it hard coping on her own.'

He banged his hand on the table.

'I'm no bloody use at all to them,' he said, putting his head in his hands. 'I don't know what I can do.'

Mikey decided that since his eighteenth birthday was only a few days away a small party on Saturday night might cheer Sean up. So he invited Mrs Hennessy, Sean and the O'Malleys to join him for a celebration, along with another couple of the men who lodged in the house.

He stopped at the shops on his way home on Friday with his pay packet and bought some crusty bread and a cake from the baker's and some ham and cheese from the grocer's. He also bought a flagon of cider and some sherry and took it all back to Mrs Hennessy's.

When he arrived at the house he was surprised to find there was no sign of Sean in the kitchen. He lit the fire and laid the food and drink on the table and when he was sure that the fire was properly alight he went upstairs to his room. As he took the bag down from the top of the wardrobe to add to his savings a puzzled expression crossed his face. His fingers became clumsy as he opened his bag and jerked the lid off the tin in a panic. It was empty! He let out a moan and sat down heavily on the bed, his head between his hands. After a moment or two he jumped up and ran along the landing to Sean's room and pounded on the door. There was no response so he ran down the stairs, his heavy work boots making great clumping noises as he jumped the stairs two at a time and hammered on Mrs Hennessy's door.

'Mrs Hennessy, Mrs Hennessy, are you in there?'

The door was opened and Mrs Hennessy looked with surprise at Mikey's wild state.

'Oh my God!' she cried. 'What's wrong?'

'My money! It's all gone! My savings! The room was locked. I don't know how it can have gone.'

'Calm down, calm down!' said Mrs Hennesy. 'It can't just have disappeared. Let's just go upstairs and check things.'

They went upstairs, Mikey running ahead of Mrs Hennessy. The bag was open on the bed. The empty tin, its lid thrown off, lay at the side of it.

Mikey pointed to the tin. 'I kept all my savings in the tin. The tin was in the bag on top of the wardrobe. I thought it was safe, the room was locked.'

Mrs Hennessy held up her hands, as though to soothe and calm Mikey. 'Look! Calm down. Let's check all the drawers.'

'There's no point. I never kept my money anywhere else but in the tin, apart from what I was spending day to day.'

'Let's do it anyway, just to be absolutely sure. You might have put it somewhere else without thinking'

'There's no point, no point,' said Mikey. 'It won't be there. It won't be anywhere else in the room.'

But he submitted to her request and they searched the room, opening drawers, looking on shelves and under the feather mattress on the bed but there was no sign of any money.

Mrs Hennessy said quietly, 'I may be doing the man an injustice, but Sean Kelly left today. He'd given me no notice. He said that he was going back to look after his family. I wondered how he could afford the fare when he's not been working.' She paused and shook her head. 'God! What a terrible thing I'm saying about the poor man.'

There was silence. Then Mikey spoke quietly. 'It was him! He knew I had a fair bit saved and he knew where I kept it.' He shook his head. 'It's my own fault so it is. I gave him my key last night. He asked if he could have a look at a copy of "The Western People" that a fella at work had lent me. I was too lazy to go and get it for him, so I was, so I gave him the key to my room. He knew I only went into the tin on a Friday night when I got my pay.'

He slumped down on the bed and put his head in his hands.

'I trusted him, so I did! I wanted to help him! Ah, what's the use,' said Mikey. He shrugged his shoulders. 'We can't do anything about it. He'll be well gone by now.'

'Come downstairs, Mikey, and I'll make you a cup of tea. It'll help calm you,' Mrs Hennessy said, her hand on his arm. 'Don't stay up here fretting by yourself.'

'If I ever set eyes on Sean Kelly again,' said Mikey, 'his life won't be worth living. All my money gone…!' he said despairingly, shaking his head from side to side. 'All my money gone!'

Mrs Hennessy patted him on his shoulder. 'I'll go and make some tea.'

Mikey felt exhausted. He thought about the two years of working and saving since he had arrived in Liverpool, which now counted for nothing. He repeated over and over again, 'What an idjit! What an idjit!'

He was as annoyed with himself as he was with Sean Kelly but found it hard to believe that someone whom he had thought of as a friend could have done such a thing. He sat for a while thinking about what he could do to salvage the situation and eventually said aloud, shaking his head as though to clear his mind from what had happened, 'What the hell......' and went downstairs.

The O'Malley brothers had already arrived home and Mrs Hennessy had made them aware of the situation. Frank stood as Mikey walked into the kitchen and put a comforting arm around his shoulders.

'Ah God! Mikey! We're sorry about all this. Who would have thought it? Poor man. Sure he must have been desperate to do a terrible thing like that, so he must. What a thing to happen and on your birthday an' all.'

'Ah well! What's happened has happened. It would have been a bad thing even if it wasn't my birthday, sure as anything. Anyhow,' he paused, 'there's no point in crying about it. We may as well pour ourselves a drink and have a bite to eat.' He laughed bitterly. 'And celebrate my birthday.'

Chapter 7

During the time that Mikey had worked as a porter, if there were slack periods, he had used the time to acquaint himself with the docks. He spent hours watching the horses and carts and the lorries with clouds of steam belching forth, arriving at the docks either fully laden with goods to be loaded onto the ships, or empty waiting to be loaded high with barrels, crates, bales of cotton and all manner of things, which were then transported to the various factories or warehouses in and around Liverpool and Manchester. He often spent time chatting to the men who came with these vehicles and had sometimes helped them with the loading or unloading.

On the Monday after Mikey discovered that his money was missing, he made sure that he had plenty of opportunity to talk to as many of the lorry drivers on the docks as he could. The loss of his savings had given him the impetus to look for work which would be more financially rewarding. He knew that the work that the lorry drivers did earned a higher wage than portering. He told the men that he met that he was looking for other work and that if any jobs as second-man on any of the lorries became available, he would be interested. He wanted to recoup his losses as quickly as possible.

A few months went by, with Mikey trawling around as many haulage companies as he was able in his spare time, before there was an offer of work. He was told that a man working as second-man on one of the lorries had been badly injured whilst unloading a bale of cotton which had slipped its hook and fallen on top of him from a great height, crushing him and he was likely to be off work for some time. Mikey rushed off as soon as he could to visit the office of John Carter's haulage company, where the man had worked, and a week later he began his new job.

John Carter owned a fleet of six lorries and had an office and large yard about five miles from the docks, where Mikey had to report each morning. He was given a time sheet on which he had to record the hours that he worked each day. The time sheets were handed in at the end of each week and his pay was based on the number of hours that he had worked in the course of the week.

Mikey was used to hard work but this was work which required particular skills, where each different load required its own particular handling technique. Barrels were rolled, timbers flipped and tossed and even the operation of fastening the bales of cotton and silk onto the crane hooks was all new and exhausting work and Mikey went home to Mrs Hennessy's each night and fell asleep in the chair beside the fire.

One thing which pleased Mikey was that there was plenty of opportunity to work overtime which increased his earnings, and slowly his savings started mounting up again. But now, instead of putting his money in the biscuit tin at the end of each week, Mikey had taken Mrs Hennessy's advice and opened a savings account at Martin's Bank on Stanley Road.

Saturday night was a night when, with often no work to go to on the Sunday, the men at Mrs Hennessy's felt that they could relax. A routine became established where the O'Malley brothers would sit and play music in the kitchen. Ted played the piano accordion and Frank, the fiddle. The other occupants of the house would often join them and on occasions also Mrs

Hennessy, drawn to the kitchen by the music, singing and laughter.

Because of the high number of Irish in the area, they tended to seek their own to socialise with and the music evenings had only been functioning for a few months when Ted and Frank were joined by two other musicians, both also Irish, who lived a few streets away: Jamie, who was another piano accordionist and Peter, a very good whistle player, and they all crowded into the kitchen which soon filled with cigarette smoke and loud music.

One Saturday night, when the music was in full swing, Father Fitzpatrick the parish priest called in and, after sitting and listening to the music for half an hour or so, he stood up. 'Now then, lads. I have an idea! You need more space than you've got here, all crammed into this room. Would you be interested in playing from time to time in the church hall? It could work to all our advantages. We'd charge an admission fee and you'd all be able to spread yourselves out a bit. It would be a way that we could get some more funds for the church and you'd be getting paid for your music.'

The four musicians were enthusiastic and after some discussion it was decided that a ceilidh would be held on the first Saturday of each month.

The following Sunday, a notice was placed inside the door of the church advertising the ceilidh. At the end of Mass and after the announcements of births, marriages and deaths in the parish, Father Fitzpatrick made another announcement inviting people to attend the ceilidh on the Saturday two weeks away.

When the Saturday night arrived, Mikey, with the help of some of the men of the parish, set up tables and chairs around the church hall leaving the centre of the floor free for dancing. There was no stage but an area was kept clear at one end for the band. At the other end a bar was set up which sold jugs of beer, glasses of lemonade and cups of tea.

When the doors were opened, a steady stream of people

flowed into the hall. The men soon congregated around the bar, chatting and drinking, whilst the women caught up on the local gossip and danced with each other or their children. It was only when the reels were called that some of the men joined the women on the floor and whirled them around and around to the music.

When the band took a rest, one of the old men of the parish stood up and started to sing. Gradually others took the floor, singing songs about Ireland and all that had been left behind.

'Wouldn't ye think that it was a grand life that they'd all left behind, instead of scratching out a living and with no food in their bellies,' Mikey said to Ted.

'And you're mighty cynical for a young lad, so you are,' Ted replied. 'D'ya really think that most of them would be here if they'd had any choice.'

The ceilidhs became popular, providing a respite and release for many after a hard week's work. They were occasions to be enjoyed by all the family and provided a place where the young men and women of the parish had the opportunity to become better acquainted.

One Saturday night when the band had their break, Ted introduced Mikey to a middle-aged couple and their daughter, Hannah, a young girl of eighteen.

'Sure wouldn't the two of you make a grand picture dancing together,' Ted said, a broad grin on his face. 'Isn't it about time, Mikey, that you took a young lady in your arms for a dance?'

'You've no need to talk,' Mikey muttered to Ted. 'I've yet to see a woman on your arm.'

'Ah! Well,' said Ted, 'I can't play in the band and dance at the same time, now can I?'

But having been put in a position where it would be churlish to turn his back on Hannah, Mikey asked her to dance.

'You'll have to take me as you find me,' Mikey explained to Hannah. 'Sure I've never had a dancing lesson in my life and haven't I two left feet to make it worse!'

'This one's easy,' Hannah said. 'It's called "The Waves of Tory".' Mikey had seen people dancing it many times but had never had the courage to try it himself. 'Just do what I do and you'll be fine.' She pushed Mikey into position and showed him how the waves were represented. Each couple held hands and marched down the row of fellow dancers, alternately ducking under joined hands and then raising their hands so that the next couple ducked under theirs and so the waves were formed.

And Mikey found that he was enjoying himself. They made an attractive couple: Mikey, tall and muscular, his red hair making him stand out from many of the other young men, and the slim girl with the long flowing chestnut hair.

At the end of the dance, Mikey escorted Hannah back to her parents who were laughing and chatting to a man whom Mikey had never seen before at any of the ceilidhs.

'Mikey, come and let us introduce you to Paddy. If you want to meet a rogue, there's one standing right in front of you,' Hannah's father said.

'Paddy Grady's the name,' Paddy introduced himself.

Paddy was a short, rotund man who, it turned out, had a scrap metal business in Kirkdale. A heavy gold chain spanned the front of his corpulent belly, a gold watch at one end and a slender snuff box attached to the other, both ends of the chain were tucked into the slim pockets of his waistcoat. Chunky gold rings bedecked fingers on both hands and, for one so short, when he spoke an unexpectedly rich, deep voice spilled out of his mouth.

'If there's anything that you need, I'm the man to get it for you,' Paddy said. And as the conversation continued and Paddy told Mikey a little more about himself, a seed of an idea was planted in Mikey's mind.

Paddy had a big barn on the patch of land from where he ran his scrap metal business. The barn was standing empty and Paddy was looking for someone who might want to rent it.

'If you're in no rush to rent it out, will you bear me in mind?' Mikey asked. 'I've an idea of how it might be of use to me but I need a bit of time to think about it.'

'Take your time,' Paddy said. 'It's been standing empty long enough. If anyone else shows any interest in it I'll let you know so that you can have first refusal.'

After the ceilidh, when Mikey arrived back at Mrs Hennessy's, he went straight upstairs to his room instead of staying chatting as he usually did. He needed time to organise his thoughts, in peace and privacy.

Despite Mikey now earning more money than he had earned previously, he had gradually become more and more dissatisfied with his life. He saw people such as John Carter, for whom he worked and whom Mikey reckoned was of no greater intelligence than himself, running a successful business.

'If John Carter can do it, then so can I,' he reasoned.

He knew that with the money that he was now earning, even after he had paid his rent and sent a small amount home to Bridie and JJ, he could afford the rent of Paddy's barn. But what he really wanted was his own lorry to put in it.

Over the next few weeks, Mikey's spare time was spent investigating the cost of new lorries and he soon realised that he was being far too ambitious even thinking about a new lorry which was way beyond his means, so he began to look at the price that second-hand lorries were fetching.

He also knew that he would not initially be able to afford the wages of a second-man even if he bought a second-hand lorry and would have to work on his own. The thought of hard work had never worried him and he began to feel more and more enthusiastic about his new idea.

He spent a long time in conversation with Maude, the girl who did the office work for John Carter, finding out what sort of income he was likely to be able to make once he had established himself. Maude had a soft spot for Mikey and divulged the information with pleasure, only too glad of a smile of thanks.

He arranged a meeting with Mr Pierce, the manager of Martin's Bank, to present his plan and invested in a suit, which he bought from the pawnbroker's. The suit, which was scarcely worn, was black with a fine grey stripe and consisted of three pieces, a jacket, trousers and a waistcoat. The trousers were a little too large around the waist, so he bought some braces along with a leather belt to hold the trousers up. He also bought himself a shirt, white with a separate, stiff, hard collar, which was held together at the front by a brass stud. The shirt was smart but uncomfortable, rubbing his neck and leaving a red line of abused skin.

'Ah well, it's all in a good cause,' he said to Frank. 'A little bit of discomfort did nobody any harm from time to time.'

A pair of highly polished shoes and a cap completed the picture. He thought, as he viewed himself in the pawnbroker's mirror, that he looked well in the outfit and it was obvious that Mrs Hennessy thought so too when she saw him the following morning as he set off to meet with Mr Pierce.

Martin's Bank stood on a corner in Stanley Road and Mikey arrived soon after it had opened. He swung open the big oak door and entered. A large mahogany counter faced the door and Mikey, holding his cap in his hand a little nervously, told the young man behind the counter that he had an appointment to see Mr Pierce.

Mr Pierce, who had seen Mikey on more than one occasion when he was depositing money usually dressed in his working clothes, was impressed by the young man who entered his office. He realised that Mikey had made an effort to present himself well and was even more impressed by the fact that Mikey, at so young an age, had taken so much trouble to research and present his business plan. After a long discussion, his eyes twinkling in amusement at the verve and vigour of the young man who sat in front of him, he told Mikey to go off and look for a lorry, to come back when he had found one and he would see what he could do to help.

Mikey was pleased with the outcome of the meeting with Mr Pierce, and thought that the loss of his morning's pay was well worth it. His mind was occupied with the next stage of his plan but he remembered with a feeling of frustration, that he had used up the last of his writing pad on his last letter to his parents, so stopped on the way home to buy a replacement. When he arrived home, he ran upstairs to his bedroom and thankfully changed out of his suit. He took a pen and some ink from the top drawer and returned downstairs where he sat down at the kitchen table, with his newly purchased writing pad and very carefully and slowly wrote,

'Wanted. Second-hand lorry in good condition.'

He put his name and address at the bottom of the page and wrote another dozen.

'That will do for starters,' he said and, satisfied with his labours, he took the small bundle of leaflets that he had created and returned with them upstairs where he left them at the side of his bed, ready to distribute the following morning to some of the lorry drivers.

'Can you put these anywhere that might be useful for me and will you keep your eyes open for me yourselves?' he asked, handing over some of the leaflets. 'If you hear of anyone wanting to get rid of a lorry, will you let me know as soon as you can?'

'Maybe you're running before you can walk,' Brian, the lorry driver that Mikey worked with as second-man, said. 'You're a young lad to be wanting to set up in business on your own, but I can't fault you for trying. Good luck to you, but I'd keep quiet about it in front of John Carter, if I were you. He won't be best pleased.'

Mikey's search for a lorry coincided with his wooing of Mrs Hennessy.

The evenings of music in the kitchen had made Mikey more and more aware of his feelings for her but, since the advent of the ceilidhs, those evenings had more or less ceased as the O'Malley brothers and their band now also did their practising in the church hall. It caused Mikey a great deal of disappointment to have the social contact with Mrs Hennessy lessened.

However, he did enjoy the ceilidhs and Hannah had become established as his main dancing partner. He had no stronger feelings for her; she was simply his dancing partner, but it was obvious to Ted and Frank that Hannah hoped differently. When Mikey was around, Hannah could hardly take her eyes off him.

One Friday night, after he had been paid, he arrived home with a bunch of violets. He told Mrs Hennessy that he had just happened to pass the flower seller on the corner and this was her last bunch so he had bought the flowers from her so that she could get home out of the cold to her family. The O'Malley brothers knew that this was not true, having seen Mikey purchasing the flowers from a well-stocked basket. They watched with interest and joked with Mikey about his sweethearts.

'Is it two of them you're after then,' Ted said. 'You've young Hannah and now you're after Mrs Hennessy as well.'

'Ah! I've no interest in Hannah. Isn't she simply a dancing partner. As for Mrs Hennessy, she's not my sweetheart yet but I hope that she soon will be.'

It was Mikey's suggestion to Mrs Hennessy that, since she had appeared to enjoy the musical evenings in the kitchen so much, she ought to join them at one of the ceilidhs. Her friends had also been trying to persuade her that the time of mourning for her husband should have finished long ago.

'You're not surely trying to be like Queen Victoria after Prince Albert died, are you, wearing black for the rest of your life and never looking at another man. You're only a young woman and you ought to get out and about a bit more and meet other people,' one of them had said.

'Is it people you mean because, if it is, I meet plenty of them.

Or is it men that you mean?' she asked dryly, but she had to acknowledge to herself that she did miss the social events that she no longer attended since the death of her husband.

Mikey's suggestion that she joined them at the ceilidhs happened at a fortuitous time, as it coincided with a change in her own needs and Mikey was delighted when she agreed to join them at the next ceilidh.

The four of them set off for the ceilidh the next Saturday night; Ted and Frank carrying their musical instruments and Mrs Hennessy walking along beside them, her arms linked on one side through Mikey's and on the other through Frank's.

When they arrived at the church hall the bar was already set up, so Mikey went to buy some beer for the three men and a glass of lemonade for Mrs Hennessy. As he waited at the bar, Hannah arrived with her family and Mikey acknowledged her with a nod and a smile. Her smile slowly faded as her eyes followed him back to the table where Mrs Hennessy sat. Mikey sat down beside her and Hannah realised that his attention was focused entirely on Mrs Hennessy and he appeared oblivious to everything and everyone else around him.

When the music started a few couples began to move onto the dance floor and Mikey stood in front of Mrs Hennessy, holding out his hands.

'I'm not the greatest of dancers, Mrs Hennessy,' he paused, then said awkwardly, 'but I'd be honoured if you'd have this dance with me.'

'I'd like that very much, Mikey,' she said smiling at him, 'and seeing that you're going to be my dancing partner, perhaps you'd better call me Eileen.'

'So be it...Eileen.' Mikey held his arm out to her and they walked onto the dance floor. It was an effort for Mikey to maintain his composure. He felt that her hand was burning through the sleeve of his jacket. He turned and his arm encircled her waist; she felt light in his arms and he could feel the warmth of her body. He thought of the women that he had picked up on the dock road and had gone with to relieve his natural yearnings and vowed that, if he could win Mrs Hennessy, then that was the last of them. No more back alleys or grimy rooms where fatherless children sat and watched their mothers earn a few coppers to buy food.

As the evening progressed, the atmosphere became livelier; jackets were removed, thrown over the backs of chairs, shirt collars were loosened, ladies twirled with flowing skirts and Hannah watched unhappily as Mikey danced time after time with Eileen. When the last waltz was called, Mikey once again escorted Eileen onto the dance floor. When the music stopped, they stood close to each other whilst the Anthem was played. Mikey sighed. What a grand evening it had been!

'Oh! I did so enjoy this evening. It's so long since I've danced that I'd forgotten how much I used to enjoy dancing,' Eileen said.

'We must do it again then…soon,' said Mikey

'Indeed we must,' Eileen replied.

They walked back to the house together laughing and joking where Mrs Hennessy, who now insisted that they all must call her Eileen, left them in the kitchen, telling them that she was exhausted but thanking them and repeating what a great night it had been.

After she had left the room, Ted said to Mikey, 'She's a lovely lady and I wouldn't want to see her hurt. She's not had an easy time.'

'There's no way that I'd harm a hair on her head,' said Mikey. 'I'm going to marry her one day if she'll have me.'

Chapter 8

Weeks went by and Mikey was patient. He knew exactly what he wanted. Firstly, he wanted a lorry and his own business and, secondly, he wanted Eileen. He thought that a proposal of marriage would stand a better chance of being accepted if he had a little more to offer her and so he bided his time.

Mikey's savings in Martin's Bank continued growing but he still had not managed to find himself a lorry that was an acceptable price. He had looked at a couple of lorries but they were older than he had wanted and he knew that he would be landing himself with a load of trouble and expensive repairs if he was too hasty and purchased one of those, but one day, whilst loading bales of silk onto the back of the lorry, a man approached him.

'Are you Mikey Whelan?' he asked.

'I am,' said Mikey. 'What business is it of yours?'

'I've a lorry to sell and I hear that you might be interested in buying one?'

Mikey called to Brian, 'I'll just take a break for a minute, if that's OK, Brian. I need to speak to this fella here.'

The man introduced himself as Alastair McLoughlin. He said that he had tried to start a haulage business for himself but it hadn't worked out and he needed to sell the lorry to pay off his debts.

'Ah! Well! I'm sorry about that and that's a fact but I suppose one man's misfortune is another man's luck,' Mikey said. 'When can I have a look at the vehicle?'

Arrangements were made for Mikey to see the lorry at the end of the day when he had finished work.

The lorry was in good condition. The cab had a flat roof of a reasonable size to carry the fuel that was necessary to power it. The only drawback was that it didn't have a rear tipping facility but Mikey decided that was not essential for, after all, it was only the newer vehicles which had them. He knew that he could manage without, but if he was really honest, he knew that he had no choice. There was no way that he could afford a lorry with a tipper. As the lorry was already stoked up, Mikey had a test drive and decided that the vehicle was ideal for him if the price was right. Eventually, after much haggling, a price was agreed and the next day, a trip to Mr Pierce at Martin's Bank followed. A loan was agreed, a loan account opened and Mikey made arrangements for repayments to be made on the first Friday of every month. Mr Pierce watched Mikey walk away from his bank, interested in how this ambitious young man would progress.

The black and red lorry was deposited at Paddy Grady's yard and Mikey thought hard about which colour he should paint it. He wanted his own personal stamp on the vehicle and he decided to change the colours to dark green with gold lettering.

'I think that it will give it some class,' he told Ted and Frank.

He had asked Paddy if he could use his telephone number as a contact number until such time as he had a telephone of his own. Paddy had agreed and had also agreed that the girl who worked in his office as a secretary could take messages for him.

The words on the cab doors were to say:

Michael Whelan
Haulage Contractor
Telephone: Kirkdale 1320

With the acquisition of the lorry, it was now time for Mikey to leave the protection of John Carter's and to stand alone. Brian, who had become a good friend of Mikey's in the time that they had worked together, tried to persuade John Carter to keep Mikey on part-time until he had built up his business.

'Do you think I'm some sort of fool,' John had replied to Brian. 'He'll work for me full-time or not at all. I'm not going to encourage someone setting up in competition against me.'

And so Mikey and Brian shook hands and parted company.

The weeks and months that followed were hard for Mikey with little money coming in, but it was not unexpected. He had known that he would have a hard time until he could become established and build up a band of regular customers. There were some days when there was no work at all and he was glad that he had held back some of his savings in the account in Martin's Bank, instead of using it all as a deposit on the lorry. It was this which helped him over the difficult period and allowed him to continue living at Mrs Hennessy's until, gradually, the work began to increase and the money began to come in.

Some of the companies that he had worked for earlier, when he had worked for John Carter, had been some of those that Mikey had targeted when he had been looking for customers and a number of them, remembering that he had been a hard worker and was trustworthy and reliable, placed work in his direction, particularly as he had deliberately set his rates lower than many others. He knew that once he had the business, he could always increase the rates later.

But it wasn't all easy. The sun shone on Mikey most of the time, but occasionally there were problems. One night as he returned the lorry to Paddy's yard he realised that the lorry had been followed into the yard by a couple of men.

As Mikey climbed down from the cab of the lorry, the two men approached him.

'Is it Paddy you're wanting?' Mikey asked.

'No! It's you we're here to see. We've a message for you from John Carter,' the taller one said.

'Oh! Yeah. And what might that be?' Mikey asked.

'He said to tell you to keep away from his customers.'

One of them had raised his arm to reveal an iron bar in his hand.

'He said that you might need some persuading.' He approached Mikey, swinging the bar around and around in front of him.

Mikey backed away in the direction of Paddy's office, realising that both the men were bigger and more powerful than he was. He carefully positioned himself behind a large cylindrical drum that housed thick lengths of rope that were used for securing the loads on the back of his lorry and, quickly pushing it on its side, he rolled it in the direction of the men. As they dived out of its way it crashed into a pile of scrap metal sending it flying in all directions. Taking advantage of the situation, Mikey turned and ran towards Paddy's office. As he approached the wooden steps that led up to the office the door was flung open and a large bundle of snarling fur exploded past him.

'Thank God! I thought you must be still here, when the dog wasn't out in the yard. But when you didn't appear I thought I must have made a mistake,' Mikey said as he saw Paddy in the doorway.

There were yells and shouts of pain as one of the men unsuccessfully tried to pull the large Alsatian away from the other who was rolling on the ground with the dog's teeth firmly fastened around his arm. Paddy waited a couple of minutes before calling the dog off.

'Wolf! Wolf! Here, boy,' he shouted.

The dog, after much barking and snarling, reluctantly moved away from the two men and, as they staggered to their feet, Paddy yelled at them, 'Get the hell out of here. Now! Before I set the dog on you again.'

The two wounded men made a hurried departure, half

stumbling, half running out of the yard.

'What the hell was that all about?' Paddy asked Mikey.

'It appears that John Carter is none too happy about me taking business away from him,' Mikey replied. 'He sent those two bastards to teach me a lesson.'

'Well,' Paddy said, 'If they're the sort of friends you have, I think that you ought to be thinking about carrying something in the cab with you to protect yourself.'

'They say that forewarned is forearmed,' Mikey said, breathing a deep sigh of relief. 'I'll not allow myself to get in that sort of situation again.'

As Mikey's business began to thrive he was able to gradually put up his prices and eventually decided that he needed a second-man to help him as the work was becoming too much for one man to handle. He had been working illegally since he had owned the lorry. Legislation stated that any steam vehicle which carried goods of over five tons in weight required two people to man the vehicle and Mikey, driving alone, had been stopped on a couple of occasions by the police and his pocket was lighter and theirs heavier, as a result of them "turning a blind eye". He knew that his luck would not last forever and so he contacted his old friend and training partner, Barney Gallagher, and asked him if he would be interested in coming to Liverpool to work with him as second-man.

The work situation in Ireland had not improved since Mikey had left and when Barney received the letter with Mikey's suggestion it provided a welcome opportunity for him. With his parents' blessing and a loan from his uncle to cover his fare, he set sail for Liverpool.

Mikey met Barney off the boat and the two friends greeted each other affectionately.

'God! You've grown to be a fair size!' Barney said, throwing his arm around Mikey's shoulders. 'You must have been eating some mighty powerful stuff. So! You've obviously been doing well for yourself with your own lorry and everything. Who'd have believed it when you were running in all those races with your trousers halfway up your legs, trying to scrape together your fare to Liverpool, that you'd end up your own boss.'

'Well, didn't we all know that if you were willing to put your nose to the grindstone you could have a far better life here than in Ireland?' Mikey commented. 'Anyway, I've found a place for you to stay. It's not in the same place as me, because there are no rooms empty there but it's not too far away. Let's get you settled in and then I can catch up on all the news from back home.'

It was Friday and, with no work over the weekend, Mikey was able to spend some time with Barney, proudly showing him the lorry at Paddy's yard and telling him about the incident with John Carter's two henchmen. Barney was very impressed with the lorry with Mikey's name emblazoned on the doors and suggested to Mikey that he ought to have sent for him earlier.

'Sure, if I'd been here keeping an eye on you, you would have been alright. Haven't I always been your guardian angel?' he said, laughing.

On Saturday night, Mikey asked Barney to join them all at the ceilidh and introduced him to Eileen and the O'Malley brothers.

'Well, you're a quiet one,' Barney said with a grin when Eileen was deep in conversation with one of the other women of the parish. 'You didn't tell me in any of your letters that there was a woman on the scene.'

'Ah! Sure, we only go to the ceilidhs together,' he told Barney, 'but I'm hoping that now that the business is getting well and truly off the ground that she'll marry me. Mind, I haven't asked her yet.'

'Well, you'd be on to a good thing there,' Barney said. 'She's a good-looking woman, so she is and with her own house and everything, you'd be well set up.'

'The house has nothing to do with it,' Mikey said, his voice sharp. 'I'll have my own house eventually. I don't want to live off anyone else, let alone a woman. I'll be the one to provide for her, not the other way around.'

'No offence!' Barney apologised. He grinned. 'I see that you've not changed then. You're still as tetchy as ever.'

The business went from strength to strength and after a few months with Barney at his side, Mikey decided that it was time for him to make known his intentions to Eileen.

The ceilidhs still took place once a month on a Saturday night and, as Mikey always accompanied Eileen, many of the regulars already thought of them as a couple. One Saturday night after the ceilidh, when everyone else had gone to bed and Eileen had departed to her rooms, Mikey plucked up courage to knock on her door. He had been thinking all day about how he would approach her, what he would say, his thoughts were racing around and around in his head and he was nervous.

'Is it alright if I come in?' he asked her. 'I've a few words I'd like to say to you in private.'

Eileen stood to one side and indicated to Mikey to go into the parlour. She offered him a chair and waited for him to speak.

'I'd rather stand, if you don't mind,' Mikey said and cleared his throat.

'You look rather serious, Mikey. Do you have some sort of problem? You're not planning to leave us, are you?'

'No! No! It's nothing like that. I've wanted to talk to you for a long time but I had nothing to offer you. Now that I have a lorry and the business is going well…..' he paused, 'I'm nearly twenty-one and you're only six years older than me. And sure what's six years…..'

There was a long silence as Eileen waited for Mikey to continue.

'And the business is beginning to get going big style!'

'Yes!' Eileen said, beginning to anticipate what Mikey was

about to say. She suddenly had no wish to encourage him further but Mikey continued to say what he had intended.

'And.....I'd be deeply honoured if you'd consider marrying me.'

He stumbled with his words as they came pouring quickly out of his mouth. 'Eileen, I have loved you from the first moment that I set eyes on you, young as I was. I will look after you and provide for you and treasure you forever.' Never a man of great eloquence, the words were difficult for Mikey to utter.

Eileen looked at him, flustered. She could feel herself blushing.

'Mikey, I wasn't expecting anything like this. Thank you for asking me.' Eileen wasn't sure what to say. 'I'm flattered and grateful but I've been a long time now on my own and I don't know how I'd cope with having someone around me all the time again. You have been a good friend and a good lodger but I had never thought about marrying again.'

'Look! I know that. Take as much time as you want to think about it. I'm not asking you for an answer straight away. Sure, I don't want to rush you. I know that it will be a big step for you.'

There was an uncomfortable silence as they stood and looked at each other.

'I'll say goodnight now.'

He leant forward quickly and kissed her on the lips and then turned around and left, closing the door quietly behind him.

Eileen stood where he had left her, her hand pressed to her mouth, wondering how things had managed to escalate to this situation. It was true that she had never thought about remarrying and, even if she had, she was not sure that Mikey would have been the one that she would have chosen. She knew that other women found him attractive but, as far as she was concerned, the only feeling that she felt for him was friendship.

Mikey returned upstairs to his room and lay on his bed

staring at the ceiling. He wasn't sure what he had expected but he had been unwilling to allow the possibility that Eileen might say 'No' to enter into his mind. He spent a restless time, tossing and turning before he eventually drifted off to sleep.

The next days were painful for Mikey as he waited for Eileen's reply. She acted as if nothing had taken place between them. Mikey desperately wanted to ask her what her decision was but waited for her to approach him. Eventually on Friday night, two weeks after his proposal, when Mikey arrived home, Eileen was waiting for him in the kitchen. She closed the door behind him and put her hand on his arm.

'Mikey, I've decided that I can't marry you. I'm just not ready to share my life with anyone else yet, and I am not sure that I ever will be.' She paused. 'I am so sorry, Mikey.'

Mikey stood and stared at her, his face pale.

She said again, 'I'm so, so sorry, Mikey,' she went on, 'you've been a good friend. I didn't think that you would read anything more into our friendship. I'm sorry if I've led you to believe otherwise. It wasn't deliberate. I wouldn't have wanted to hurt you.'

He made no attempt to persuade her to change her mind but shook her hand off his arm and walked back upstairs to his room, experiencing a mixture of emotions: anger, humiliation and confusion. He had been so sure of himself and couldn't believe that he could have so totally misjudged the situation.

The following day he told Barney that he was going to move out of Mrs Hennessy's. The dark look that he gave Barney warned Barney not to question him. Barney expressed no surprise, merely raised his eyebrows and said nothing except, 'There's a room free at my place.'

Leaving two weeks' rent in an envelope pushed under Eileen's door, with a note telling Eileen that he was moving out, Mikey packed his few articles of clothing into his canvas bag and the remainder of his possessions into a couple of large, brown paper bags and left.

Chapter 9

Mikey had never before experienced a setback such as the one that he experienced as a result of his rejection by Eileen. Although he had felt betrayed by Sean Kelly's dishonesty and the theft of his money some years earlier, at least after the initial shock he had felt that he was in control. He had known that with hard work he could salvage the situation. But now he felt that he had exposed himself, had allowed himself to become vulnerable and, as a result, he felt a fool. He knew that if Eileen did not want him, there was nothing that he could do about it. He loved her and had even allowed himself to imagine them living together and even having children together. His self-confidence and arrogance had not allowed him to think about the possibility of being rejected and the pain that he was now experiencing made him determined that he would never allow the same situation to occur again.

Mikey still continued attending the ceilidhs but studiously avoided Eileen. When contact was unavoidable he was polite but cool towards her. His black mood communicated itself to his friends. Ted and Frank watched the situation without comment, as did Barney, but they all guessed at what had happened and all of them were aware that Mikey's pride was hurt and that any show of sympathy from them would not be appreciated.

Neither Eileen nor Mikey made any mention of Mikey's proposal and rejection. Mikey, because his pride was hurt and he didn't want anyone to know about his humiliation, and Eileen, because she felt guilty and thought that perhaps she had encouraged Mikey to believe or at least hope that their relationship could be something more than friendship.

Mikey began once more to pay attention to Hannah. He wanted to show Eileen that he had no need of her, that there were other woman who were only too happy to spend time with him.

Hannah also had no idea what had gone wrong between Mikey and Eileen. She had watched unhappily as Mikey had switched his attentions from her to Eileen and had become even more unhappy when the relationship between Mikey and Eileen had appeared to blossom. She had asked no questions when Mikey turned his attention back to her. She didn't feel the need to know anything as long as Mikey was showing interest in her once again.

The card playing for which Mikey had displayed a talent, on the boat journey from Ireland to Liverpool, had continued to play a part in Mikey's life all the time that he had been in Liverpool and, in an effort to help him forget his rejection by Eileen, he now spent more and more time playing cards and smoking and drinking.

Initially, because the group with whom he had played had consisted of fellow dockworkers, the stakes had not been particularly high but gradually the group had expanded to include some local businessmen who met in a back room of one of the hotels on the outskirts of Liverpool. Consequently the stakes had become higher.

Barney watched Mikey's behaviour unhappily. He knew that part of it must stem from disappointment about his failed relationship with Eileen but Mikey had never spoken to him about it and he knew that he would be unwise to raise the subject. He did not approve of Mikey's gambling, particularly when there were large amounts of money at stake. He was also unhappy about Mikey's level of drinking and regularly had to undress him and help him to bed when he staggered home to his lodgings after one of his card-playing sessions.

One Saturday morning, after Mikey had come home the previous night particularly drunk, he challenged him. 'For God's sake, Mikey. Will you get a hold of yourself. What in God's name has got into you? You're going to wreck yourself and the business. And what about young Hannah?' he added. 'She'll want nothing to do with you if you carry on like this.'

'She can take me as I am or not at all! There are plenty more where she came from,' Mikey replied with a snarl. But he had already realised that the way he was behaving was not sensible. He knew that the business was already suffering when he turned into work late after a heavy drinking night and that some of his customers had already expressed dissatisfaction at work not being completed on time. He knew that it was stupid to allow the break-up of his relationship with Eileen to ruin what he had worked so hard to achieve, so he began to control his level of drinking, but the gambling still continued.

When Barney questioned him, puzzled about why Mikey found it so necessary to gamble, Mikey tried to explain what it meant to him. He ran his fingers through his hair and closed his eyes, as though trying to picture what it was that he gained from the gambling.

'Sure, it gets a hold of you, so it does. It's not about drawing the best cards in the pack, it's about knowing when to bet high and when to ease off. It's about being able to bluff and beat the fella sitting next to you. It's about chancing it.' He laughed. 'And sometimes it's just about getting something for nothing.'

'Well if it's all about bluffing, you're a master at that,' Barney replied, having regularly sat in on the card games and watched Mikey's impassive face as people stacked their cards only to find that Mikey often had nothing worthwhile in his hands as he raked in the money.

Barney was not averse to having an occasional bet on the horses himself but had no great wish to spend hours in a smoke-filled room with people he scarcely knew, seeing his hard-earned money disappear into the air like the smoke from the cigarettes and he still could not fully understand the hold that the gambling had on Mikey and some of his other card-playing compatriots.

But despite everything, he had to acknowledge that Mikey was a winner. Other people lost money time and time again but although Mikey occasionally had a run of bad luck, overall he had a winning streak.

'Lady Luck spends a lot of time smiling on you, so she does. Let's hope that she doesn't turn around one day and desert you,' Barney said.

One of the men who played regularly with the group of card players, was a man called Phillip Corcoran who, on the death of his father, had inherited various pieces of property and land. Because of his inheritance, Phillip had no need to work and spent a lot of his time drinking and gambling and, over a long period of time, had become more and more in debt to Mikey, amongst others.

'There's no problem, Phillip. Pay me when you're ready. You're not going to run off anywhere, are you?' Mikey had said laughing, but at the same time keeping a careful note of how much he was owed in a small black bound notebook that he kept in his inside pocket.

'You shouldn't be encouraging him to play, Mikey, when you know that he's only going to lose his money to you,' Barney said one evening after Phillip had lost even more money than usual to Mikey.

'For God's sake, will you stop acting like an old woman,' Mikey replied. 'Isn't he a grown man and more than able to make his own decisions without you hovering over him and me like a mother hen.'

It wasn't accidental that Mikey had allowed Phillip's debt to him to mount up and soon Mikey felt that the time was right to call in the debt.

He had been grateful for the opportunity to park his lorry in the shed on Paddy Grady's land but had decided that the time had come when he needed to look for his own premises. He wanted to buy another lorry and if he did that he would need more parking space and an office of his own.

He knew that one of the properties that Phillip owned was a good-sized house not far from where he was lodging, in Springfield Road. The house and the possibility of owning it had figured large in Mikey's plans and was one of the reasons that he had felt few scruples about relieving Phillip of his money.

It was a large, detached house with gardens which lay to all four sides. The house had been unoccupied for a number of years and was in a sorry state. Some of the roof slates were broken and missing; the peeling paintwork only partly disguised the rotten woodwork beneath, damaged by the sun and rain. Shards of glass littered the garden from the broken and boarded up windows.

It must once have been an impressive house, its proportions quite elegant, but Mikey knew that because of its dilapidated condition the house would not fetch a high price if put on the market. He equally recognised its potential as business premises for himself.

The front door was flanked on one side by a veranda and on the other by a large bay window which overlooked the front garden. Double wrought-iron gates, rusted and hanging from broken hinges, led from the road at the front to a wide path, large enough to allow a lorry access, which ran up the side of the house to an extremely large garden at the back. The back garden was one of the reasons that the house was of interest to Mikey. Once levelled and paved it would provide a yard for his lorries.

'I have a suggestion to make to you, Phillip,' said Mikey when he approached Phillip with his proposition one evening as they left the hotel room, after yet another card-playing session. 'I know that you have a house in Springfield Road that's of no use to you and I'm needing to move from Paddy Grady's and get my own place. Would you consider selling it to me? What you owe me could be part payment and I'd see if I could get a loan from the bank for the rest.' He paused. 'We'd need to get it valued to make sure that the price was fair, of course.'

Phillip did not take long to make up his mind. He had no use for the house and if he sold the house to Mikey then his debt would be cleared and he would also have a sum of cash in his hand to pay off some of his other debts, so it provided a good solution to his problems.

An agent was called to give a valuation of the house and another trip to see Mr Pierce at Martin's Bank was arranged.

Mikey went along to the bank with his carefully worked out plans for expansion, explaining how having premises of his own, with more space, would increase the potential of the business. He presented the case plausibly as before and Mr Pierce sat back in his chair and eyed the youg man in front of him. Mikey had been a good customer, always repaying promptly.

'You're doing well for yourself, Mikey. You're careful with your money and your existing loan is almost paid off, so I can't see any problem. I'll have the necessary papers drawn up.' He stood up and held out his hand to Mikey. 'Call in at the end of the week and they'll be ready for you to sign.'

Once the loan was official the next stage was to legalise everything to do with the purchase of the house. Phillip went with Mikey to the solicitor's office, where Mikey handed over the money as agreed and Phillip signed over the house and piece of land to Mikey. Mikey left the solicitor's office jubilant at having become a property owner.

Work continued as usual; Mikey and his lorry trundled backwards and forwards to the docks but now Mikey, in addition, spent more and more time with a pad and pencil, taking measurements and working out what he was going to do with Springfield Road.

He asked Barney to help with some of the basic work on the new house and Barney agreed to do so, despite his reservations about the way that Springfield Road had ended up in Mikey's hands. He had not built up many other friends since he had been in Liverpool and Mikey had given him the opportunity to escape from his constricted life in Ireland and, because of this, he felt loyalty towards him.

They started work initially on the inside of the house at weekends, as Mikey had no extra money for the equipment required to level the yard. Walls were plastered, windows repaired and Barney and Mikey acquired skills which they had never possessed before. They returned to their lodgings each weekend evening tired but satisfied at what had been accomplished.

The relationship with Hannah was still ongoing despite the fact that he had little time to see her. He had explained to her that he was busy working on the house and, although she was disappointed that she was not seeing much of him, Hannah recognised that the work on the house was necessary.

One Sunday afternoon, Mikey decided that he needed a break from all the building work and he met up with Hannah for a walk in Derby Park. On the way home it began to rain. Mikey grabbed Hannah's hand.

'C'mon,' he shouted, 'the house is just around the corner. I've got the keys with me. I was planning to do a bit of work there later. We can shelter there until the rain eases off.'

Hannah had been curious about the house in Springfield Road, which was taking up so much of Mikey's time, and was pleased that circumstances were creating the opportunity at last for her to see it.

They arrived out of breath at the front door and while Mikey fumbled in his pocket for the keys, Hannah held her hat firmly on her head to stop it blowing away.

Mikey unlocked the front door, which led straight into a long wide hall with high ceilings and a terracotta tiled floor. At the end of the hall was a large square area totally open from the ground floor to the cracked and dirty skylight above, where the rain now unceasingly drummed out a tune. An impressive staircase led to the first floor, where a landing swept around three sides of the house, with doors opening off at regular intervals.

'Goodness me!' said Hannah, staring about her. 'It's far, far bigger than you would ever imagine from the outside.'

After taking off their sodden outer garments they wandered up the stairs and through the house, stepping over piles of bricks, timber and tools, where some of the rooms were showing evidence of Barney and Mikey's efforts.

Hannah looked about her at the high ceilings and tall windows, some laced with cobwebs, their shutters hanging drunkenly from broken hinges.

'I can understand why you thought the place had possibilities,' said Hannah, 'but it's going to take a lot of hard work and money.'

'Would you be interested in helping me make something of the place?' Mikey asked and Hannah began to laugh, glancing around her.

'I'm not sure that I'm cut out for building work, Mikey.'

'No, that's not what I'm saying. I'm asking if you would be interested in…being part of it, making something of this place……with me.' Mikey paused, not sure how to continue.

What he said next had not been planned, but it suddenly seemed to be a good idea. 'I'm asking if you'll marry me.'

For a brief moment, as Hannah paused, Mikey wondered if he was about to meet the same response from Hannah as he had from Eileen.

'I'm not suggesting that we get married straight away,' he said quickly. 'It's going to be a little while before any of it will be fit to live in, but we could get engaged now and set a date for the wedding later when we see how things are going.' Suddenly concerned at Hannah's silence, he said, embarrassed, 'If you're not interested, it's of no consequence.'

'Sorry, Mikey. I was only hesitating because I was taken by surprise. It was a bit of a shock!' She glanced at him smiling. 'I'd be very happy to marry you.'

It was not the sort of proposal that Hannah had envisaged as there was no declaration of love or undying devotion from Mikey. It was all very matter-of-fact but Hannah was intelligent enough to realise that this might be all that was on offer and she thought that, even if Mikey didn't love her now, maybe he would grow to love her in the future.

They sat on one of the deep, low window sills which Mikey carefully dusted down with some old rags and watched the rain falling outside as Mikey told her his plans for Springfield Road.

They sat and talked like two friends, not lovers, but Hannah was scarcely able to conceal her excitement at what had just happened to her. When the rain gradually eased they wandered out to the back garden where roses grew wildly, intertwining with the brambles and convolvulus, a damp freshness in the air despite the rotting fruit which lay around the bases of the neglected apple and pear trees. Hannah could immediately see the sense in Mikey's ideas. It was a big space and once cleared and levelled could house many lorries.

By the end of the afternoon Mikey had accompanied Hannah to meet her parents and officially asked for her hand in marriage.

Part Two

HANNAH

Chapter 10

Hannah was the only child of Jack and Maisie and had been born after many years of marriage, when they had almost given up any idea of having a child and, consequently, she was greatly treasured. She was dependable and reliable, worked hard at school and had always been a loving and obedient daughter. After school she had attended a secretarial school and subsequently had found work at the Town Hall as a secretary.

Jack and Maisie had met many of the friends that Hannah had made at work who were mostly what Jack and Maisie thought of as "respectable", but Mikey was an unknown quantity to them and although they liked him well enough, liking him was a different matter to him marrying their only daughter, particularly as they had observed Mikey's switch of attentions from Hannah to Eileen and their daughter's subsequent unhappiness.

But it was, perhaps, the very qualities that Jack and Maisie recognised as a little worrying in Mikey which fascinated Hannah because he was so different from any of the young men that she already knew.

Having at last gained Mikey's interest and attention, Hannah set about making herself indispensable to him and within a few weeks of accepting his proposal had offered to attend to his accounts, a chore which she knew he detested because he complained about the task regularly. Her offer was gratefully accepted.

The accounts were in chaos. Mikey had no interest in something as mundane as bookkeeping and Mary, Paddy Grady's secretary, who had sometimes helped him with his accounts, had only been able to spare a very limited amount of time to work on them. So Hannah set to work, determined that they would soon be in some sort of agreeable order.

She persuaded Mikey that they needed official invoice and receipt pads, instead of the scrappy bits of paper on which Mikey had previously jotted down transactions.

'You need your name and address on the pads so that people can refer to them quickly,' she thought for a minute, 'and maybe you ought to have Paddy's telephone number on them as well. I'm sure Paddy won't mind Mary taking messages for you for a little while longer.'

So with Mikey's agreement, she paid a visit to the printers. A typeface was chosen and the pads were duly printed and delivered.

Hannah also purchased two large ledgers and, as business was transacted, it was recorded in the books. She had pamphlets printed echoing the information on the invoice and receipt pads and the slogan "No job too big. No job too small", and they were distributed about the town.

The building work on the office was soon completed and a desk, a chair and, eventually, Mikey's own telephone were installed. The invoice and receipt pads were then replaced with new ones with Mikey's new telephone number replacing that of Paddy's. A proper filing system was still needed but, as a temporary measure, documents were carefully stacked in labelled trays on the floor in the corner of the office. Mikey was delighted with the way that things were progressing. He sometimes sat in the office and surveyed his domain, smiling to himself as he remembered some of Barney's words, 'Who would have thought that you would ever be in a situation like this, when a few years back you didn't have two farthings to rub together.'

Once the office was completed Hannah began to work on the accounts at Springfield Road on a Saturday, instead of working on them at home in the evening. This suited her well because it gave her more contact with Mikey.

The office, where she did her work at Mikey's desk, had two large sash windows which overlooked the yard. Mikey, looking to the future when he hoped to have a fleet of lorries, had decided that it was important for him to be able to see what was happening in the yard if he had work to do in the office and now Hannah was able to work on the accounts and watch Mikey and Barney out of the window as they worked in the yard, where great lorry loads of earth were taken away and a base was laid for some paving stones, which Mikey had acquired cheaply from Paddy Grady.

'A friend over-ordered,' Paddy said, with a knowing wink at Mikey. Mikey laughed and thought that it was no business of his where Paddy had obtained the paving stones as long as they did the job for him.

The paving was laid and Mikey's lorry was moved from Paddy's yard. Mikey recognised that there was still a great deal of work to do before the house and yard would be completed and, in an effort to conserve money, decided that he ought to move out of his lodgings and into Springfield Road, where he slept on a straw mattress on the floor and washed under a tap in the back yard. Living in these primitive conditions brought his early life in Ireland to mind but the difference was that this time he knew it would only be for a short time.

Mikey was still playing cards, the amount that he was prepared to risk increasing in size as his business grew. But sometimes caution left him and when the mood took him, he was not beyond betting his total evening's profit on what he considered a winning hand. Occasionally he went home with less than he had started with, but sometimes he went home with substantial sums of money.

Hannah had no idea that Mikey was gambling. He kept that well hidden from her. She assumed that he didn't see her during the week because he was too tired as a result of the long hours he was working which was, in fact, partly true. He worked long and hard but, when he wasn't too tired, he played cards.

As money became available, work was eventually started once again on the interior of the house. The large room at the front of the house with the big bay window was to become the sitting room. A door from this room adjoined another large room that Mikey and Hannah had decided would be ideal for a large kitchen where they would also take their meals. Hannah had insisted that the rooms in which they were to live were at the front of the house away from the office, so that there would be some privacy for them away from the business but was a little dismayed, despite recognising the logic behind Mikey's decision, when Mikey said that he wanted these all completed before they even set a date for the wedding. She had visions of a stooped, greying old lady in a wedding dress standing at the altar.

Hannah began to join Barney and Mikey whenever she could, sometimes in the evenings after work or occasionally on a Sunday, to work with them. She was still attending to the accounts on Saturdays, so most of her free time was spent in the company of Barney and Mikey. Although it was useful to have an extra pair of hands, Mikey found her presence a little frustrating because it curtailed his card-playing.

There was nothing that Hannah was unwilling to do, no matter how dirty or time-consuming. She became adept with a paintbrush, with a scarf tied over her head to protect her hair and even tackled some plastering, much to the amusement of Barney. Clothes destined to be thrown away found a new use as work overalls.

Gradually the downstairs rooms were completed and

Hannah chose furniture for them. And then began the renovation of the upstairs rooms with the priority being a bedroom for her and Mikey. She enjoyed making the house hers and was happy to spend as much time and energy on it as she had available. As she walked through the completed rooms and saw what had been achieved, she was delighted and decided that the delay had been worthwhile.

Eventually, two and a half years after Mikey had proposed to Hannah, a date was set for the wedding. Mikey hired the church hall for the reception and Ted and Frank and their band were asked to play for the guests.

There had not been a lot of contact between Mikey and the O'Malley brothers in the years that Mikey had been engaged to Hannah. The two brothers had become involved in anti-English activities and Mikey did not want to be too closely connected with them as he thought that it might affect his business but they were a good band and he knew that they would provide lively entertainment for the wedding guests.

The day of the wedding was a crisp and clear November day and, despite the time of year, Hannah insisted on wearing a traditional wedding dress. This was her special day and she wanted to be beautiful for Mikey. The dress was of ivory satin over which there was a layer of ivory lace studded with tiny pearls and, when Mikey saw her in her wedding dress at the church, he congratulated himself on his choice of bride.

When Barney, who was Mikey's best man, saw Hannah he couldn't take his eyes off her. He had always thought that she was an attractive girl but in her wedding gown he thought that she was beautiful.

'You're a lucky man, so you are, Mikey. You've got a treasure there. I hope that you'll take care of her.'

Despite his friendship with Mikey, Barney had some misgivings about the wedding. He had become very fond of Hannah and was aware that she knew nothing of Mikey's gambling activities. He felt that since the time when he had first met Mikey, there were changes in him and they weren't for the better and he hoped that Mikey would not cause Hannah any unhappiness. And he was not alone in worrying about Hannah. Jack and Maisie, although they had not interfered in Hannah's choice of partner, also had misgivings about the marriage.

The wedding guests were mainly from Hannah's side of the family. None of Mikey's family, who did not even know that the wedding was to take place, were present. Hannah had known that there had been a rift between Mikey's parents and himself and had hoped that the wedding would have helped heal the wounds, but it appeared that it was not to be.

She had tried to persuade Mikey to tell his parents about the marriage but Mikey had stood firm.

'Sure, they couldn't afford to come over here for the wedding anyhow,' he had told Hannah, who couldn't help but think to herself that this was just an excuse. Mikey could have afforded to pay the fare for his mother and father, even if he couldn't afford to pay the fares for the whole family.

The nuptial Mass was at eleven o'clock in the morning and it was a nervous Mikey and Hannah who made their vows to each other. Afterwards, a horse and carriage took them to the church hall for the reception. Speeches were made, drinks were consumed and the band began to play. Once the music was well under way, the bride and groom posed for photographs before changing out of their wedding finery and leaving the assembled guests to enjoy the remainder of the day.

The horse and carriage was waiting to take them to Kirkdale Station where they were to catch the train to Southport and spend one night in The Prince of Wales Hotel on Lord Street in the centre of the town. This was a concession to Hannah, who wanted a "proper" honeymoon. They were then to return to begin their married life in Springfield Road.

When the train arrived at the station, Mikey ran down the platform until he found an empty carriage. He called to Hannah, 'C'mon, Hannah, quick! There's an empty one here,' and she rushed down the platform to join him. He helped her up the step and into the carriage and lifted their bag up onto the luggage rack above the mahogany-framed sepia photographs of the Lake District. He sat down beside Hannah, pulling her towards him. She put her hand through his arm and snuggled against him, resting her cheek on his shoulder and sighed with contentment.

'What does it feel like then to be Mrs Whelan?' Mikey asked, smiling.

'It feels wonderful! Oh Mikey, I know that we are going to be so happy together.'

He kissed her and held her close. They jumped apart as the next station was reached and a large, elderly lady entered the carriage and, huffing and puffing, settled herself on the long velour-covered seat opposite. Mikey pulled a face at Hannah and muttered, 'So much for having a carriage to ourselves.'

Hannah had to try hard to prevent herself from giggling. They sat slightly apart for the remainder of the journey, casting occasional smiling glances at each other until the train pulled in at Southport station.

Southport was the last station on the line and Mikey helped the large lady down the step from the train before they headed towards their hotel, Hannah, giving an occasional skip, trying to match her pace to Mikey's long stride.

The hotel was a large, imposing, red-brick building and as they approached the large oak reception desk Hannah twisted the new gold band around her finger. Mikey entered the names Mr and Mrs Michael Whelan in the large red book and the porter collected their suitcase and showed them to their room, where Mikey didn't need Hannah's reminder to tip the lad who stood waiting expectantly. He remembered his own days as a porter on the docks and, feeling generous, gave the young boy a sizeable tip.

'It's been an absolutely wonderful day,' Hannah said as she removed her coat and kicked off her shoes. Plumping up the pillows, she sat on the bed using them as a back-rest, her legs stretched out in front of her.

'Mr and Mrs Michael Whelan,' she said. She liked the sound of it. She repeated it over and over again, giggling, until Mikey too was laughing. She threw a pillow at him and smiled as she watched him remove his coat and tie and unloosen the stud on his shirt collar.

'God! It's good to get out of these clothes and get a bit more comfortable,' he said as he too kicked off his shoes.

He moved towards Hannah and pulled her to her feet, pressing his body against hers. He eased her jacket from her shoulders and, after throwing it over the back of a chair, began to undo the buttons of her blouse, which then joined the jacket on the chair. He started kissing her neck and then her breasts.

Her breathing quickened as he began to undo her skirt and pull it down over her hips.

Her mouth sought his as he lowered her onto the bed and she felt a little nervous, remembering her mother's warning that the first time might be painful and that there may be a little blood. She lay watching Mikey as he removed the remainder of his clothes and stood before her naked. He returned to the bed and was soon astride her. She felt him enter her and gave a small moan of pain. He climaxed quickly and rolled away onto his back, his eyes closed as he stroked her belly. She lay and enjoyed the sensation of being stroked until the movements slowed and she realised that Mikey was asleep.

She lay for a little while propped on one elbow, watching Mikey as he slept, then eased herself out of the bed, trying not to waken him and began to hang her clothes on the hooks in the wardrobe. She poured some water from the jug on the washstand and sponged herself. When she turned around, she realised that Mikey was awake again, lying on the bed watching her, his hands behind his head. He patted the bed beside him, smiling. 'Come here,' he said.

She approached him shyly and laughed as he grabbed and tussled with her, pulling her down onto the bed once again.

Much later they had dinner in the hotel and a bottle of

champagne, which Mikey had ordered as a surprise for Hannah, was brought to the table in a bucket full of ice.

'Oh, my God, Mikey! Champagne!' Hannah said, her hand to her mouth.

The waiter opened the bottle and poured two glasses, smiling as he wished them health, wealth and happiness.

'Do you think that he knows that we've just got married?' Hannah whispered to Mikey as the waiter moved away.

'I think he might at that,' Mikey said. 'I'm sure you must get to know the look of people who've just got wed after seeing them week after week in the hotel.' He took a couple of mouthfuls from his glass, pulled a face and said, 'I don't know what all the fuss is about this stuff. I'd much prefer a glass of port or whiskey. But anyway here's to us.' He clinked his glass against Hannah's.

Hannah caught the eye of an elderly gentleman at the table next to them, who raised his glass in their direction. She blushed and said to Mikey, 'I think that everyone in the place knows that we've just got married.'

'Is it ashamed of the fact that you are?' said Mikey laughing. 'If you are we can get a divorce in the morning.'

'You know that I'm the happiest woman in the world,' said Hannah. 'I'll never divorce you.'

The following morning they had a leisurely breakfast in the hotel before they departed to the station to catch the train which would take them back to Liverpool and to Springfield Road.

Chapter 11

Back home at Springfield Road, life became very busy, so Mikey suggested that Hannah gave up her job as a secretary at the Town Hall to work with him in the business and Hannah was happy enough to do this as it would mean that she would be able to spend even more time with him.

Taking telephone messages and making phone calls, organising the work schedules and the accounts now became part of Hannah's routine, as well as taking care of all the cooking and cleaning. The office work did not keep her fully occupied so she coped fairly easily with the domestic chores; however she was aware that the house was a big one and when all the refurbishing was completed, things might have to change as there would be a lot more to look after.

Twelve months after they were married, Mikey was able to purchase another lorry and employ another driver, a man called Albert Stansfield, and a second-man to accompany him whose name was George Devlin.

Mikey continued working as a driver, as he was unwilling to immerse himself in the office work, and Barney continued to work as Mikey's second-man. The confines of office work bored him and although he didn't particularly like driving, he found life far more interesting out and about on the road, meeting new people. He also found that it was easy for him to adopt this attitude because Hannah was so well organised.

Hannah found the work satisfying. She knew that she had become invaluable to Mikey and some of the tales Mikey or Barney told when they returned from their day's work gave her an insight into their working day and often caused her much amusement.

Although the gambling and drinking had been tempered upon Mikey's marriage to Hannah, there were still instances when Mikey demonstrated that there were elements of the rebel within him. He had not become a man who totally conformed, as Barney witnessed on more than one occasion.

One incident which illustrated this took place not long after the two new men, Albert and George, had started working for Mikey. One cold and wintry night they arrived back at the yard, handed in their time sheets to Hannah and then hurriedly made their way home to escape the extreme weather conditions. Hannah had already prepared the evening meal. It was in the oven at the side of the fire which blazed in the black-leaded hearth, awaiting Mike's return. After a while, when they still had not returned, she thought that the meal was going to be ruined so she took it out of the oven intending to reheat it when Mikey arrived home. As time went on and Mikey and Barney still had not returned home, Hannah became a little concerned, particularly because of the poor conditions of the roads.

At eight o'clock she began to panic a little. At nine o'clock when they had still not arrived home and there had been no telephone call from them explaining the delay, she decided that they must have had an accident and she had better contact the police. As she went into the office to make the phone call, she heard the lorry drive into the yard and ran out to meet them.

'Thank God!' she said. 'I was so worried about you, what with the roads being like they are. I thought that you must have had an accident.'

'C'mon, let's get in out of the cold,' Mikey grabbed her hand

and ushered her into the house out of the cold and sleet. She was surprised that both he and Barney were in such good spirits, given the time that they had been out and the poor weather conditions. When they were inside and had taken off their jackets and warmed themselves by the fire, Barney began to tell her what had happened, shaking his head and laughing.

'You've picked a fine one there,' he told Hannah. 'He'd manage to get himself out of any situation so he would.'

It transpired that because of the weather the journey that they had undertaken to Manchester had been particularly slow and the lorry had run out of fuel. They had been forced to stop at the side of a road in a country area surrounded by fields and little else. With quite a few miles further to go before they reached home, Mikey had jumped out of the lorry and called to Barney, 'C'mon! Give us a hand.'

Barney was not sure what he was supposed to be doing until he saw that Mikey had taken an axe from the back of the lorry and was proceeding to chop down a fence which bordered one of the fields nearby.

'For God's sake, Mikey!' Barney yelled. 'What the hell are you doing?'

'Do you want to get home tonight or not?' Mikey replied, scarcely pausing in his act of vandalism.

And as the wind blew stronger and the driving sleet soaked them through, Barney decided that it was not the right time to start an argument. So, as Mikey chopped the wood from the fence, Barney loaded it onto the lorry and eventually with the engine stoked up and blazing away, they set off for home.

'You needn't worry,' Mikey said, looking at Barney sideways and grinning at Hannah. 'As soon as I'm able, I'll go back there to get the fence repaired or pay for the damage.'

And, true to his word, that was exactly what he did two days later, when the weather improved.

Although initially, after the purchase of the new lorry, there was not enough work to justify the wages of two extra men, it wasn't long before work began to increase and Mikey began to break even and soon the business was once again going from strength to strength.

Hannah, Mikey and Barney used to meet every morning in the office, where the lorry runs for that day would be discussed and allocated. Hannah then cooked breakfast for the three of them, which was eaten around the large kitchen table before the men departed to work. It was as she was preparing breakfast one morning, after eighteen months of marriage, that Hannah thrust the frying pan at Barney who was standing at her side.

'Here, Barney, look after this for a minute,' and with her hands across her mouth, she rushed upstairs.

'What's wrong?' said Mikey, jumping to his feet and staring at Barney. 'What's wrong with her?'

'What do you think, you great idjit,' Barney replied, a big grin on his face. 'Isn't she going to have a baby.'

Mikey ran up the stairs two at a time.

'Hannah, are you alright? Are you alright?' he shouted, hammering on the bathroom door.

Hannah came out of the bathroom, pale and sweating, her eyes large and dark in her white face.

'I don't know what's wrong with me,' she said, shaking her head and leaning against the wall. 'I feel sick all the time these days.'

'I think that you'd better go and have a talk with your mammy,' Mikey said, smiling, 'and then I think you should see a doctor.'

What he was saying suddenly registered with Hannah.

'Oh my God! Oh my God, Mikey! Oh, isn't that just wonderful.'

She flung her arms around his neck and hugged him, then they went downstairs to tell the waiting and grinning Barney the news of which he was already aware.

After she had cleared away after breakfast Hannah went,

almost immediately, to see her mother, who agreed that there was a strong possibility that Hannah was pregnant. The two women then went to see Dr Clarke, who confirmed the fact. Hannah returned home where she waited impatiently for Mikey to finish work so that she could tell him that he was definitely going to be a father.

Mikey wanted a son.

'And what if it's a girl?' Hannah asked.

'It's a boy. It's definitely a boy. I can feel it in my bones!' Mikey replied.

'And since when did you become such an expert?' Hannah said laughing.

'You just wait and see if I'm not right,' Mikey said, waltzing her around the kitchen.

Over the next few months Mikey was very attentive to Hannah, not allowing her to do anything too strenuous and Hannah thought that she wouldn't mind being permanently pregnant if it meant that she would always receive this amount of attention from Mikey. She carried on working despite her increasing size but took regular rests and moved more slowly as her bulk increased.

Although they were now working on organising a room for the baby, Hannah decided that she would feel more relaxed if initially the baby was immediately within hearing. So a cot was bought and installed in their bedroom.

As Hannah's pregnancy continued, her mother called in regularly to check that everything was well and the two women would sit in companionable silence as they knitted or crocheted bonnets, bootees and mittens, needles clicking away furiously.

It was only about half an hour after one such visit from her mother that Hannah went into labour.

The pains started, first as small twinges. Maisie had told Hannah what to expect and so Hannah knew that it was a little too soon to call her mother or the midwife. She screwed her face up with the discomfort as each pain came and went, but sat and waited patiently, her hands resting on her stomach, trying to remain calm until Mikey returned home. As soon as she heard Mikey's lorry drive into the yard she stood and waited for him at the door.

'I think it's time, Mikey, the pains are coming more and more often and they're getting stronger and stronger,' she said grimacing.

Mikey ran into the yard and shouted to Barney, 'The baby's coming. Can you go and get Hannah's mother?'

When Maisie arrived, she immediately took control of the situation having already sent Barney off for the midwife.

'C'mon, let's get you upstairs. Here, Mikey. Let her rest against you whilst we get her up to the bedroom.' Mikey and Maisie helped her upstairs, one on either side, her face now strained and her hair sticking in damp strands to her forehead. Maisie undressed her and plumped the pillows up behind her in the bed.

'Are you alright, Hannah? Are you alright? Can I get anything for you?' Mikey was hovering anxiously around her. Despite having been present on numerous occasions when his own mother had gone into labour, this was his own child and he wanted to make sure that nothing went wrong.

'Stop fussing, Mikey. Go downstairs. Women have babies everyday.' Hannah's mother steered him away from the bedroom and guided him to the top of the stairs. She gave his arm a gentle squeeze. 'Hannah's in good hands. We'll call you if she needs you.'

Whilst the women were ensconced in the bedroom above, Mikey and Barney sat downstairs with a bottle of whiskey, smoking cigarette after cigarette. They were soon joined by Hannah's father, who had returned from work and found the note Maisie had left him, and the three men sat drinking and waiting. Mikey occasionally went to the bottom of the stairs and, his head cocked to one side, listened to the sounds from the room above.

'God, it's taking a terrible time, so it is,' he said.

'Well, you may as well sit down and stop the pacing,' Barney replied. 'It's not going to come any faster because of you walking up and down.'

A little after three o'clock in the morning, Hannah's mother appeared in the kitchen. Barney had gone home to bed and Mikey slept at the kitchen table, his head resting on his arms. Hannah's father was also asleep, snoring gently in the armchair at the side of the fire. Maisie took hold of Mikey's shoulder and shook him.

'You can go up now,' she said smiling, 'Oh, Mikey! You've got a lovely little baby boy.'

Mikey rushed up the stairs and into the bedroom where Hannah lay on the bed, pale but smiling, her hair combed and tied back with a ribbon, the baby at her breast.

'Look, Mikey,' she said, pulling the blanket away from the baby's face. 'We've a son. Isn't he beautiful? '

'I told you!' he said triumphantly. 'Didn't I tell you it would be a boy. He's a grand lad, so he is,' Mikey said, with tears in his eyes. 'And you're a grand woman. And hasn't he got the hair of his da',' he said laughing. He sat down on the bed and encircled them both with his arms.

The baby was to be called Patrick Jack. Patrick, because they both liked the name, and Jack after Hannah's father.

'And sure isn't he just a little king, so he is,' said Mikey in delight.

The celebrations started that night at Springfield Road. Barney had told Ted and Frank the news and they insisted on joining him and Albert when they called to see the new baby and to congratulate Mikey and Hannah. They were soon joined by Paddy Grady and his wife, Elizabeth, and Hannah's uncle and aunt. Eventually, Maisie ushered them all out of the room.

'Away with you all now. Hannah has to feed the baby and she needs some peace and quiet.'

Hannah was left to rest, whilst everyone else went downstairs where the music, singing and drinking started in grand style. She sat, propped against the pillows, watching her son as he grunted and snuffled, suckling from her breast. She stroked his head and smelt his lovely smell and smiled to herself thinking how lucky she was.

Meanwhile, Mikey was in his element downstairs, bursting into song at every opportunity and repeatedly telling everyone what a great son he had.

'And hasn't he got a grand head of red hair just like his father,' he kept repeating, laughing.

Each evening, for the remainder of the week, the celebrations continued. If anyone called to offer congratulations they were immediately encouraged to have a drink.

'To wet the baby's head,' Mikey said.

As soon as Hannah was able, she returned to work in the office, and life settled into a more stable routine. The "little king" was carried in a wicker basket from room to room. The basket was placed beside Hannah's desk whenever she was working there as she didn't want to be separated from her precious baby for one minute. Mikey came in and out of the office throughout the day, often stopping to stroke his son's face or dropping a kiss onto Hannah's head.

They were blissful and happy days for both Hannah and Mikey but it wasn't many months before Hannah's sickness returned. Mikey had made sure that she fulfilled her wifely duties as soon as she was physically able and just over twelve months after Patrick's birth she went into labour again.

Although Hannah was pleased to be pregnant again, she was still tired after the previous pregnancy and birth and wished that there had been a little more time between the two. She enjoyed baby Patrick and had never felt closer to Mikey who worshipped his son.

As with her first pregnancy, she often felt nauseous. It made her feel wretched but she knew that it would all be worth it if the new baby gave them as much joy as Patrick. Names were

124

discussed and eventually Mikey and Hannah agreed that if it was a boy, he would be called John James, after Mikey's father, JJ. Mikey was reluctant to call his son after his father, for the wounds were still not healed, but Hannah insisted on it.

'If we called Patrick Jack after my father, it's only fair that if it's a boy, we call him after your father.' They agreed that if it was a girl, the baby would be called Oonagh Maisie.

The birth was shorter and easier this time and a second son was born.

With the birth of John James and with the baby's name a constant reminder of his father, Mikey began to feel a little nostalgic. He thought often about the farm, his parents and his brothers and sisters. Although Hannah's parents were very good to them and spent a lot of time looking after the children, Mikey wanted his children to know their other grandparents and something of the country where he had been born.

He began to regret not having told Bridie and JJ about his marriage and decided that it was time for him to attempt to heal the breach, so he wrote to them and told them what had happened to him in the years since he had left home.

Within a few weeks a letter arrived from Ireland, written by his brother Anthony on behalf of his parents, saying that they were pleased to have heard from Mikey and were excited at the idea that they had a daughter-in-law and two grandsons. At the end of the letter, as a postscript, Anthony had asked if there was any way that he could get across to visit them with his family. *'It would mean the world to Mammy and Daddy,'* he had written.

'Oh, Mikey!' Hannah said. 'Surely we could manage to get across to see them. Just think how they must feel, not having seen hide nor hair of their son for so many years. Just think how you would feel if it had been Patrick or John.'

Mikey thought about it for only a short time before he took a decision. He wrote to Bridie and JJ telling them that, as soon as Hannah felt that she could cope with the journey, they would like to visit them. The tickets were purchased and Mikey wrote to ask if they could arrange for someone to meet them off the boat in Ballina.

A shopping spree was organised to purchase new clothes for Mikey, Hannah and Patrick and also to buy presents to take with them for all the family in Ireland. Mikey was determined to impress everyone with how well he had done. He smiled to himself. He intended to go home wearing a better suit than Joseph Flynn had worn so many years before.

Chapter 12

The crossing from Liverpool to Ballina was a miserable one for Hannah. It was stormy and rough and she was violently ill for most of the trip. It took all her energy and concentration to feed and change the children, although Mikey helped by keeping Patrick occupied and out of mischief, but it was a great relief when the boat finally docked and she knew that the worst part of the journey was over.

Anthony was waiting to meet them at the docks with the horse and cart.

'My God! Mikey! Haven't you grown and just look at the state of you. If it wasn't for the red hair on you, I wouldn't have known you at all.'

He shook hands with Mikey and slapped his back.

'It's grand to see you, Mikey, so it is. It's been far too long. And so this is Hannah. Welcome to Ballina. What two grand boys you've got there. Two little redheads an' all,' he said, rumpling Patrick's head of curls. 'Let's be getting you home and we'll get something to eat inside of you.'

The porter helped load their bags onto the cart and Anthony climbed up to sit in front with Mikey, who held Patrick on his knee. Hannah sat in the back, cradling John in her arms and listening to the banter between the two men. Mikey was asking questions about the family and the farm, hardly giving

Anthony a chance to reply before firing the next question at him.

It was not quite dusk and Mikey looked around as the cart trundled on its way, noticing some of the changes that had taken place. But as the cart turned into the long track between the fields of flax, Mikey felt a lump come into his throat. He had always loved this part of the journey home from the fields, no matter how tired he had been. He thought about the number of times that he had sat in the cart, returning from the fields at the end of a day's work and the number of times that he had raced up and down the track, stopwatch in hand, preparing for the races at the fairs.

Soon the farmhouse was in sight and, as the cart slowly approached, he saw the two figures of Bridie and JJ who had been listening for the sound of its approach, waiting at the door to greet them.

Anthony jumped down and went to the back of the cart to take the baby from Hannah so that she could climb down. JJ had already lifted Patrick down and Bridie, scarcely giving Mikey time to climb down himself, ran to him flinging her arms around him, tears running down her cheeks. 'Oh my God, Mikey, would ya just look at yerself! How you've grown. Sure you're a man now, not the young lad who went away. Many's a time I've thought about you and wondered if you'd ever come back home and now here you are. Sure it's a great thing altogether to have you back with us.'

'Stop the chattering, Bridie.' JJ blew into his handkerchief and wiped a tear from his eye, as emotional as his wife. 'Let them get inside. They'll be wanting a sit down and a rest.'

Mikey had half expected that the reception from his parents would be a cool one but it was as though there had never been a problem, had never been any anger or animosity. He looked at his mother and father. JJ's hair was almost white, his shoulders stooped and curved. The years of hard physical work had taken their toll since Mikey had last seen them. Bridie's face was lined and worn, her once wonderful red hair was now more grey than red.

JJ ushered them in through the porch. It was as though time had stood still. The old wooden bench and the tin bath, although both looking more battered and worn, still rested in the same place.

Mikey stood aside to allow Hannah to pass inside where the remainder of the family stood waiting. He looked at his brothers and sisters. Annie and Lily were young women, no longer little girls, and Annie rushed towards him and flung her arms around him. He hugged her as he looked at his brothers. The picture he had held in his mind was of them as they had been when he had left, young boys in short trousers, urchins with bare feet, not the young men that they were now. They were lined up: Kieran, Declan, Shamus and Brendon.

'God! Would you look at you all!' Mikey said in amazement. 'Sure you're all young men and women and wasn't I expecting to see a crowd of children.' He shook his head in disbelief.

It was Anthony who broke the silence. 'Well! It has been over ten years, ya know, Mikey, and time doesn't stand still. I'm to be married in September and the girls are both courting. It took you a long time to come back but it's great to see you.' He put his arm around Mikey's shoulders and squeezed affectionately. 'The prodigal son returned so you are, but I have to say, it's been nice having the bed to myself instead of you kicking me all night like an angry mule.'

'Let me have the babe while you take off your coat and hat,' Bridie said, holding out her arms towards Hannah, who passed over the sleeping John to his grandmother.

'And isn't young Patrick the picture of his da' with the Donehue hair and all!' she said. 'Come on, son, let's introduce you to your uncles and aunts.'

Patrick clung to his mother's skirt, his thumb in his mouth.

'He'll be alright in a little while,' Hannah reassured Bridie. 'He just needs a little time to get used to everyone. He's not used to meeting so many people all at once.'

The table was set, and the smell of freshly baked soda bread filled the air. Annie and Lily brought more food to the table, thick slices of ham on a plate along with slabs of cheese and butter, hard-boiled eggs, a bowl of steaming potatoes, a pot of Bridie's bramble jam and a big bowl full of apples and pears. In all the sixteen years that Mikey had lived on the farm, he had never seen such a display of food as this on Bridie's table.

'Would you look at this now,' Mikey muttered to Anthony. 'Sure they'd no need to get all this stuff in for us.'

'I told you. You're the prodigal son returned. They wouldn't have it any other way. Don't make a fuss. It's what they wanted to do,' Anthony replied quietly.

'Take the bags upstairs, boys,' said JJ. 'Bridie's put you all in Brendon and Declan's room. You'll be more comfortable there than anywhere else. We've no crib for the baby but Bridie's taken out a drawer from the chest of drawers and lined it with bedding, so the little one will be comfortable enough.'

'I hope that we've not put you to too much trouble...... Mrs Whelan,' Hannah found it strange calling someone else by the same name that belonged to her.

'Sure, it's no trouble at all,' said Bridie. 'What trouble could there be providing a bed for my very own son and his wife and my only grandchildren? And you may as well call me Bridie,' she said smiling. 'There'll be no standing on ceremony in this house.'

Mikey, who was deep in conversation with his father and Anthony, heard enough to think to himself 'beds?' This was certainly a step up in the world for Bridie and JJ.

The men carried on chatting, paying little attention to the women, too busy catching up on all the news and gossip on both sides of the Irish Sea and, on Bridie's command, they moved across to the table to continue the conversation. Baby John, who was still asleep rolled up in a blanket, was placed on the sofa in front of the glowing turf fire. There were lots of questions about Liverpool and what Hannah and Mikey did with their days and how well Mikey's business was doing, Bridie regularly shaking her head in astonishment at the idea of Mikey being his own boss and, more than that, actually employing other people.

Lily and Annie were fascinated, scarcely taking their eyes away from Hannah in her smart new clothes, very much aware of their own worn, unstylish clothing. When the meal was finished Bridie refused offers of help from Hannah.

'The girls and I will wash up in good time. Sure sit down and take the weight off your feet. You're a visitor and you'll be more than tired after the journey. An early night would do you no harm. Sure, travelling is tiring and you not long having had the baby an' all.'

Hannah was only too pleased to agree. She had been unable to eat much of the food that Bridie had offered, her stomach was still unsettled after the journey, but she had forced some down so as not to offend and she was most definitely feeling the effects of lack of sleep.

Mikey, anxious to continue reminiscing with his family but realising that Hannah was tired, added his persuasion to that of Bridie.

'You look tired, Hannah love. You'll feel a lot better once you've had a decent night's sleep, so you will. I'll stay up for a little while longer but I'll follow you up shortly.'

Hannah and the two boys went upstairs with Bridie who tucked John into the drawer that was his cot, while Hannah settled Patrick into the extra bed, which had been brought into the room. Hannah and Mikey were to sleep in the bed normally shared by Declan and Brendon, who were to sleep downstairs in front of the fire on the sofa.

'It's a might cramped,' said Bridie apologetically, 'but at least the beds are comfortable.'

Hannah put her arm around Bridie's shoulder. 'It's very good of you and I'm sure that I will sleep well. So don't you worry now. It's fine for us all.'

'Goodnight and God bless,' said Bridie as she left the room, 'and may the angels watch over you.'

Hannah sighed and looked at her two sleeping children. She stroked their heads and kissed them both before climbing exhausted into her own bed, where she was soon asleep, only waking briefly to feed John when he stirred. Mikey was still not in bed but she could hear the chatter and laughter from downstairs and smiled to herself thinking how pleased he was to be home.

Hannah awoke the next morning feeling refreshed and Mikey, despite his late night, was awake and already out of the house. He had sought out Annie, who had always been the favourite of his brothers and sisters. They sat side by side on the big farm gate.

'How are you getting on?' he asked her.

'Ah! I don't suppose things have changed much since you were here. The money you send Mammy and Daddy home has made a big difference to them but there's still not much work for the rest of us.'

'There's plenty of work in Liverpool for young women. Aren't they crying out for nurses in the hospitals. If you ever fancy coming over to Liverpool to find work, you can always stay with us,' he told her.

'That would be grand but Mammy's getting older and needs a bit of help around the place so I couldn't leave her. And, besides, there's Joseph. We've been courting now for more than a year,' she said, blushing. 'But maybe I could come some time for a holiday?'

'Has the auld fella calmed down a bit or is he still handy with the belt?' Mikey asked.

'Well, he never had the same need of it after you were gone. Sure weren't you the only one who drove him crazy with your antics. Poor Daddy, half the time with you around he didn't know what had hit him. You were always wanting something better than you had, not that I blame you, mind. It was a hard life for a young lad.'

Mikey was surprised to hear Annie talking in such a mature

way. She had obviously seen and absorbed a lot more than he would have given her credit for, given her age at the time.

When Mikey went back into the house, his arm around Annie's shoulders, Hannah was in the kitchen with Bridie and the two boys.

'Sit down now and get your breakfast,' Bridie told Mikey, 'and then I'll look after the babies whilst you show Hannah around the farm. You've a good day for it, to be sure.'

Anthony and JJ were already out working in the fields and Mikey knew that, unless things had changed dramatically, they wouldn't have had the slices of bacon and eggs that were set down now in front of Mikey and Hannah.

'You shouldn't have put yourself out like this, Mammy,' Mikey said. 'Sure a bit of bread and butter would have been fine for us.'

'Isn't it the first time that my daughter-in-law is visiting and I'm not going to have her thinking that we don't know how to feed her properly!' Bridie replied.

Bridie poured tea from a big brown teapot, a new acquisition since Mikey had left home, and then cut great slices of soda bread. She had boiled an egg for Patrick and sat down beside him dipping thin slices of bread into the runny yolk.

'C'mon, my lovely boy, open wide,' and as he obligingly did so, she chuckled. 'What a grand lad you are!'

When they had finished breakfast, Mikey and Hannah left Bridie in charge of the children and went to look around the farm. Mikey showed Hannah the river where they had played as children, the bogs where they had cut the turf and the fields where the flax grew. He explained how the flax was picked and loaded onto the cart and taken off to Ballina where it was made into bolts of linen.

'The fields of flax are not JJ's. Sure, that would have been too lucrative a crop for the Englishman to have left with my da'.'

He painted a picture, not remotely similar to the one that he had described in earlier years to Hannah. Even the bogs, where Mikey had ended up blistered and bruised on so many occasions, were romanticised. Hannah was amused to see how the story had changed. The previous picture of poverty and misery had now become almost poetic but Hannah knew that he would never truly want to return to the previous existence which he had fought so hard to escape. There was a world of difference between Springfield Road and being his own boss and the work on the farm.

Bridie and JJ were determined that Mikey and his family would have a good time; all previous antagonism was forgotten and a series of visits had been arranged to friends and relatives. Wherever they went they were welcomed, everybody was impressed by the lad who had run away from home so many years ago and was now back visiting with his fine clothes and his smart-looking wife and beautiful children.

Mikey had achieved what he had wanted, despite the grief that he had caused his parents at the time. He had escaped the poverty and made a new, more affluent life for himself and had returned home to demonstrate to everyone how well he had done.

And for Bridie and JJ, it was truly, as Anthony had said on Mikey's arrival, the prodigal son returning home; everything was forgiven and although "the fatted calf" had not been produced, Bridie and JJ, in terms of their own meagre earnings, had produced the equivalent and it would take them a long time to recover financially from the visit of their son.

It was a tiring ten days for Mikey and Hannah. There were lots of late nights and socialising. Mikey was in his element, enjoying being the centre of attention. Bridie and JJ had wanted to ensure that their son had a homecoming to remember but, despite JJ's and Bridie's kindness, Hannah just wanted to be back home on familiar territory.

As an only child, she was not used to being part of such a large and noisy group as Mikey's family. She also found it difficult to cope with the primitive sanitary and washing conditions and felt a little guilty, knowing that Bridie and JJ were providing the best that they could. She still felt that she hadn't had a decent wash since she had left Liverpool, being too embarrassed to strip and bathe in the tub in front of the fire. She would only wash when the men were all out of the house and she could shut the kitchen door and wash as best she could at the sink.

When the time came to say their goodbyes, Hannah kissed her parents-in-law fondly and said that she hoped they would visit Liverpool soon, an invitation which was genuinely meant.

'Ah! Now!' said Bridie, 'wouldn't it be a grand thing if we could visit you, to be sure, but we have all the children to look after. We couldn't be leaving them. And then there's the farm and the animals. There'd be no one to look after them.'

Bridie omitted to say that there was no way that they could afford a trip to Liverpool for many years to come, having spent every bit of savings they had to provide a welcome home for Mikey and his family.

Tearful farewells were said, Bridie clutching each of her grandchildren to her in turn and JJ clinging on to the little boy that they had named after him for as long as he could.

Anthony hugged his brother. 'Don't leave it so long 'til next time,' he said. 'Maybe you'll be able to come back for the wedding in September?'

Annie came running out of the house as they climbed into the cart and thrust a bag into Mikey's hand. 'I forgot to give you this,' she said.

It wasn't until they were on board ship and the children were settled and sleeping that Mikey opened the bag.

'Look, Hannah,' he said. 'The bag Annie gave me. There's a load of my medals in it. Ah God! So Annie kept them all these years. I asked her to keep them for me but I thought they'd be gone long since.'

Chapter 13

Back in Liverpool work progressed on Springfield Road. More rooms were completed and furnished. Hannah continued to work in the office but now was helped in the house and with the children by a young woman from Connemara. Her name was Kitty and she was seventeen. Mikey had placed an advertisement in "The Western People" for a young woman to help in the house, offering to pay the fare to Liverpool, provide food and lodging and pay a small salary in return for housework and care with the children.

Within a couple of weeks he had received a reply from Kitty's mother anxious to lose one mouth to feed from a home already overcrowded. Kitty herself had jumped at the opportunity and subsequently occupied one of the newly completed rooms next to the children's bedroom. She was allowed Sunday off and one half day during the week.

Kitty was an innocent and simple girl, poorly educated and far more innocent than most seventeen-year-old girls. She had never experienced anything other than life on the farm where she had lived with her family and five other brothers and sisters, a background not so dissimilar to Mikey's.

Hannah found that Kitty could do simple jobs but could not be trusted to do anything which required her to take any major decision, but nevertheless she shouldered a great deal of the physical work which Hannah had previously undertaken and so eased Hannah's burden of work. Kitty's naivety caused Hannah great amusement, particularly when, standing with Kitty in the grocer's one day, a West Indian sailor from one of the ships that had docked in the port had entered. Hannah had to control her laughter when Kitty, with her hand in front of her mouth, whispered to her, 'Missus, missus! Would you look at the state of that fella over there. He needs a good wash. Wouldn't you just want to be taking a scrubbing brush to him.'

When they were back home, Hannah tried to explain to Kitty that the man was not dirty and that he came from a country far away where everybody had that colour of skin. Because Liverpool was a busy port, Hannah was well used to seeing people with all shades of skin but to poor Kitty the idea was almost unbelievable.

'Sure you're pulling my leg, so you are, missus.'

After a short time, Hannah gave up trying to convince Kitty. She was sure that, even when the conversation had ended, Kitty had not really believed her.

When Hannah told Mikey of the incident he laughed uproariously. 'Well, isn't she from Connemara. What else could you expect?'

But Kitty was a kind girl; she worked hard and loved the children.

She had only been with Mikey and Hannah for a few months when Hannah realised that once again, she was pregnant. As Hannah's size increased, Kitty uncomplainingly took over yet more of the household tasks. Hannah managed to continue to work in the office because the work allowed her to sit down during the day, but she felt that she had put on a great deal more weight with this pregnancy and had become a great deal more tired. She thanked God that Kitty was around to help. She felt awkward and clumsy as she moved about slowly, holding her aching back. Kitty, well used to her own mother's pregnancies, tried to do what she could to ease Hannah's burden.

'You should be sitting down, missus. Sure I'll sort out what needs to be done.'

Although Hannah's pregnancy had initially been welcomed by both Hannah and Mikey, as the pregnancy progressed Hannah became increasingly unhappy. Her constant tiredness was something that Mikey could not understand, having always been strong and fit and healthy himself. He appreciated that she must feel some element of tiredness as a result of being pregnant but was impatient with her lack of energy which was so different from her normal, lively self.

'For God's sake, Hannah,' he exclaimed, 'you've had two bairns already. You should be well able to cope with the situation.'

Hannah's reply that she still felt far more tired, two more babies or not, did not ease Mikey's attitude towards her. He began to spend more and more time out of the house in the evening and Hannah began to realise after she questioned him that he was out playing cards.

'What would I want to be staying in for, when all you do is complain or go away to your bed? I may as well be out enjoying myself. Sure, you're no company for anyone these days.'

'I can't help it, Mikey!' she said unhappily. 'Do you think I like feeling the way I do?'

Hannah's feelings of unhappiness were compounded by the fact that she knew that Mikey was also frustrated because she was often so tired that she could not be bothered to respond to his advances in the bedroom.

Having had no knowledge of Mikey's previous gambling history, she was now suddenly made very aware of it. Mikey had now decided, in response to Hannah's complaints about the time that he spent away from home in the evenings, that the card schools, which before their marriage had been held in the back room of the hotel in Liverpool, would occupy a room in Springfield Road once a week.

Hannah hated those evenings, when men she didn't particularly like came into her home. There were loud voices and raucous laughter. The air was thick with cigarette smoke and whiskey fumes. Mikey started to drink regularly and to excess and Hannah wondered how much the drinking and gambling had been a part of Mikey's life before their marriage.

She complained but, when she was met with belligerent resistance, she could not summon the energy to complain any more. She was too tired, this pregnancy was certainly taking its toll.

Despite Hannah's bulk it was a great surprise to everyone when two babies were delivered, a boy and a girl. The girl was called Oonagh Maisie, after Hannah's mother and the boy was called Anthony after Mikey's older brother. They were both dark-haired and brown-eyed, taking after Hannah in appearance this time, rather than Mikey.

Mikey was so proud to be the father of twins. It was almost as though he thought that he was totally responsible for their creation. As soon as Hannah was able, they attended Mass as a family, Mikey with Anthony in his arms, Hannah with Oonagh in hers and Kitty following behind with the two older boys, each clutching one of her hands.

Mikey had donated some money to the church and so the family now had their own pew with a brass plate on the side inscribed with the name "Michael Whelan and Family". The family followed Mikey in procession, down the aisle to the front of the church and took their places there.

Hannah was now feeling stronger and decided that she had to rid the house of the card schools, particularly now that two more children were involved.

It was not only the presence of these men in her home to which Hannah objected; it was the fact that she was expected to provide sustenance for what she thought of as a group of foul-mouthed drunkards. She refused to set foot in the room where the card-playing took place whilst the men were there because she knew that she would find it difficult to hide her disapproval and it would only serve to make Mikey angry. So it was Kitty who used to take the tray of food through to the men. Fortunately, in her innocence, the lewd and suggestive comments that came her way had no effect on her. She just smiled, dumbly unaware.

Although Hannah's protests continued, it reached the point where she knew that there was no way that Mikey was going to stop. He justified his gambling to her by saying that it was the gambling that had provided a great deal of the funds which had helped create such a successful business and such a good home.

She asked why the card evenings always had to take place at their home and never at the homes of any of the other participants. She had decided that she could tolerate his card-playing anywhere, as long as it was away from Springfield Road. But Mikey would have none of it and, particularly after a few drinks, would become aggressive if she raised the subject, insisting that he would do what he bloody well liked in his own home.

It was not just the card evenings themselves that were a problem to Hannah; it was also Mikey, staggering up to bed in the early hours of the morning and collapsing in a drunken stupor. If he wasn't too drunk, he would demand his rights as a husband and Hannah would turn her head away from his whiskey breath, just waiting for it to be over.

She was sad, because her love for Mikey was still strong but she wondered why he couldn't see that his actions were hurting and upsetting her or, if he could see, why he didn't appear to care.

Her distaste of these activities was shown not only on the actual evenings when the men were present, but in a frostiness and aloofness towards Mikey which she couldn't help, but which often lingered on for days afterwards. And their relationship slowly deteriorated.

One night, after one such evening, Mikey staggered upstairs to bed as Hannah came out of Oonagh and Anthony's bedroom in her dressing gown, her long hair loose down her back. Anthony had been restless and his cries had woken Hannah. She had tended to him but was concerned because he was feverish and distressed. She had eventually managed to settle him and was on her way back to bed when Mikey stumbled up the stairs and into the bedroom, cursing as he bumped into furniture.

'Do we have to have this carry-on every single week?' she said angrily. 'The drinking is bad enough but I don't want the children to hear all the cursing and swearing. It's not a good example to be setting them.'

'Well, aren't you the Holy Mary then,' Mikey slurred mockingly. 'For God's sake, stop nagging, woman. This is my house and they are my children and I'll do what I bloody well like.'

'They're my children as well,' Hannah replied, 'and I don't want them to think that it is acceptable to curse and swear. I don't know what's got into you these days, Mikey. I hate it when you're like this.'

She took off her dressing gown and hung it on the hook on the back of the bedroom door. Mikey had removed his trousers and was standing in his underwear and socks, swaying. He stumbled across the room towards Hannah and grabbing her, threw her onto the bed, falling half across her.

'For God's sake, Mikey! Is that all you ever think about?' Hannah yelled as she tried to push him off. 'Anthony isn't well and I'm tired.'

As she struggled to free herself, Mikey raised his hand and slapped her across the face. Her head jerked back with the force of the blow and she felt tears come to her eyes. She put her hand to her face where Mikey had hit her, the red prints of his fingers across her cheek. Her tears flowed even more as Mikey grabbed her hair and forced himself upon her and then pushed her drunkenly aside.

Hannah lay still, sobbing quietly, finding it hard to believe what had actually happened. She lay until she thought that he was asleep, then eased herself gently out of bed so as not to wake him and went quietly downstairs to the kitchen where she made herself a cup of tea to calm herself. She was shaking, her hands unsteady as she filled the kettle. She drank her tea, her fingers flying back to her face from time to time, feeling the heat from her throbbing cheek She stayed downstairs until she had calmed herself and finally stopped shaking, then reluctantly she went back upstairs stopping at Oonagh and Anthony's bedroom to check once more on Anthony before she settled down for the night.

As soon as she entered the bedroom, she knew that something was wrong. Anthony's breath was coming in irregular, jerky gasps and his whole body was shaking violently. His face was flushed. She put her hand on his forehead, which was burning, then rushed into the bedroom where Mikey lay on his back, his mouth wide open and snoring.

Grabbing hold of his shoulders, she shook him furiously. 'Mikey! Mikey!' she cried. 'We need to call the doctor, Anthony's not well.'

The only response was a grunt as Mikey rolled onto his side. She shook him again but there was still no response, apart from an arm out-thrust to push her away. In exasperation and panic, she ran downstairs into the office where she found Dr Clarke's telephone number. With shaking hands she dialled.

'Come on! Come on!' she pleaded as she waited for the telephone to be answered. When it was finally answered, by Dr Clarke's housekeeper, she gasped out, 'It's Hannah Whelan here. Baby Anthony is ill. He's very hot and his breathing is strange. Can I speak to Dr Clarke?'

She waited impatiently while the housekeeper went to fetch Dr Clarke who spoke calmly and instructed Hannah to bathe Anthony with tepid water to try and lower his temperature and told her that he would be with her as soon as possible. Back upstairs, Hannah lifted Anthony out of his cot and went with him into the bathroom where she filled a bowl full of water. Kitty, who had been awoken by the noise, stood beside Hannah as she sat on a stool and started to undress Anthony, his body lying limp in her arms, offering no resistance to her actions. She started to sob, cradling him to her as she sponged down his tiny body. He gave a great shivering sigh and was quiet. In a panic, she shook him, trying to get a response from him.

'Anthony! Anthony!'

But there was nothing. She ran back into the bedroom with him in her arms.

'Mikey! Mikey! For God's sake, wake up!' she yelled, holding Anthony with one arm and punching Mikey violently with her free hand, tears streaming down her face, Kitty standing behind her, not sure what to do.

'For God's sake! What's the matter, woman?' Mikey slurred, putting up his hands to protect himself.

'It's Anthony! He's ill, really, really ill.' Her voice changed to a wail. 'I think he's stopped breathing. For God's sake, help me! Do something!'

She heard the staccato sound of the front door knocker and Kitty ran downstairs. Hannah followed with Anthony in her arms. As Kitty pulled open the door Hannah thrust Anthony towards the doctor.

'I think he's stopped breathing,' she wailed.

The remainder of the night passed in a haze for Hannah. Despite Dr Clarke's attempts to revive Anthony, it was all too late. Hannah sat cradling Anthony in her arms, talking to him and stroking him. Mikey sent Kitty to fetch Hannah's mother. He felt useless, his brain was still not functioning properly because of the effects of the alcohol. He was unable to help or comfort Hannah who sat and wept, pushing him away when he went near her.

It took all Maisie's strength when she arrived, to prise Anthony away from Hannah whose hands desperately held onto him, talking to him as though he were still alive. Maisie placed the tiny body, now wrapped once again in a blanket, on the big bed in Mikey and Hannah's bedroom, tears running down her cheeks.

Mikey too wept. Great heaving sobs. His whole body shaking with grief and guilt.

Dr Clarke stayed a while, trying to comfort the distraught parents but telling Maisie as he left, 'I am so sorry! There was nothing that I could do. Comfort them, but let them cry.'

Dr Clarke called again the following morning to see if there was anything that he could do for the family. He told them that there was an epidemic of scarlet fever and many children had been affected but that was no comfort to Hannah or Mikey.

A few days passed and the tiny wooden casket was lowered into the ground. It was almost more than Hannah could bear. Her baby, Anthony, alone in the dark, cold ground.

It was almost as if the weather echoed the grief of Hannah and Mikey. The sunshine left Springfield Road and dark clouds appeared in the sky. The rain started and went on for days, not that Hannah was aware or even cared. She would not allow Mikey near her. He was not allowed to offer her any comfort. And she gave him none.

She neither knew nor cared that he was full of guilt and remorse. She was convinced that if the events of that night had not taken place, Anthony would not have died. If Mikey had not demanded her attention, if he had not been drunk, Anthony might have been attended to earlier.

Each time she held baby Oonagh in her arms, tears filled her eyes. They had looked so alike, Oonagh and Anthony. Hannah insisted that Oonagh's cot was moved into their bedroom so that she could keep watch over her. She was terrified that the same thing that had happened to Anthony might happen to Oonagh. She found it difficult to sleep, listening for every grunt or snuffle, constantly getting out of bed to check that Oonagh was still breathing. She took to leaving all the bedroom doors open, wandering up and down the landing so that she could also hear the two older children if they stirred in their sleep. She was like a ghost figure, pale and thin, her face grey and drawn.

At first Mikey was patient with Hannah, because of his own feelings of guilt, but after a while her constant tears and unhappiness began to make him impatient with her. He too was grieving, but life had to continue. He wanted Oonagh back in her own bedroom so that there was a possibility that normal relations could be resumed between them for, with Oonagh in their bedroom, Hannah would not allow him near her in bed, afraid that any noise might disturb the baby.

But life did eventually begin to assume an element of normality. It was Patrick who was the instigator of the change. Coming upon Hannah in the kitchen, weeping one day, he climbed upon her knee and stroked her face with his chubby hand trying to wipe away her tears.

'I'll kiss you better and take the hurt away,' he had said.

They were the words of comfort that Hannah used whenever one of the children had taken a tumble. Now the situation was reversed. Hannah smiled despite the tears and hugged Patrick to her, realizing that she had been sorely neglecting her other three children, wrapped up as she was in her own grief.

'Mummy's alright, my darling,' she said. 'The pain has started to go away already.'

But nevertheless, although things improved and she began once more to pay more attention to the children and the house, Mikey would still sometimes come across her as she sat in the kitchen, her elbows on the table and her chin resting in her hands, staring blankly. He did not dare to ask her what her thoughts were, in case the question let loose tears or recriminations. On summer evenings after the children were in bed, she would often sit in the front garden, reading or sitting silently by herself, in a little corner where she had created a peaceful haven away from the house and telephone.

Chapter 14

The card schools at Springfield Road had stopped as Mikey had realised that it wasn't appropriate, in the circumstances, to have a group of loudmouthed, heavy-drinking men in the house. But Mikey had not given up gambling entirely. The card-playing was replaced by another hobby, one in which he had indulged from time to time in the past.

Near to JJ's farm in Ireland, there were large stables owned by a man called Martin Buchanan. The horses were all bred for racing and the man who trained the horses was Danny O'Donnell who had become a good friend of JJ, Mikey's father. Mikey's brother, Anthony, had written to ask if Mikey and Hannah could accommodate a couple of jockeys who were to visit Liverpool to race in The Grand National at Aintree racecourse and Mikey had welcomed them.

The two jockeys who had arrived to stay that first year were Tommy McLaughlin and Jamie Spencer who were both quiet and gentle men, and the evenings were spent chatting and reminiscing about Ireland or telling stories about some of the joys and disappointments that they had experienced in their lives as jockeys.

It soon became a regular event that if Tommy or Jamie were racing anywhere in the area, they would visit Hannah and Mikey. They always arrived with a gift of some sort, a bottle of Irish whiskey for Mikey, a length of linen for Hannah and one year, a painting of a horse named "Lough Conn" after a large lake in County Mayo near to the stables where the horses were trained and where Mikey had spent his childhood. Hannah hung the painting in pride of place in the hall, just inside the front door where it could be seen by everyone who visited.

Hannah always enjoyed the times when Tommy and Jamie stayed. She appreciated their company far more than the loudmouthed card-players who frequented the house and Mikey always moderated his drinking when they were around, not wishing to appear brash and vulgar in front of these two softly spoken men.

They had long conversations with Mikey telling him about the background, breeding and training of many of the horses and Mikey began to consider himself something of an expert. He began visiting race meetings throughout the north of England whenever he had the opportunity. Although Hannah intrinsically disapproved of gambling, she found this new pastime far more acceptable than the card-playing and the people associated with it.

But this distraction lasted only a short time before Mikey became bored, and the card schools started up again, much to Hannah's distress. They were now firmly linked in her mind with Anthony's death but she knew that it was futile to try and persuade Mikey to stop, so she closed her eyes to what was going on and kept the children well away from the back room where the card-playing took place.

Hannah soon realised that she was pregnant again. There was no joy in her heart over this pregnancy. She was nervous about having the responsibility of a tiny baby again and the three other children, despite Kitty's help, were still hard work. Patrick, at five was full of mischief and she sometimes felt that John was in competition with Patrick to see who could wreak the most havoc. She often felt that if she took her eyes off them for one minute there would be a problem. Oonagh, however, was a calm and sweet child and replaced Patrick as Mikey's favourite. He would allow Oonagh to take liberties that he would never have dreamt of allowing the two boys.

She had a mop of dark curly hair and followed her father everywhere. He would sit bouncing her on his knee while she played with his waistcoat buttons or carry her on his shoulders when he went to speak to the men in the yard. Wherever he went she was never far behind.

It was around the time that Hannah realised that she was pregnant that she also realised that Kitty was struggling to do the work that she had previously coped with easily.

'Are you alright, Kitty? Am I giving you too much to do?' Hannah asked one day, aware that when she had been so wrapped up in her own grief that Kitty had been forced to take over most of the work.

'I've not been feeling too good, missus, for a few weeks now,' said Kitty. 'Ah! I'm sure I'll be alright, in another couple of days, so I will.'

'In what way have you been feeling unwell?' Hannah's face showed concern.

'I've been awful tired and I keep being sick.'

'Do you mean that you've been vomiting?'

'Yes, missus,' Kitty nodded. 'I thought it must have been something that I'd ate but it's taking a long time for the sickness to go away, so it is.'

Hannah looked concerned and hoped that what she was thinking was not correct.

'Do you have a man friend at all, Kitty?' she asked gently.

'I was seeing a young fella six or seven months back. Ah, but sure it came to nothing. Wasn't he seeing someone else behind my back.'

Hannah tried to think of the best way to ask the next question.

'Have you ever been with a man?' she asked softly, putting

her hand on Kitty's arm. 'Don't be afraid to tell me if you have.'

'What do you mean, missus?' Kitty was puzzled. 'Haven't I just told you, missus, that I was seeing a fella a while back.'

Hannah was struggling, not quite knowing how to express her next question.

'What I mean is..... has any man...' she rushed the words out quickly, 'put any of his parts inside you?'

Kitty looked worried and looked away.

'What is it, Kitty? Don't be afraid to tell me. I won't get angry.'

Kitty still didn't answer but Hannah persisted.

'Kitty,' she said gently, 'tell me. I promise I won't be angry.'

'Only the master, missus,' Kitty blurted. 'It was only the master and it was just to help him, so it was.'

Hannah's chest felt tight. She felt herself go cold and clutching at the back of a chair to steady herself, she asked, 'What are you saying, Kitty?'

'It was only the master, missus,' she said. 'He told me not to say anything to you because you'd be too upset, what with the baby dying and everything. He said that you didn't have the strength to comfort him and it would do him a power of good if I comforted him instead.'

Hannah had to continue despite the pain that she felt. 'Was it just the once that you.....comforted him?'

'No, missus.' She shook her head. 'There was one time just after the poor baby died, I was only trying to help him, sure I was, and you and him so upset with baby Anthony dying and everything. I knew that you couldn't help him because you were that upset yourself.' She paused and looked anxiously at Hannah. 'I didn't do anything wrong did I, missus?'

'Ah! Kitty love.' Hannah sighed and shook her head. 'How often did you....comfort.. the master?' Hannah asked wearily.

'I don't know, missus. But a fair few times since the baby died, so I did,' Kitty replied.

Hannah's emotions were in turmoil. She felt angry and near

to tears. How could Mikey have betrayed her, like this. She knew that she had been distraught after Anthony's death and that they had drifted apart but surely he should have been trying to heal wounds, not create more. But she was not only angry about his betrayal of her; she also found it hard to believe that he could have been so despicable to take advantage of poor, simple Kitty.

'Kitty, love, will you go off now and get the children ready for bed? As soon as I've seen to the master's dinner, I'll be up to have a talk to you.'

Kitty turned and left the room glancing at Hannah as she did so. 'Sure, I was only trying to help, missus, so I was,' she said with a worried expression on her face.

Hannah busied herself, automatically setting the table and then sat down to wait for Mikey. When he arrived home, Barney was with him. They walked through the door, both laughing at a story that Barney had been telling. Mikey pulled out two chairs and indicated to Barney to sit down. He glanced in Hannah's direction.

'I've asked Barney to eat with us tonight, Hannah.'

Hannah stood, knuckles white, her hands clenching the side of the table.

'I'm sorry, Barney, but I don't think that it's a good idea tonight. I need to have a few words with Mikey,'she said in a tight voice.

Barney glanced at Hannah and realised that there was something very wrong.

'Sure. Look, no problem, Hannah. Let's forget it for tonight. There's plenty of food needs using up at home. I'll catch up with you later, Mikey.' He nodded to them both and left.

'What's all this about then?' Mikey asked angrily. 'What's wrong with you? I asked Barney to have something to eat with us and you treat him as though he's a leper.'

'There's nothing wrong with me, Mikey, apart from being pregnant, but more to the point, it's what's wrong with Kitty that's the problem.'

Hannah tried to keep her voice from shaking. She watched his face as she spoke. 'I'm going to have to take Kitty to see Dr Clarke tomorrow. She's not well.'

'What's the matter with her?' Mikey bent to untie his bootlaces.

'I think the poor girl's pregnant.'

His head jerked up and he looked at Hannah.

'What makes you think that?' He glanced away, unable to hold Hannah's gaze.

'She's been vomiting and haven't you noticed the extra weight she's put on?'

'Ah! Sure. That could be anything at all,' said Mikey. 'Sure, she's a good appetite on her, that one, so she has.'

Hannah exploded and banged her hand down on the table.

'For God's sake, Mikey. What on earth got into you? The poor girl doesn't even know how babies are made.'

'What do you mean? What got into me?'

'Don't, Mikey! Just don't say anything else! The poor girl's upset because she let it slip to me that she'd been "comforting" you.' She gave a hard laugh. 'She told me that you had asked her not to tell me.'

Mikey blustered, 'What's a man supposed to do? You wouldn't let me near you, Hannah. You wouldn't even perform your duties as a wife. Sure a man has to find comfort somewhere, so he does.' He paused. 'Anyway, how do you know the baby's mine? It could be anybody's!'

Hannah's voice was harsh. 'Don't say anything else to make the matter worse, Mikey. We have to help the poor girl and move her away from here before tongues start wagging. And the first thing we have to do is take her to see Dr Clarke and make certain that she is pregnant. She doesn't have any idea that she might be yet. I didn't want to say anything to her until you and I had spoken and sorted out what we are going to do about it.'

The following morning Hannah took Kitty to see Dr Clarke who confirmed that Kitty was indeed pregnant. It was not the first time in his working life that he had come across a situation such as this where an employer took advantage of a young girl in his employment and made her pregnant. Although Hannah had not told him the exact situation, he had guessed and he felt sorry for her. She had suffered pain enough already, he thought. And as for poor Kitty, he silently shook his head, poor innocent that she was.

After a further discussion with Mikey, Hannah visited a convent in Preston, far enough away for it not to be an embarrassment and arrangements were made for Kitty to spend her confinement there. She would stay there until the baby was born and the baby would then be taken from her and placed in the orphanage run by the convent to await adoption.

Hannah had carefully explained everything to Kitty. How it was best for the baby to have both a mother and a father, and that if Kitty kept the baby she would be unable to work and look after it. For the sake of the unborn baby, Kitty had agreed that it was for the best. She knew that she couldn't take the baby back home to Ireland as, despite her innocence, she knew that to have a baby out of wedlock was a bad and wicked thing. She knew that she would be called a "loose" woman and she couldn't bring that disgrace on her mammy and daddy. She still didn't understand that her predicament was of Mikey's making and Hannah did not enlighten her.

While Kitty was at the convent Hannah visited her regularly. She had been put to work sewing and darning, for the nuns would not allow anyone to be idle.

'You must tell me, Kitty, if any of them are unkind to you.'

Hannah knew that some of the convents which took in unmarried mothers were not necessarily "Christian" places, but had reputations for being places of cruelty where the young women in their care were punished for their sins and she was determined that Kitty was not going to suffer any more than she had done already as a result of Mikey's wrongdoing.

Hannah was with Kitty when her baby son was born and

Hannah, remembering the loss of her own child, felt the pain that Kitty must have felt when, after a few weeks, her baby was taken away.

After Kitty had fully recovered from the birth, Mikey and Hannah paid her fare back to Connemara. They had managed to find employment for her in a country house owned by a wealthy Irish family. The references that Hannah had written for her could not have been more flattering and Kitty couldn't thank them enough.

'I'll never forget this, missus,' she told Hannah tearfully, 'the way you've looked after me and been so good to me. I don't know how you're going to manage with the little ones all on your own, but I wish you and the master the best of luck, so I do.'

Hannah's own baby was due a couple of months after Kitty left for Ireland but she moved out of the bedroom that she had shared with Mikey and into the room that Kitty had occupied. As far as she was concerned the marriage was over apart from outward appearances. She would continue keeping house, working in the business and looking after the children but she was never going to share a bed with Mikey again.

Their baby, David, was born and, like the two older boys, had the O'Donehue red hair. She remembered the feeling of relief that she had felt when she had seen the dark head of Kitty's baby appear. It would have been just too much for her to cope with if Kitty's baby had also had red hair. She puzzled that Mikey expressed no interest in his other son, now taken away to be cared for by complete strangers, and it made her feel even more guilty when she thought about the baby who would probably spend his early years in an orphanage with no mother or father to offer him love and comfort.

With four children to look after, work still to do in the office and no Kitty to help, Hannah decided that she needed to employ someone to help her in the house once again. But she was determined that she would not make the same mistake twice.

This time she selected a mature English woman, a widow in her fifties. She was a large woman, who wore long, heavy, dark clothes, her grey hair scraped back from her plain face into a bun. Hannah wanted no repeat of the situation with Kitty and was not going to put temptation in Mikey's way.

The lady's name was Mary White and she moved into Springfield Road and was given a room on the attic floor. She was soon efficiently in charge of the household, leaving Hannah more time for the children and the business. Hannah knew that Mary would stand no nonsense from Mikey and it amused her to think that he would not even have been tempted to try.

But Hannah knew that Mikey was finding satisfaction elsewhere. He often stayed out late at night and she knew that it was not because he was drinking or card-playing. She no longer cared, as long as it wasn't under her roof. She had hardened her heart against him and had decided that she could hardly complain if he did find sexual satisfaction elsewhere, but she hoped and prayed to God that he'd take care and not make any other poor girl pregnant.

To outside eyes, the relationship between Hannah and Mikey was one of mutual respect and, within certain parameters, that was so. Hannah ran a competent and efficient home and office and worked hard and Mikey respected that. Equally, Hannah knew that it was Mikey's flare and willingness to take chances, where others might not have done, that had made the business so successful.

Hannah knew that Barney suspected that there were problems between herself and Mikey, although she was sure that Mikey had never discussed anything with him. She knew that Barney couldn't have helped but notice Kitty's increase in weight and subsequent disappearance and he knew that Hannah made regular visits to the convent in Preston. It would not have taken a genius to work out what the situation was.

But Barney said nothing to either Mikey or Hannah; he merely watched and felt sorry that the marriage of two people who meant a lot to him and whom he classed as friends was in disarray.

Hannah was also aware that Mrs White must wonder about their sleeping arrangements but she knew that Mrs White was discreet and, from comments that she had made to Hannah, that she herself had experienced a less than perfect marriage.

With Hannah's rejection of him, Mikey's drinking and gambling increased even more. He had become a member of the Royal Order of Ancient Buffaloes or "the Buffs" as Mikey called them. It was a charitable organisation which had many prominent local businessmen as members and Mikey began to spend more and more time at the clubrooms where there was a bar.

Sunday became a day which was increasingly devoted to drinking. The family no longer went to Mass together. Hannah would go to an early Mass with the older children, Patrick and John, whilst Mrs White looked after the younger ones.

Mikey would set off for the later Mass at eleven o'clock, black prayer book in hand, but he never arrived at the church nor even intended to. His church-going days were over.

Hannah knew what he was doing but said nothing. As far as she was concerned, as long as the children didn't know that Mikey was not attending Mass, there was no problem. He could do as he liked.

Instead of Mass, Mikey would go to the bar at "the Buffs" where he would join his hard-drinking friends and stay drinking well into the afternoon. He would then stagger home for Sunday lunch, where Hannah had the food prepared and she and the children waited his arrival. On one occasion only, Hannah, when Mikey had been particularly late returning, had started lunch without him because the children were fractious and hungry. It was an event not repeated. His drunken shouting and swearing had terrified the children and Hannah had been relieved that it was Mrs White's day off and she was not there to witness the outburst.

After Sunday lunch Mikey would usually settle in his armchair at the side of the fireplace and sleep, the children tiptoeing about so as not to waken him. As long as he was asleep, there could be no angry words. When he had slept off the effect of his dinner and the alcohol he would set off for the local public house where he would stay until closing time. Hannah always made sure that she was in bed before he came home, her door closed, to avoid his drunken behaviour.

Sunday was not Hannah's favourite day!

Chapter 15

One day, at the beginning of August 1914, Hannah looked out of the window and saw that there was a commotion in the yard. The neighbours who lived on either side of the haulage company had gathered in the yard and were talking excitedly to Mikey.

Mikey glanced towards the house and, noticing Hannah at the window, gestured for her to join them. As she appeared at the back door Mikey rushed towards her.

'It's war! It's war! England has declared war on Germany,' he called. 'The Government's decided that they can't stand by and do nothing now that Germany has invaded Belgium.'

'Oh, my God! That's terrible news.' Although there had been rumours of war for many months, Hannah was shocked. She had hoped that war would not materialise and she immediately wondered what it was likely to mean, most importantly to the family and, to a lesser degree, the business.

The neighbours stood around and discussed what was likely to happen to those members of the forces who were already enlisted and whether there would be more recruitment. Some of the younger members were excited at the prospect of war and there was much talk of 'sorting out' the Germans and 'We'll show 'em!'

Hannah left them to their discussions, concerned that they

appeared to be glorifying the situation. She shook her head, wondering if any of them realised what war really meant. She was not sure that she did herself, but she knew from her history books that it only boded ill. She went inside to tell Mrs White the bad news knowing that the daily newspaper, when it arrived the following day, would have more information than she would be able to impart for the moment.

Four days later, on August the eighth, under the Defence of the Realm Act, the Government assumed direct control of many resources and communications, including railways, docks and harbours and imposed many other restrictions on the citizens of Great Britain. Mikey and Hannah were concerned at this development, particularly the part relating to the docks. They were not sure how it was going to affect their livelihood, as most of Mikey's work involved going backwards and forwards to the docks.

In addition to this worry, there were reports that in many of the factories throughout the country, particularly those that produced non-essential or luxury goods, orders had already been cancelled and employees placed on a reduced working week. Mikey and Hannah were both aware that if the factories were not producing the goods, there would be less need of a means to transport them and that Mikey still had money outstanding on a further loan from Martin's Bank for two more lorries and the wages of five extra men to pay. He had employed two extra drivers and two second-men to man the two new lorries and a further driver to replace himself. He had given up driving only six months earlier and had planned to spend the released time canvassing for more business but now he wondered if perhaps he hadn't been too hasty and should have taken more heed of the rumours. He had trusted to luck, as he had for most of his life but now wondered if his luck might not have run out.

It wasn't long before leaflets and posters appeared everywhere, the result of a massive recruiting campaign under the direction of Lord Kitchener, the War Secretary, asking for volunteers from men between the ages of nineteen and thirty-eight and more than five feet three inches tall. The response to Kitchener's appeal was dramatic with thousands of young men, from all walks of life, queuing at recruiting offices to offer their services.

'Well! I for one won't be rushing into it,' Barney said and Hannah thanked God that none of her three sons were anywhere near old enough to participate.

The main war industries, however, began to thrive. Women were being encouraged to work in the munitions' factories doing the work previously carried out by men, many of whom were now away fighting, and further factories were commandeered to help with the manufacture of weapons and aeroplane parts.

Hannah, because of the children, was unable to contribute to the war effort directly by undertaking any of the work in factories as many other women were doing and she also had to support Mikey in the business but, determined to play her part, she organised a group of women in similar circumstances to knit blankets and socks for the menfolk away on active service.

Towards the end of the year all men between the ages of fifteen years and sixty-five years were required to enrol on a national register, so that the government had an accurate idea of what its fighting force might be and also to inform the government of how many of these men were employed in vital work.

As the level of voluntary enlistment dropped, many thought that it was inevitable that enforced conscription would occur, particularly as many of those who had previously volunteered were returning from the war injured and many more had been killed in action. It was clear that a larger fighting force was needed.

In January 1916, a Military Service Bill was introduced which required all single men between the ages of eighteen and forty-one years of age to present themselves for action and it wasn't long before Barney arrived at Springfield Road to tell Mikey and Hannah that he had been conscripted.

'It's a pity I haven't a wife. Sure, I'd have gone and got myself any auld biddy if I'd known this was going to happen,' Barney told Hannah. 'The tales you hear wouldn't make anyone want to take part in this damned war.'

But it would have made no difference to Barney whether he had married or not, because only a short time after, in May 1916, all males between eighteen and forty-one years, whether married or not, became liable for service.

Mikey's business was still managing to survive. Lorries were still essential, often used to back up military vehicles in the transportation of goods within the country. He had managed to obtain a contract for work transporting munitions from some of the factories which had been taken over by the government to make weapons and armaments. This meant that the work that he was doing was classed as essential work, with the result that Mikey was not conscripted.

'If Barney had been a driver as opposed to a second-man,' Mikey told Hannah, 'he might have got away with it.'

At the beginning of the war there had been panic buying as people stocked up and hoarded food but, by the end of 1916, people had settled into a routine and food shortages were not a problem. However, problems were to come.

A large amount of food was imported from America on merchant ships. Early in the war, the ships transporting these goods were not targeted by the Germans but, in 1917, the Germans introduced unrestricted submarine warfare and merchant ships were sunk with great frequency. This meant that vital goods such as grain were in short supply. Those with money were able to buy what they wanted but those without the means to do this had reached a point where many began to suffer from malnutrition.

'If you're able to pay the price you can get anything you want, war or no war,' Paddy Grady said, and this was indeed true as Hannah and Mikey experienced, for Paddy, with his dealings on the black market, remembered his friends and helped them out when he could. But the Government, aware that many were suffering hardship and were unable to pay the large sums of money that were often demanded for vital supplies, introduced rationing which ensured that everyone had a fair share of food. In January 1918, sugar was rationed, followed by meat, butter, cheese and margarine. Ration cards were issued and everyone had to register with a butcher and grocer.

Meanwhile, Hannah had dug over the front garden and had started to grow vegetables in an area hidden from the view of passers-by, screened by a privet hedge on three sides. The roses that she had planted when she had first married Mikey were now replaced by the more essential cabbages, potatoes, peas and beans.

Hannah and Mrs White worked hard at economising and saving money. The small amount of meat that they were allocated was turned into stews and bulked out by the vegetables that Hannah grew in the front garden. Collars and cuffs on shirts were turned and resewn and worn sheets were turned, so that the outer edges replaced the worn centres. Because of the scarcity of alcohol, Mikey's level of drinking reduced and life between Hannah and him became a little easier.

During the war years, Mikey's business flourished as a result of the contract that he had managed to secure but it was nevertheless with relief that the news that an Armistice had been signed on the eleventh of November 1918 was received and finally, in June 1919, The Treaty of Versailles was signed and the war was over.

Life very slowly returned to some normality. Within a few weeks Barney, who was one of the lucky ones, returned home but the tales that he told of the horrific sights that he had experienced were to live with him for the remainder of his life and cause him many sleepless nights.

'I think that I must have had the luck of the devil,' Barney said, 'to escape without any injury at all. Sure, some of them have suffered terrible injuries and thousands have died. It's strange, you can be talking to a man one minute and the next he's beside you with his head blown off.'

'Did that really happen to you, Barney?' Hannah asked in horror.

He nodded. 'There were some awful sights. Dead and injured bodies with rats crawling all over them.' He shuddered. 'And some of the poor lads who couldn't stand any more and were off their heads with the fear and horror of it all were shot as cowards.' He shook his head. 'Sure, war's a terrible thing and I wouldn't wish it on anyone. Let's hope that that's it for our lifetime at least.'

It became a common sight in the following months to see war veterans, some horribly maimed, about the streets of Liverpool, and many more, whose mental stability would never recover from the things that they had witnessed, were in hospitals or looked after by members of their families

Barney gradually settled back into his former role as second-man but also as a friend to Mikey who had missed him whilst he had been away.

There were many discussions long into the night, when Barney recounted the horror of his experiences.

'You were well out of it, Mikey. Don't ever let anyone try to tell you that war is glorious. It does things to some men …..it turns them into animals.' Barney sat quietly. 'But there are others it turns into heroes. People you wouldn't think had any backbone at all, doing amazing things when they have to.' He shook his head. 'But it's a bad, bad business. You were definitely well out of it.'

It was a strange experience for Mikey. He suddenly felt insignificant beside Barney.

With the war over the business started to prosper even more, and Mikey acquired more lorries and staff. If they were short of a driver or second-man, Mikey, never afraid of hard work, would step in and man one of the lorries. He was a hard man who demanded hard work from his employees and would not tolerate shirking.

It was Paddy Grady who put the idea that he should have a car into Mikey's mind. 'Now that you're such a big shot,' Paddy had said, 'why do you want to be walking or getting a tram everywhere you want to go? I know where you can get a real bargain. It's a black Wolseley and in perfect condition. It'll suit you down to the ground because it's big enough for the lot of you and it's got a big trunk as well for luggage.'

Mikey and Paddy went to look at the car and Mikey made a quick decision. He liked the look of it and he thought that Paddy was right. It was about time that he bought himself a car. He had not told Hannah of his search for a car and when he arrived home in it, he left it parked outside the front of the house and went through to the office where Hannah was working.

'Will you come outside with me for a minute?' he asked her.

She looked puzzled and asked, 'What for?'

'I've a bit of a surprise for you.'

He walked ahead of her and down the front path without saying anything.

'Well, what am I supposed to be looking at?' she asked.

'What do you think of it?' Mikey asked, pointing to the car.

'It looks very nice.' She was about to say 'Whose is it?' when she realised by the grin on Mikey's face what the surprise was.

'Oh, Mikey!' she exclaimed. 'Have you bought it? Is it ours?'

'Indeed I have and indeed it is.' Mikey was still grinning.

'It's wonderful.' Hannah opened the front passenger door and slid into the seat. 'Just think of all the places we'll be able to go. We'll be able to take the children into the country or out to the seaside and we'll be able to go shopping in it.'

'Hey! Wait a minute.' Mikey laughed. 'If we're to do all

those things, there'll be no time for work. We'll be too busy chasing all over the countryside, so we will.'

Mikey was pleased at the display of excitement from Hannah. It was a long time since she had shown much enthusiasm for anything that he had done, but Hannah's enthusiasm was more for what this might mean to the children than it was for anything to do with Mikey. It took her quite an effort to take four children anywhere and she could immediately see all sorts of opportunities opening up for her and them.

The children were growing fast and Patrick, now nine years old, and John, eight, were both doing well at school. John had inherited his mother and grandfather's ability with numbers. Oonagh was still her father's favourite and could do no wrong but David, who at four and a half was small for his age, received little attention from his father and the small attention that he did receive was often in the form of a rebuke. Hannah sometimes wondered if Mikey linked and blamed David in some strange way with the final breakdown of their relationship. But whatever the reason, she was determined that David would not suffer as a consequence and went out of her way to compensate for Mikey's disinterest.

As Patrick had grown older, it had become obvious that he did not have the same flare for numbers as his younger brother. Instead his talents lay with things mechanical and, from the age of seven, he began to spend time in the yard with his father. By the time that he was eleven or twelve his interest had become almost an obsession. He followed Mikey and Barney around asking questions about anything to do with the lorries. The steam lorries had originally fascinated him but some of these were now replaced by petrol-driven lorries and added another dimension to his interests.

He spent time pottering, connecting, disconnecting and checking how things worked. He was constantly covered in dirt and grease, but loved every minute of it. Hannah complained when he arrived home, supposedly straight from school, with his white school shirt and his grey trousers smeared with grease, having gone in through the back gate to the yard to avoid being stopped by his mother. After the war, the back gates had been constructed of heavy wrought iron, with letters fashioned in an arc above the gates, "Michael Whelan, Haulage Contractor" and painted the same shade of green as the lorries.

'I despair of you, Patrick,' Hannah often said. 'Why on earth can't you come in and get changed first before messing about in the yard?'

But Patrick's response, accompanied by a grin, was always the same, 'Sorry, Mammy, I keep forgetting!'

Patrick now, in addition to tinkering with the lorries, had a new toy added to his collection, namely the black Wolseley which he spent a great deal of his time cleaning and polishing until he could see his reflection in it.

Chapter 16

Soon after the war ended Mikey and Hannah visited Ballina again with the children, but Hannah, despite being fond of Bridie and JJ and despite some minor improvements which had been completed on the house, still found the cramped conditions uncomfortable, especially with four growing children. But the worst aspect of all was that she had to share not only a bedroom, but also a bed with Mikey. Hannah disliked being pushed into Mikey's company at night as he still made the occasional advance towards her, but she felt that an unspoken bargain had been struck. She would keep house and look after the children and the business, even turn a blind eye to Mikey's liaisons but in return he must not force his attentions on her.

Whilst they were on holiday in Ballina, Mikey persuaded JJ and Bridie to visit them in Liverpool.

'C'mon now,' he said to Bridie. 'The boys are perfectly capable of running the farm for a couple of weeks while you're away. Surely Anthony manages well enough on the times that Daddy has been ill, and the girls are more than capable of running the house for a couple of weeks. And you needn't worry about the cost. I'll look after all that for you.'

He wanted them to accompany the family when they returned to Liverpool, but they wouldn't be persuaded.

Eventually Mikey gave in and said, 'Right! I'll drop it for now, but only if you promise that you'll come over for my birthday. The hay will be in and things will have quietened down here on the farm for you by then. Is that a bargain?'

They had agreed and a few months later, after Mikey had left them little choice by sending them the money for their fares, Anthony had bought the tickets for them and they had arrived in Liverpool.

They had both been nervous about the journey, never having travelled outside Ballina before, but Anthony saw them securely on board the ship and settled them before leaving them.

'Well, you'll be one step ahead of me,' he told his parents. 'I've never been further than Mayo in my life. You'll have a grand time so you will and don't you worry about a thing. We'll look after everything here. Sure it's about time that you started taking things a bit easier now anyway.'

The journey was a long one for JJ and Bridie, who were both quiet and retiring people outside their own immediate circle of family and friends. They kept themselves very much to themselves on the journey and they were both relieved when they eventually docked in Liverpool.

When Mikey, accompanied by Patrick, met them off the ship and escorted them to the large black Wolseley, their nerves had subsided and they were suitably impressed by the vehicle which waited for them.

'My God, Mikey, now isn't this a fancy vehicle!' said Bridie when she saw the car and, as Mikey helped her into the back, she stroked the gleaming paintwork and the leather seats. She sat back proudly as Mikey and JJ put the scant luggage into the boot and slammed it shut.

The journey to Springfield Road was interspersed with, 'Oh! Would you just look at that now! Did you ever see such a thing in your life before?' and 'Oh! My God! Isn't that a marvel.'

Mikey was amused and delighted at their excitement and he

stopped repeatedly, proudly pointing out landmarks or answering questions.

When they arrived at Springfield Road, Hannah, Mrs White and the other three children were all waiting to greet them. They had heard the car arrive and were standing outside the front gate.

'Is it this that's your place?' Bridie asked as they drew up outside. 'It's a grand big house, so it is.'

Mikey winked at Patrick as he opened the car door for Bridie.

'Indeed it is my place, Mammy,' he said. 'Sure, we wouldn't be taking you to stay with anyone else, now would we? And what do you think Hannah would be doing here if it wasn't my place?'

'Come in! Come in!' Hannah said as she helped Bridie from the car. 'Patrick, take the bags up to Grandma and Granddad's room. It's great to see you both,' she said, hugging and kissing them.

Bridie's eyes opened wide as she looked about her and repeated what she had said to Mikey. 'It's a grand big house, so it is.'

She followed Hannah into the house and down the terracotta-tiled hall. Hannah pointed out the picture of Lough Conn on the wall. 'That's the painting that Tommy McLaughlin and Jamie Spencer, the two young jockeys, brought out to us. The one that Mikey wrote and told you about,' she said.

'It's grand, sure enough. And isn't it the spitting image of the horse himself?' JJ said, admiring the picture before glancing around the spacious hallway.

Mrs White appeared from the kitchen with a tray in her hands and carried it through to the sitting room, where Mikey now stood fidgeting. He knew that his parents needed refreshment but he was impatient to show his father the yard and the lorries with his name emblazoned across the doors.

When they had taken their tea and eaten the warm scones,

spread with cream and jam, which Mrs White had prepared for them, Mikey left Hannah to show Bridie the house and office whilst he took his father outside to show him the yard.

'Well, Mikey, you've certainly done well for yourself,' JJ commented.

'It was a lot of hard work,' Mikey agreed, 'but I'm more than happy with the way things have turned out.' He glanced at his father to see his reaction as he said, 'And wasn't it all worth the running at the fairs for.'

JJ shrugged. 'Well, it's easy enough to say that now, but at the time your mammy and myself were struggling just to put food in our mouths, so it's not surprising we thought differently then. But that's all forgotten now, so it is, and we've been grateful for all the help that you've given us.'

They stayed outside for some time chatting and Mikey opened the cab doors so that his father could climb up and inspect the insides of the vehicles.

'And what sort of stuff do you transport in the lorries?' JJ asked.

'All manner of things,' Mikey replied. 'Whatever anyone asks me to. During the war it was often aircraft parts. Sometimes even parts of guns...the big stuff, you know, not handguns or anything like that but there was a fair bit of security. Everything was checked and double-checked. You can come out with me tomorrow, if you fancy it. We've a load of bales of cotton to collect from the docks but we'll have to be away early.'

'Now, am I not used to getting up early,' JJ replied. 'Have I ever been known to have a lie-in?'

Meanwhile, inside the house, Bridie was like a child as Hannah showed her around all the rooms including the bedrooms with, as Bridie said, "the fancy furniture".

'Is it fires you have blazing away in every room?' she asked.

Hannah laughed. 'It's not like this all the time, Bridie. This is a special occasion. We normally just use the kitchen to sit and to eat in, except when we have visitors and then we use the sitting room, like today. That's why the fire's lit there. And the room that's your bedroom hasn't been used for a while, so it needed a bit of airing.'

Hannah laughed again when she saw the expression on Bridie's face when they all sat down at the table for their dinner and Bridie and JJ saw the display of food on the table.

'It's a meal fit for a king,' Bridie said, 'and aren't you a good cook an' all.'

'I tell you, Bridie,' Hannah said again smiling, 'we don't eat like this all the time but, as I said before, this is a special occasion, the very first time that you have visited us. And didn't you put on a great spread for us whenever we visited you. Anyway, it's our Mrs White, our treasure, who's done most of the cooking.'

The following day JJ and Bridie went their separate ways, JJ joining Mikey as he went about his work and Bridie staying with Hannah and the children. Although JJ was not a drinking man, it became established that at the end of each day he sat with Mikey and Barney and had a glass of whiskey and a chat in one of the bars.

It was some of the political events that JJ spoke about which interested Mikey most. Ted O'Malley's comments, many years earlier, about Mikey's lack of knowledge about the background to some of Ireland's problems still rankled a little with Mikey.

He had no wish to be active politically but he sometimes felt embarrassed, when questioned about Irish affairs, at how ignorant he was and it was a strange feeling for Mikey, now so confident and in control of his life in Liverpool, to be tutored by his father about the history of his homeland.

The conversations continued from the bar to the dinner table and Mikey became amazed about how much his father knew about the political mongering in and about Ireland, when he had always considered him to be living in a backwater and totally out of touch with current affairs. He looked at his father with a new respect. This was a totally different man to the man who had taken the belt to him as a young lad.

Mikey knew that, during the war, a lot of the antagonism that had existed between the English and the Irish had abated. There had been many Irishmen who had enlisted in the British Army prior to the war. In cities such as Liverpool, Newcastle and London there were large populations of Irish people and some regiments had been set up which actually incorporated the word "Irish" in the title, such as the "Tyneside Irish" which was formed within two months of the war starting, comprising four battalions of the Northumberland Fusiliers. In Liverpool there was "The King's Liverpool (Irish) Regiment" based at Seaforth and "The London Irish Rifles" were based at Chelsea.

'Although many people supported the English during the war, there's still a lot of people against the English, back home, so there is.' JJ then told Mikey about the British consular agent, Sir Roger Casement, who had championed the cause for Irish Independence. He had been convicted of treason and hanged in Pentonville prison in London after a consignment of German guns which he had organised for The Easter Rising in 1916 in Dublin was intercepted by a British Naval ship, "The Aud". The uprising had gone on anyway without the guns and was eventually quashed with the resulting executions.

'I read about Casement in the newspapers when he was tried and executed, but I suppose you only hear one side of a story, and that will have been the English side,' Mikey said to JJ.

'Well! After Casement was executed, the other fifteen were shot after the Easter Rising.' JJ reeled off the names of the fifteen: 'There was Padraig Pearse, Thomas MacDonagh, Thomas Clarke, Joseph Plunkett, Edward Daly, Michael O'Hanrahan, William Pearse, Sean McBride, Con Colbert, Eamonn Ceannt, Michael Mallin, Sean Hueston, James Connolly, Sean McDermott. And then there was Thomas Kent, executed at Cork jail, for God's sake!' He shook his head in disgust. 'One of our own and killed by his own, and there was even Thomas Ashe, kicking and screaming against it all, who died on hunger strike in 1917.

'Lots of folk who weren't in favour of the rebellion, like me, were disgusted at the executions. There was a lot of ill feeling when Connolly was shot by the firing squad while he was sitting down. He couldn't stand 'cos he was injured. That's no way to treat anyone, no matter what he's done.' JJ went further, 'They were fighting for what they believed in and isn't that what any man is entitled to do?'

'And hasn't it made martyrs of the lot of them,' Bridie said. 'The English did themselves no favours.'

Mikey listened to his father, amazed at the passion of his feelings. But then he wondered how much he knew about the feelings of his own wife and family.

Bridie spent her days with Hannah. She sat in the office with Hannah each morning whilst she completed her daily office chores. In the afternoon Hannah took Bridie out on a tram, sometimes into Liverpool where they went around the shops and had tea and sometimes she took her on the train to Seaforth or Waterloo, where they walked along the shore.

On the first Sunday that Bridie and JJ were in Liverpool, they all piled into the black Wolseley and Mikey drove them to Southport.

'That's The Prince of Wales Hotel where Hannah and I spent our honeymoon night,' Mikey said. 'I was terrified because I'd never stayed in a hotel before.'

'Well, you certainly didn't show that you were scared,' Hannah commented. She suddenly felt depressed, thinking about how happy she had been at that time, so full of expectation. And now she lived in a marriage which was more a business arrangement than anything else. She shook herself. She was being foolish. If she was honest and thought back to the days of Mikey's proposal, she knew that he had never professed to love her. It was she who had wanted more and for a time she thought that she had got more.

They had lunch at a café in Southport and JJ and Bridie loved it. Bridie particularly had revelled in the white damask tablecloths and napkins, not quite knowing what she ought to do with the napkins and the rows of cutlery, but following Hannah's lead.

The second Sunday they drove into the country towards Preston. Hannah shuddered at Mikey's choice of venue, her mind running back to memories of Kitty and her baby. But Patrick, with great glee and having no such memories, recounted the day when Mikey had bumped the car and the eggs, which they had bought from a farm as they had travelled, had ended up spattered all over both of them.

'You'd have thought that we'd both been sick on ourselves.'

Hannah laughed. 'I tell you it was a job that I could have done without, clearing up that mess!'

The holiday was soon over, but not before Hannah's parents were introduced to Bridie and JJ. Both pairs of grandparents took great delight in extolling the virtues of their communal grandchildren and it was a sad moment when it was eventually time for JJ and Bridie to return to home, laden down with presents from Mikey and Hannah for them and the rest of the family in Ballina.

'Don't worry!' said Mikey, as he hugged his mother and shook his father's hand as they boarded the ship. 'We'll be over before too long to see you again.'

With the departure of Bridie and JJ, Hannah was unable to stop thinking about the conflicting sides to Mikey's character. Whilst his parents had been staying he had moderated his drinking, had spent long periods of conversation with his father and had been gentle and kind to her and the children. She had almost been lulled into a false sense of security, thinking that her life with Mikey could always be like this but she knew that it was expecting too much. Life with Mikey had more downs than ups, but she couldn't understand how there were times when he was able to control his behaviour and his drinking, and other times when he appeared to be totally out of control and she wondered if in some way she was responsible.

Chapter 17

As soon as Patrick was able, with Mikey's blessing and encouragement but not with Hannah's, he left school and began to work in the yard alongside Mikey. If anything required repairing, it was to Patrick that Mikey turned and he became an invaluable part of the workforce.

This was another source of conflict between Hannah and Mikey. Hannah had wanted Patrick to remain at school and further his education.

'He could have gone on to be a teacher, or anything,' Hannah said, 'instead of spending all his time covered in grease.'

'If it was good enough for me, it's good enough for Patrick,' Mikey retorted angrily. 'The two boys are going to carry on the business when I'm dead and gone, so they may as well learn what it's all about now. It's always brought us in a decent living, so I don't know what you're complaining about.'

Hannah felt that the children would be better off if they had some element of independence. She felt that they should have some sort of training behind them and should not have to rely on Mikey for a living. His moods and his temper could change in a moment and she was worried that it might well place the boys at a disadvantage in the future.

But Patrick didn't want any other sort of training. He was

happy doing what he was doing and sided with his father against Hannah.

'Look, Mum, Daddy could do with an extra pair of hands right now. And what about later on when he might want to ease off the work himself, it would be better if there was one of us to step into his place.'

'You could still have some other sort of training first and then if anything went wrong with the business you would have something to fall back on.'

'But think about the time I'd be wasting,' Patrick replied. 'There's nothing else that I want training for. I'd rather be working in the yard.'

Hannah reluctantly had to concede defeat and Patrick happily started his first day at work.

Barney thought that it was great for Patrick to be working in the yard alongside his father, particularly as he proved to be an invaluable mechanic. He was based in the yard in charge of the general servicing and upkeep of the vehicles.

The car was a big attraction to Patrick and it wasn't long before he persuaded his father to allow him to learn to drive, initially driving in and around the yard until he was confident enough to be allowed out on the road. At first it was a hair-raising experience for Mikey, sitting beside Patrick with no control of the car, but Patrick was a good and confident driver and soon became Mikey's right-hand man, driving him everywhere.

The men were now kept constantly on their toes. There was no slacking, for they never knew when Mikey and Patrick would appear. Patrick enjoyed the feeling of importance that accompanying his father gave him, but it didn't make him many friends amongst the workmen.

Occasionally, Mikey would send Patrick out alone to check on the men. Nobody knew whether he would carry tales back to Mikey if they stopped for a smoke and chat, or stopped off at home for a cup of tea before returning to the yard.

'You're turning the men against him,' Barney said. 'He's

only a young lad and they think that you're sending him out spying on them.'

Mikey shrugged it off. 'If they're not trying to cheat me, they've nothing to be afraid of.'

But that wasn't the point as far as Barney was concerned. He saw Patrick becoming more and more arrogant and the dislike and the mistrust felt by the men towards him increasing and he felt that it was very unfair of Mikey to have put his son in that position.

A letter arrived from Anthony which said that JJ was ill and Mikey decided on the spur of the moment to visit Ballina once again.

'I don't think that I'll go with you this time, Mikey,' Hannah said. 'Now that the children are growing, I think it's best if we don't all go. It's a lot of work for Bridie and JJ having to switch all the sleeping arrangements about and it makes for a lot of extra work for her, cooking and cleaning as well.'

'Well, I'll need some company.' Mikey turned to Patrick. 'What about you; will you come with me, Patrick?'

'Do you not want me here to look after things?' Patrick asked, hoping that his father would say 'Yes.' He rather fancied being in charge of the business on his own.

'I think your mother is capable of managing. She'll have Barney to give her a hand if she needs it,' Mikey replied.

His decision was not taken without it having been given some thought. He had thought about Barney's concerns regarding Patrick and decided that a breathing space would do both Patrick and the workmen some good. He had not mentioned it to Barney but he had also become a little concerned about Patrick's behaviour towards the men. They had already lost one man, a good worker, who had told Mikey that he was not going to be ordered about by someone who was still wet behind the ears.

'And what about you, Oonagh? Do you fancy a trip to Ballina?' Mikey asked.

'She's supposed to be looking for a job,' Hannah interjected. Oonagh had left school the previous summer but had subsequently spent most of the time at home, unemployed. 'She's made precious little attempt so far.'

'Pops. I promise, promise, promise that I'll try really hard to find work when I get back,' she wheedled.

'Sure, it's not that desperate for her to find work. We're not hard up. It won't do her any harm if she comes,' Mikey said. And once again, Hannah was overruled over matters concerning her daughter.

It was decided that both John and David would stay behind with Hannah, a decision with which they were both happy. John because he had examinations looming and wanted to study and David because he had no wish to spend any more time than was necessary in his father's company and without the protection of his mother.

The three of them set off and Hannah was pleased at having more time with her two younger sons. She had a good relationship with all her sons but when she thought about her daughter she was often saddened. She had always assumed that mothers and daughters would have a close relationship, as she had with her own mother, but that was not so between herself and Oonagh. Sometimes she even felt that Oonagh deliberately created situations which undermined her authority. Hannah sighed. She had long ago recognised that Oonagh was not only spoilt but had also become very lazy and Mikey was encouraging the situation.

Hannah spent a lot of time with Barney whilst Mikey was away. They met each morning to allocate the work to the men and then again each evening to discuss the day's work, often over dinner. She enjoyed the period of freedom from Mikey. There was no need to feel constantly on edge trying to anticipate what sort of a mood he might be in, or whether he was going to arrive home drunk. The boys, particularly David, enjoyed the freedom as well.

'I wish Barney was my dad,' David said one evening after Barney had returned home.

'Don't let me hear you say anything like that again!' Hannah reprimanded him. 'Your father has worked hard for you and you should be thankful for everything that he has done for you.'

David looked at her, his gaze unwavering. 'Father has never done anything for me, or anyone else. Everything that he has done has been for himself.'

Hannah could not bring herself to answer him. She was shocked that David, so young, had such a cynical attitude towards his father but she had to admit to herself that perhaps he had good reason to feel that way and she also thought wryly to herself that it would have been a much easier life for David living with Barney rather than Mikey, so perhaps he had a point there as well.

It had not escaped some of the workmen's attention that Barney was spending so much time with Hannah.

'While the cat's away the mice will play, eh, Barney,' Joe Simpson, one of the drivers said to Barney.

'What do you mean?' Barney asked, his voice cold. 'I'm just doing my job like Mikey asked me.'

'Oh yeah!' Joe said grinning. 'And are you getting a few perks into the bargain?'

Barney was furious and before he realised what he was doing, his fist had made contact with Joe's nose.

'Don't you dare speak like that again unless you want me to have a few words with Mikey about what you've just implied. He wouldn't be past giving you a pasting.'

'I was only joking,' Joe muttered, clutching an oily handkerchief to his nose. 'I didn't mean any harm by it.'

'Well, if I hear you joking like that again, you'll live to regret it.'

Barney realised that one of the reasons that he was so angry with Joe was that he was fond of Hannah and Joe had touched a raw spot. He had enjoyed the evenings spent in the company of Hannah and the boys and it had made him yearn for the family life that he did not have. But, equally, he knew that there was no way that he would have taken advantage of his position, nor would Hannah have allowed him to.

In Ballina, Mikey was relieved to find that JJ was not as ill as Anthony had led him to believe.

'Sure didn't we think that he was at death's door a few weeks back,' Anthony said apologetically. 'He has the constitution of an ox, so he does, but I didn't mean for you to come chasing over here. Next time I won't be so quick to write to you.'

'Ah, well. I needed a holiday, anyway. And it's good to see that he's not too bad. He's getting a bit old for all the fetching and carrying anyway,' Mikey said. 'He needs to take it a bit easier.'

'I'm glad you came, Mikey,' Bridie said. 'Sure it's great to see you and we were worried about your daddy, but he's pulled around, so he has. Neither of us are getting any younger. Sure it would have been nice to have the lot of you here though. How are they all?'

'They're all well,' Mikey replied, 'but Hannah didn't think it was a good idea for us all to descend on you, with Daddy not being too good. It's a lot of extra work for you, so it is. Anyway, here's us worrying about all the work you might have had to do but what's this that Anthony was telling me, that you're having visitors tomorrow. Haven't you enough on your plate without entertaining?' Mikey laughed.

'It's not entertaining I'm doing,' Bridie said huffily. 'It's only Margaret Watson. She wants to bring her daughter, Carmel, over to meet you. Carmel is keen to find work in

184

England and she wants to ask your advice.'

'I'll help her if I can,' Mikey replied, smiling at Bridie's reaction to his comment.

The following afternoon, Margaret Watson and Carmel arrived to meet Mikey.

'Sure, I couldn't keep Carmel away when she knew that Bridie had visitors from England,' Margaret explained her visit. 'She fancies going and working there herself and wants to know all about it. Not that I want her to go but sometimes there's no stopping them when they get an idea in their head.'

'As I know only too well,' said Bridie looking at Mikey.

It soon became apparent that Carmel was more interested in talking to Patrick than to Mikey and Mikey listened in amusement as Patrick chatted to Carmel and built up his own part in the business.

'Wouldn't you think that he was in sole charge of the place?' he said to Bridie.

'Ah well! He's trying to create an impression. Sure they're only youngsters. There's no harm in it.'

The following morning Patrick told Mikey that he'd arranged to meet up with Carmel during the day.

'Is it smitten, you are?' Mikey asked. 'And you've only just met her.'

'Don't be silly, Dad.' Patrick was embarrassed. 'We're only going for a walk.'

On the subsequent days of the visit Patrick met up with Carmel every day and his grandmother watched the development of the relationship approvingly, despite the difference in their ages. Carmel was twenty-six and Patrick was twenty.

On the day before they were to leave, Patrick sat on the hillside with Carmel. He twisted a lock of her hair around his finger.

'God! I'm going to miss you. I feel as if I've known you forever.'

'I'll write. I'll write to you every day.'

'Promise.'

'I promise.'

It was dark when Patrick arrived back at the farm.

'We were just about to send the search party out for you, so we were,' Anthony said, teasing. 'You've seen Carmel safely home? Have you said your goodbyes then?'

Patrick looked embarrassed.

'She said she'd be across to say goodbye in the morning.'

When it was time for them to leave, Carmel arrived at the farm and she and Patrick said their reluctant goodbyes, watched with amusement by Mikey.

Oonagh was bored by it all. Contrary to her expectations she had not enjoyed the visit as Mikey had been involved with his parents, Anthony and the working of the farm. And Patrick, whom she had expected to be her escort and get her away from the farm, had been preoccupied with Carmel, so, as far as she was concerned, the sooner that she was back home the better.

When they arrived back in Liverpool Hannah was relieved to hear that JJ was not as ill as had been expected.

'But, you know,' Mikey said, 'every time I see them, I can see how much more they've aged. They've both had a hard life and it's beginning to show. I'm surprised that Anthony still wants to stick with it when he looks at the two of them.'

'Well, he doesn't have much choice, does he?' Hannah replied. 'He can't just leave them in the lurch.'

Letters passed between Patrick and Carmel at frequent intervals. One morning when Patrick collected his letter, instead of the usual engrossed read, Hannah saw his smile change to a frown. She reached for her mail. She was surprised to see a letter in handwriting that she didn't recognise, with an Irish stamp. It was from Carmel's parents to say that Carmel had told them that she was pregnant and that she had also told them that Patrick was the father.

'We've told no one yet about the situation but we know that the right thing for Patrick to do is to marry Carmel before it becomes too obvious that she is pregnant. The disgrace of it all in this place would be too much for us all to take.'

Hannah was shocked and dismayed as she silently handed the letter to Mikey. She had never even met Carmel and had no idea what the girl was like and thoughts of Kitty sprang to mind. She could not help but think "like father, like son" and hoped that Patrick had not taken advantage of a young, innocent girl.

A hasty visit was arranged to Ireland. If Bridie and JJ were surprised to see Mikey and Hannah, accompanied by Patrick, so soon after the previous visit, they did not say so. Oonagh had needed no persuading to stay this time at Springfield Road with John and David in the care of Mrs White. This time Barney was left in sole charge of the business.

Neither Mikey nor Hannah told either of Mikey's parents the reason for their visit.

'Let's not set the cat among the pigeons until we know what's going on,' Mikey suggested to Hannah. He had been not only angry, but disappointed with having to cope with the results of Patrick's problem.

Hannah was happy to agree, still hoping that there was going to be a way out of the situation but when she met Carmel she realised that the situation was not going to be resolved so easily. Instead of a shy and retiring, innocent young girl she found an extremely confident young woman, who insisted that she loved Patrick, that Patrick was the father of her child and that she wanted to marry him.

'Don't be pushed into this marriage,' Hannah said to Patrick. 'We'll see that she will be looked after financially and the baby taken care of.' It pained her to say it, because once again it brought back memories of Kitty and the guilt that she had felt on that occasion, but she did not want to see her eldest son tied into a marriage with a girl that he scarcely knew and at so young an age.

'For God's sake, Mother,' Patrick had replied, 'I love Carmel and even if she wasn't pregnant I would have wanted to marry her anyway.'

'Think hard about it, Patrick,' Hannah pleaded. 'You must be sure that you're not making a mistake. You're only a young lad and you've the rest of your life in front of you. For heaven's sake, you scarcely know the girl.'

'It's not so long ago, Mother, that lads younger than me were being signed up to go and fight for their country. If I am old enough for that, I'm old enough to decide whether I want to get married or not.'

And so a marriage was hastily arranged in Ballina. There had to be a three-week delay for the banns to be called before the wedding could take place. The public declaration had to take place on three consecutive Sundays in the Parish Church to allow time for any objections to the marriage to be presented and Mikey and Hannah stayed at the farm for those three weeks after phone calls had been made to Mrs White and Barney to inform them of what was happening.

Inevitably, Bridie and JJ were surprised that there was to be a wedding and, although they were not informed of the need for the haste, they reached their own conclusions. The wedding took place with only the close family present and afterwards Carmel returned with Hannah, Mikey and Patrick to Liverpool and moved into Springfield Road.

'What have you been up to?' Oonagh asked Patrick slyly when they arrived at the house. 'Who's been a naughty boy then?'

'It's none of your business,' Patrick blushingly replied, glancing at Carmel.

'What do you two think about being uncles, then?' Oonagh asked John and David, enjoying Patrick's discomfort.

'Hold your tongue.' Mikey, who had been watching the interchange, spoke angrily to Oonagh. 'It's bad enough that it's happened without the whole world knowing about our business.'

Some years earlier Mikey had purchased a plot of land with three small terraced houses on it. Two of the houses were already occupied but Hannah and Mikey decided that the third house could be renovated as a home for Patrick, Carmel and the baby. As soon as it was ready Patrick and Carmel moved in.

The renovation of the house had taken six weeks and Hannah was glad to have Carmel out of Springfield Road. She had tried at first to be kind to her, but Carmel had not responded. She had also suggested that Carmel should help Mrs White with one or two tasks but Carmel had shown little interest in doing so.

'She's a lazy madam,' Hannah told Mikey. 'You'd think that she'd want to help rather than have Mrs White waiting hand and foot on her.' She couldn't hide her exasperation. There was another factor in Hannah's antipathy towards Carmel. Hannah, no stranger to pregnancy, was puzzled by Carmel's lack of increasing size. It was no great surprise to her, therefore, when Carmel announced that there was to be no baby.

'Sure, I must have lost the baby,' Carmel said in tears, but would not be drawn any further. Hannah refrained from any comment at the time but spoke later to Mikey.

'I can't believe that Patrick allowed himself to be taken in by that girl,' Hannah expressed her dismay. 'It wouldn't surprise me if she hadn't been pregnant in the first place. There would have been more evidence of her losing the baby. She obviously thought that she was on to a good thing when she met up with Patrick.'

'Well, she's in for a bit of a surprise then,' Mikey said with determination, but did not elaborate on his statement.

The two women maintained a distance from each other. Hannah could not bring herself to show any affection towards

Carmel and Carmel stayed away from Springfield Road. She had her own home and a husband who would do anything for her and she was not bothered about Hannah's feelings towards her as long as Hannah did not interfere with her life.

But Patrick, although unhappy about the relationship between his mother and his wife, was not unhappy generally with the situation. Whether Carmel was pregnant or not was of no great importance to him. They were both young and fit and there was plenty of time in the future to have children. He enjoyed being with Carmel and loved her and was quite happy to have her to himself for a while longer, without a baby distracting her attention.

Chapter 18

John left school at the age of eighteen with flying colours and continued his education, much to Hannah's delight, by training as an accountant and following in her father's footsteps. On the recommendation of Jack, his grandfather, he had been accepted into an accounting practice in the centre of Liverpool where he had sat his exams as a chartered accountant.

Mikey had hoped that his two eldest sons would follow him into the family business and he was angry at John's decision not to. As JJ had been unable to understand Mikey's wish to stand independently of him, now Mikey also was unable to do the same with his own son. John was only repeating what he himself had done so many years earlier when he had left home to make his own way instead of following in his father's footsteps.

Mikey was particularly disappointed because he recognised that John, with his organisational abilities, would have been his true successor in the business for, despite Patrick being an excellent mechanic, Mikey had realised that he did not have the qualities which would make him a successful manager of men, nor a successful business man.

In a fit of pique and hoping that it would make John change his mind about his decision, and despite the fact that John was well settled in his profession, Mikey told Patrick that he was going to make him a partner in the business. The green cab doors on the lorries were repainted and the gold letters now proclaimed "Michael Whelan & Son" but it bothered John not at all. He had no wish to be in the control of his father.

Unfortunately for Patrick, that was as far as it went. The only share in the business that materialised was the "& Son" on the cab door.

'I've met a girl, Mother,' John told Hannah one evening. 'She's the daughter of Raymond Burns.' Hannah recognised the name as that of the senior partner of another large firm of accountants in the city. 'I'd like to bring her to meet you, I think you'll like her.'

'We'll have to think of the best time. Definitely not a Sunday,' Hannah said emphatically. 'We don't want to put the poor girl off.'

'No, definitely not a Sunday,' John agreed.

It was decided that John would collect Violet, the young lady in question, on his way home from work one Friday night, and bring her to Springfield Road for a meal.

'You'd better watch your drinking,' Hannah warned Mikey. 'I'll never forgive you if you ruin it for John.'

'Don't try and tell me what to do,' Mikey muttered. 'I've told you before, I'll do what I like in my own home.'

But on the Friday evening in question, he refrained from drinking and Violet was introduced to the family. The evening was a little strained as Mikey was not used to controlling his intake of alcohol and having to do so resulted in him being tense but, although the evening passed without any disaster, John decided that he needed to move out of Springfield Road. The fact that he had felt unable to bring his friends home because of the unpredictable behaviour of his father had been a constant problem as he was growing up and Mikey's behaviour that evening, although more controlled than was usual, allowed nobody to relax fully. John knew that Violet was probably sensible enough not to judge the remainder of the family by Mikey's behaviour but nevertheless he thought that the time had arrived when he ought to be looking for a home of his own, a home that he eventually wanted Violet to share.

He earned sufficient money to rent a small house close enough so that he could visit his mother regularly if he wished, but far enough away not to be troubled by his father. He felt concerned about David, who often turned to him for comfort when Mikey was being particularly unpleasant, and wondered how he would cope. He worried that he was being selfish, but also felt that he had his own life to lead.

'Stay out of his way,' he told David. 'If you know he's been drinking just steer clear of him. If it gets too bad you can always come and stay with me.'

'It's not always that easy to stay out of his way,' David replied. 'There are jobs that I have to do and if I'm not around to do them, I'll only end up in worse trouble.'

David could not understand why his father appeared to dislike him so much.

'He doesn't treat the rest of them the way he treats me,' he told Hannah one day. 'I don't know what I do to him to make him hate me.'

Hannah could think of nothing to say that could justify Mikey's behaviour towards his youngest son. Unlike the two older boys, who were both tall and broad-shouldered, David was small for his age and was constantly ridiculed by his father because of his small stature.

'How the hell did I ever end up with one like you!' he had said on more than one occasion to a pale and silent David. 'You're the runt in the pack.'

David never responded; all that he had ever wanted from his father was some small show of affection but sometimes all it took was a glance, a look or a question and Mikey would take offence, unbuckling the belt from his trousers and lashing out at him, repeating the same sort of behaviour that his father had used towards him, but with far less justification. Sometimes Hannah would stand between them and take the lash from the belt herself. 'For God's sake, will you leave the poor lad alone. What harm has he done? You're just a great bully!'

With Mikey often drinking during the day as well as in the evening, it was Hannah who was keeping the business going. Although he was still "the boss" and the men feared him and his violent moods, Hannah still did all the organising and scheduling, often pacifying the men when Mikey had been particularly abusive to one or other of them. She felt that most of her time was spent either pacifying the men or comforting David.

She began to find it more and more difficult to cope. She often felt unwell and always felt tired. Sometimes she would have to stop halfway up the stairs, her heart pounding and her head spinning, holding on to the mahogany handrail until the dizziness had passed. She resolved to see Dr Clarke as soon as she had time to spare.

It was Mrs White who found her lying at the bottom of the stairs one morning after she had finished cleaning the bedrooms and was returning downstairs. She saw Hannah's inert body lying at the bottom of the stairs. Her head, where it had hit the terracotta-tiled floor, was in a pool of blood.

Hannah was carried upstairs to the bedroom and Dr Clarke was called. He told Mikey and Mrs White that Hannah had suffered a stroke.

Mikey stood in the doorway of Hannah's unfamiliar room and glanced about him. Her clothes, which Mrs White had removed, lay over the back of the chair. Her silver-backed hairbrush lay on the tortoiseshell tray, the combs and pins from her hair at the side of it. Her long chestnut hair, still with scarcely a hint of grey was spread out across the pillow. Mikey sat on the side of her bed with his head in his hands. To see Hannah, who was always so capable, in this condition was an uncomfortable feeling.

It was a few days before Hannah showed a slight improvement. She appeared to have regained consciousness but, although her eyes were open, she was still not registering anything around her. Mrs White and Maisie propped her up on the smooth, white cotton pillows, so that she might be able to see around her and they both talked to her as they washed and ministered to her, but there was no sign of recognition in her eyes.

Over the years, Mrs White had watched Mikey's behaviour towards Hannah and his children but she had felt unable to express any opinion or indeed to offer Hannah any support other than to attend to her work as best she could, for Hannah had never uttered a word of criticism of Mikey in her presence. When there were confrontations she had tried to stay out of the way. She knew that Hannah would have found it embarrassing if she realised that Mrs White knew the extent of Mikey's behaviour.

Even Maisie and Jack, who had long suspected that all was not well between Hannah and Mikey, knew better than to probe, having been at the receiving end of Hannah's tongue when they had initially tried to ask if there were problems.

Each morning Mrs White attended to Hannah, washing her, changing her nightclothes and bedlinen and gently brushing her hair. She knew that Hannah had always been proud of her appearance and was determined that things would continue as she would have wanted. She fed Hannah with drinks and sips of liquid food from a spoon, as though she was a baby, wiping her chin as the food dribbled down.

It soon became obvious that Mrs White could not continue as she was, attending to all the household chores as well as caring for Hannah. It was John, despite not living at home but always the sensible one, who had been the first to observe the impossibility of the situation. He noticed how strained and tired Mrs White was looking and suggested to his father that he ought to either employ a nurse to look after Hannah, or a housekeeper to run the house to take some of the extra work away from Mrs White. It was decided after much discussion that a nurse was probably the most appropriate, as Mrs White was not getting any younger and was struggling with the lifting and turning of Hannah.

A newly opened nursing agency was approached and four ladies were sent along to Springfield Road to be interviewed by John. The nurse chosen was a young Irish girl called Molly Herbert who had completed her nursing training in the Infirmary at Walton before working for the agency. She was given a bedroom next to Hannah's, with a communicating door so that if Hannah needed anything during the night, she could attend to her. Mrs White, who was extremely fond of Hannah, had been reluctant to give up all care of her and sometimes helped Molly to attend to Hannah and, in return, Molly helped Mrs White whenever she could with tasks about the house.

It had also not escaped John's attention that the business was beginning to fall apart. Barney had approached him many months earlier, before Hannah's illness, and had spoken to him about the workload that Hannah was incurring because of Mikey's inability to function properly because of his drinking.

'I don't know why he's let himself get into this state. I've tried speaking to him about it but it's as if the devil himself has got into him. I've tried speaking to Patrick about it but he doesn't know what he can do. To be honest, I think that he's too wrapped up in his own life to be wanting to bother trying to sort your father out. Not that I'm sure that he can do anything anyway.' Barney had paused. 'I don't want to speak out of turn. You know that your father and I have been friends for years and I wouldn't be saying this if I didn't think that it needed saying. Sure wasn't I around before any of you were born, but he's a changed man from the young lad I first knew. He's drinking himself and the business to death.'

There was another pause before he had continued. 'I've known your mother since before she and your father were wed. She's a good woman but she's worn out and I just had to say something. Maybe you can say something to your father to make him see sense.'

'I don't know what I can do,' John had said. 'I've spoken to him already, but you know what he's like. He nearly bit my head off. Told me to mind my own bloody business. I've been worried about Mother as well and I've asked David to keep an eye on her but there's a limit to what he can do. He's like a red rag to a bull as far as Father is concerned.'

Barney had sighed. 'You'd think that he had everything that he needed. A lovely wife, four lovely children, a big house and a successful business. I don't know what's wrong with the man that he can't be happy. But it's not only that he's not happy, he makes everyone else unhappy as well. Your mammy and pappy have had problems for a long time. Sure Mikey's not been an easy man to live with and he doesn't get any easier.' He had picked up his cap. 'I thought that maybe you could do something as nobody else seems able to. I just thought that it would be worth a try, for your mammy's sake.'

'Thank you for speaking to me, Barney. I really appreciate your concern and I'll try to have another word with my father.' John had paused. 'As you say, it's worth a try.'

What Barney had not said to John was that his concern for his mother was far more than friendship. For years he had watched with dismay Mikey's poor treatment of her. All he could do was be there if she needed him, but he knew that she would probably never turn to him for help because of her loyalty to Mikey.

It was not long after Barney's meeting with John, and before John had had any opportunity to tackle Mikey, that Hannah had her stroke and now Barney saw that Mikey was coping even more poorly than he had done before. He appeared to have fallen apart without Hannah there to support him and the business was in an even worse state of disarray without Hannah's guiding hand.

John was not prepared to return to the fold to rescue the situation. It had been a difficult decision to oppose Mikey and not join the family business in the first place and there was no way that he was going to relinquish his hard-won freedom. Whatever he could do, he could not step back in time and protect his mother. It was too late for that; she was damaged beyond repair.

John viewed the situation objectively and tried to think of some way to salvage the situation before it became any worse. He weighed up the qualities of his brothers and sister. He knew that Patrick, although a talented mechanic, was not an organiser and Oonagh was too selfish; she was completely wrapped up in her own world of socialising and partying, so if they were not to employ somebody outside the family it only left David. The more John thought about this idea, the more he realised that it might not be such a bad thing. David was a good organiser and had shown an aptitude for figures and John thought that maybe, if his father had to rely on David, it might help to bring them a little closer together.

'What am I doing?' he said to Violet. 'He's still got a grip of me. I should just leave him to it and let him get what he deserves.'

'You're doing it for your mother, not for your father,' Violet answered.

John put his head in his hands. 'Mother's worth ten of him and look at her. She's the one who's broken. He's still carrying on with people dancing attention on him and, what's more, feeling sorry for himself while she's lying in that state in her bed. D'you know there are times when he disgusts me.'

Violet put her arms around him and tried to comfort him. 'Just do what you think is right. That's all that you can do.' She stroked his head as he leant against her. 'And remember that you're doing it for your mother and not your father.'

In the days that followed it took all of John's ability to convince Mikey that David might be able to contribute something useful to the business. Mikey, after many protestations, eventually had to acknowledge that if the business that he had created was not to fall apart completely and if he didn't want outsiders involved in the business, then he had no choice but to agree that David, now seventeen, could leave school and start working in the office.

Before approaching Mikey, John had already discussed the option with David. He wasn't sure how David would react to the idea of being in close contact each day with his father. David was reluctant about the whole idea. 'I don't know that it would work, John. You know what he's like. Sometimes I get the feeling that he hates me and can't bear me near him.'

'Do you not think that it's worth a try, if not for him, then for Mother. At least it would mean that the business would be kept going until she's back on her feet again.'

'Do you honestly think that she will get back on her feet again?' David asked, his face brightening at the idea. 'If I thought that I was doing it for Mother, then I would do it. But not for him.'

'I'll not try to persuade you if you're unhappy with the idea.'

'Just give me a bit of time to think about it, will you?' David asked.

David telephoned John two evenings later and told him that he had decided that he would do as John had asked but that he was not going to approach his father with the suggestion. He wanted John to do that. It took all John's powers of persuasion to stop David from reversing his decision when Mikey spoke to him about the job.

'It's on a trial basis only,' he had told David curtly. 'If you don't make a decent job of it, you're out on your ear.'

Mikey called into Hannah's room each morning before he started work and also each evening when he returned home. It disturbed him to see her slim body wasting away before his eyes. Her skin stretched tight and shiny across her frail bones. Her hands clenching and unclenching like shrivelled claws on the counterpane. He felt guity as he looked back on their life together. He knew that he had started associating with Hannah in a fit of pique because of Eileen's rejection and even now he cringed at the thought of having made such a fool of himself over her but, when he thought about the early years of his marriage to Hannah, he had to acknowledge that they had not really been bad years. He knew that he had never felt the same strong feelings for Hannah as he had felt for Eileen, but she had been a good wife. She was the one who had given everything to him, from the first day they had met. He tried to excuse things to himself. She had known the sort of relationship that she was getting into. She couldn't have helped but be aware of his relationship with Eileen. She must have seen that they had gone everywhere together and had been thought of as a couple. But then he had to acknowledge, however reluctantly that, even if she had understood the situation, she had still given him loyalty despite everything that he had done.

He thought about baby Anthony and the grief that Hannah had experienced at the time of his death and then he felt a great sense of shame as he thought about Kitty and her baby…his baby… and the further grief that he had caused Hannah.

He remembered Patrick trying to talk to him and later John, as things had worsened, and he knew that he had ignored everything that they had said. And this was the result.

'Hannah! Oh, Hannah!' He sat and talked to her softly, wishing that he could put the clock back and start all over again, stroking her forehead, trying to elicit some response. These were attempts at conversation that only took place behind a closed door and after the new nurse, Molly, had left the room as he was too embarrassed to show his emotions in front of her. He told Hannah that he loved her and that he was sorry for all the troubles that he had caused her, but soon he found the sight of her deterioration too distressing and he stopped calling by her bedroom, instead asking Molly to come to him each day to tell him how Hannah was progressing.

But there was no progress, only a slow deterioration in Hannah's condition until one morning Molly came into the kitchen where Mikey was eating his breakfast and told him that Hannah had died in the night.

Patrick, who had already started work, was called in from the yard and David from the office. John was contacted at home; fortunately he had not yet left for work. Oonagh was away from home staying with friends and John said that he would contact her and he would also call and tell Hannah's parents about the death of their daughter.

David was devastated. He sat at Hannah's bedside weeping and stroking her hand until Maisie, also grief-stricken and in tears, persuaded him to leave.

They were all surprised at Barney's reaction. Barney, who had been a loyal friend to Mikey over many years, was so distraught that he could barely bring himself to offer any sort of condolences to Mikey.

For the first time, John realised that Hannah had probably meant more to Barney than she had ever meant to Mikey.

A day's holiday was given to the men in the yard on the day of the funeral.

The immediate family gathered in Springfield Road, a subdued group all in dark clothes. Mikey had contacted his mother and father but had told them that he did not want them to make the journey for the funeral, as he doubted that they could even arrive in time. Mrs White looked out of the front window as the coffin was loaded into the hearse. She spoke quietly to John, 'I think that you had better have a look outside.'

John was astonished to see all the drivers and second-men, kitted out in their Sunday best clothes gathered in the street outside the house in Springfield Road. He tapped his father on the shoulder.

'I think the men are here to pay their last respects to Mother. Do you want to have a word with them or shall I?'

Mikey felt unable to speak to them and asked John to thank them on his behalf.

'You'd best ask them back to the house afterwards.' he said.

The hearse left the house on the way to the church for the requiem mass and the men lined up behind the family and followed, caps in hands.

'She was a good woman, Mikey,' Barney said and, unusually for him, followed it with words of criticism. 'You led her a hard life and she deserved better.'

After the Mass, the family, friends and the men from the yard returned to the house where Mrs White had laid out food and drink. The men didn't stay long and John was aware that they had little sympathy for Mikey in his grief, but had simply come to pay their respects to Hannah and the rest of the family.

Mikey was still not functioning properly and John once again assumed command. He asked Molly if she would be prepared to stay on for a while after the funeral to help Mrs White as she attempted to reorganise the house and tried to establish some routine once again.

'I know it's not nursing work,' said John, 'but Dad is prepared to pay you the same money and it would help us out if you would do so.'

Molly agreed to stay on. She felt sorry for Mikey, this big man who appeared to be so heartbroken by the death of his wife.

'She was always there,' Mikey said in bewilderment. 'Steady as a rock. I never thought that she would be the one to go first.'

Maisie was little help. She found it hard to accept that she had outlived her daughter and John tried to comfort her as best he could. Like John, she too was concerned about David whom she knew would find it hard to cope without his mother, on whom he had depended greatly, but she was relieved that, at least for the moment, Mikey had appeared to calm down and was not drinking.

John, older and more aware than David, had known for a long time that it was Hannah who had kept them united as a family by attempting to minimise Mikey's aggression and selfishness and compensating in excess herself. He wondered if it was all the extra strain that had been placed on her by Mikey's behaviour which had precipitated her death. David also found it hard to suppress his angry feelings towards Mikey for he, like John, felt Mikey was partly responsible for his mother's early demise.

In contrast, although Oonagh was overwhelmed with feelings of guilt when she first heard the news of her mother's illness, it was not long before her own personal requirements took precedence. She now found that her father was relying more and more on her and found his need uncomfortable and oppressive. She felt that she had her own life to lead and did not want to be a prop for her father and she began to spend more and more time away from the house.

It was a few weeks before Molly, with grateful thanks from the family and Mrs White, returned to the nursing agency. Mrs White, who was now well into her sixties, continued to look after the family carrying on much as she had before Hannah's illness with the cooking and cleaning and general household tasks.

The house was strange without Hannah bustling about, preparing vegetables one minute, immersed in the accounts the next, but always there when she was needed.

David, despite feeling deeply resentful towards his father, settled into his role in the office and proved competent in his own quiet way. Mikey came to depend on him more and more, but David was not entirely at ease with the situation and was constantly under the scrutiny of his father, who was a hard taskmaster.

Oonagh, still her father's favourite, continued living her own life as usual, cajoling money from Mikey whenever her allowance was spent and generally doing as she liked.

John watched and said nothing, but six months after Hannah's death and after what they felt a "decent" time had elapsed, John and Violet announced their intention of marrying.

At the same time as the wedding was announced, Carmel revealed that she was pregnant.

Patrick had still not officially been made a partner in the business but he and Carmel thought that the baby might prove to be the deciding factor that would spur Mikey on. But it was not to be. Instead, Mikey's present to celebrate the pregnancy was a larger house for Patrick and Carmel.

Patrick was frustrated. He had worked in the business since he had left school but felt that he was treated as little more than another employee.

Carmel was constantly pushing him to speak to his father about his promise of a partnership but Patrick was afraid of his father's anger and would only go so far before retreating.

'He's given us a new house, Carmel! For God's sake! It's more than most fathers do for their children.'

'Yes! But it's still in his name, not in yours so he could turn us out whenever he had a mind to and what would you do then? You've worked hard for him in the business; you're entitled to more than that.'

But Patrick knew that there was no point in pushing his father over the matter. He would make Patrick a partner when it suited him and not when Patrick or Carmel decided.

As time went on, Mrs White was finding the work in the house harder to cope with. Oonagh, particularly, was a problem. Always untidy and very spoilt, her room was in a constant mess. She would sometimes change her clothes two or three times a day and expected them to be washed and ironed almost immediately, throwing a tantrum if they weren't ready. Mrs White felt unable to seek support from Mikey. She had in the past seen Hannah's constant battle with her daughter and the lack of support that she had received when she had appealed to Mikey to help impose some sort of discipline on her.

Mrs White had met Molly on a few occasions since Hannah's death and had confided in her that she was finding the work at Springfield Road a little too much for her as she was getting older, but she didn't want to leave the family with nobody to look after them. However, she had decided that the time was fast approaching when she must speak to Mikey and tell him that she felt no longer capable of doing the work and wished to leave his employment.

It was a strange accident that a few days after Mrs White had spoken to Mikey and told him of her decision to leave, Mikey met up with Molly in the grocer's shop in the town. Mrs White, who had fallen and injured her leg, had asked if Patrick could collect some provisions for her on the way back from the docks in the car. Mikey was with Patrick and they had stopped at George Inch, the grocer's, to collect the groceries and Molly happened to be in the shop.

As soon as Mikey saw Molly he saw a solution to his problems and asked her if she was working. When she said that she had just finished a contract with the nursing agency and was having some time off, Mikey took the opportunity.

'I have a proposition to put to you, Molly. Mrs White is about ready to retire and I need someone to take her place. I wonder if you might be interested in the position. I would pay you the same salary as you would get nursing and your food and lodging would be free.'

It was a very tempting proposition but Molly asked Mikey if she could have a few days to think about it. It did not take long for her to make up her mind. She realised that if she didn't have to pay for food and lodging she would be able to save more of her wages and, two days later, she called at Springfield Road to tell Mikey that she was willing to take the job. Her wages and days off were agreed and it was decided that she would start in one month, which would give Mrs White time to organise herself and prepare for her move to

Coventry to live with her sister, and would also give Mrs White time to show Molly the tasks that would be required of her.

Mikey was pleased with the solution to his problem. It meant that he didn't have to get used to a complete stranger in his home and he knew that the boys had liked Molly when she had been looking after Hannah. Oonagh, he knew, was another story but he would face that situation when he had to.

So Molly moved into Springfield Road and started work.

Part Three

MOLLY

Chapter 19

Molly folded some clothes and put them into a suitcase. She thought that it would probably take three trips on the tram to Springfield Road before she had transferred all the belongings that she had acquired since she had been in England.

She knew that she should write soon to her parents and let them know how things had progressed. A smile came to her face as she thought of them. She sat on the bed and allowed her mind to wander back to her childhood.

From a young child, she had watched her father at work at the big table in the workroom at the side of the house. There was a connecting door which went through from the house into the workroom, and a separate door, half-glazed and painted maroon, the outside weathered by the sun and the rain, which led from the workroom to the street outside. The words "James Patrick Herbert" were written in an arc in gold letters on the glass. And below that "Tailor" was written in black. This was the door through which customers came and went.

Molly had loved being there with her father in the workroom, his linen tape measure around his neck, a padded band around his left wrist into which he stuck the slim silver-coloured pins with their flat shiny heads. He would fetch a bolt of cloth from the shelves that lined one wall and expertly flick it over and over, each flick making a loud thump on the table as the cloth was unwound. Molly had tried on many occasions to copy her father but had always failed, the cloth usually ending up on the floor.

'Sure, you haven't the knack or the strength yet,' he would say, laughing, 'but give it time and practice and it'll come.'

Then when the cloth was laid out he would take the silver grey tailor's chalk and the tape measure and draw out the rough shape of the garment on the cloth, constantly referring to his notebook where he kept all the measurements.

Molly had loved the smell of the fabric. It was a strange smell that she had never smelt anywhere else. Her father said it was "the dressing". She didn't know what that meant but she knew that it was only the new cloth that smelt like that.

He would then take the big, heavy scissors, which were nearly as long as her forearm, and with decisive snips would cut through the fabric, the scissors crunching as they followed the chalk lines.

This was the part that always worried Molly. What if he made a mistake?

But he never did!

Her mother would come in with two cups of tea on a tray, one for Molly and one for her father and sometimes her father would burst into song, particularly if he had taken a tot of rum that morning.

'Oh Kathleen Mavourneen! The grey dawn is breaking,

The horn of the hunter is heard on the hill,

The lark from her light wing the bright dew is shaking,

Kathleen Mavourneen. What slumbering still.....'

If there were customers there her mother, Kathleen, would blush and pretend not to hear the song he sang to her and he would wink at Molly and smile at her mother's discomfort, knowing full well that this display of affection would forestall the lecture that she might have in store for him, for the money that he had wasted on the greyhounds the previous night.

'You're a rogue, James Patrick,' her mother would say, smiling.

Without thinking, Molly looked down at her ringless finger. If everything had gone to plan she would have been married now. She had thought that she would have a marriage as happy as that of her parents, but that was not to be.

She had been engaged to Eamonn for two years and they had planned to marry in the spring. They had found a small two bedroomed house at a rent that they could afford, not far from where her parents lived and they had spent many happy hours renovating it. It appeared that everything couldn't have been more perfect. Everyone said that she and Eamonn were perfectly matched, both young and attractive, both extrovert and full of life. An ideal couple.

Molly remembered the discomfiture of Maura, her best friend, as they had sat in Maura's bedroom only three months before the wedding. Molly had taken some fabric samples around to show Maura what she had in mind for her bridesmaid's dresses. Maura was to be Molly's matron of honour and Molly had been surprised at her reluctance to discuss the fabric when suddenly Maura had blurted out.

'Look, Molly. I don't know what the best way of telling you is,' she paused. 'Sure there's no easy way, but Eamonn's been seen around with Rhona Finnegan.'

'Good try, Maura! But Eamonn has better taste than that,' she laughed. 'Sure didn't he choose me?'

'I'm not jesting, Molly. It's true. I know that you'll find it hard to believe.' She looked miserable. 'I'm sorry, but you needed to know. I thought it'd be better coming from me than from anyone else.'

'Don't be foolish, Maura. Isn't she an old boot, anybody's for a farthing,' Molly said with a little less certainty, as she looked at the expression on Maura's face.

Maura persisted. She was embarrassed and distressed, her feelings showing all too clearly on her face.

'It's common knowledge, Molly. No one wanted to tell you. He's been seen with her and not just once, but on more than one occasion'

Molly had felt as though the smile was frozen on her face. She couldn't believe what she was hearing. Eamonn and Rhona Finnegan. She put her head down, pressing the palms of her hands against her eyes, and rocked backwards and forwards, her stomach churning.

'God, oh God,' she had whispered to Maura. 'Are you sure it's true?'

Maura put her arm around her shoulder. 'There's no doubt about it,' she said gently. 'Loads of people have seen them together….and like I said, not just once. I thought Rhona might come round to see you. She's been mouthing it off all over the place, saying that Eamonn and her are to be wed, and I wouldn't have put it past her to come knocking on your door. God knows what story he's spun her or whether she's just out to make trouble! I don't know how Eamonn thought he could keep it hidden from you.'

There was a tap on the bedroom door and Maura's mother opened it.

'I just wanted to check that everything's alright?' She looked at Molly and raised her eyebrows. Molly flinched. So, even Maura's mother knew.

'I told Mammy,' Maura explained apologetically. 'I didn't know what to do and she said the best thing was to tell you and then you could decide what you wanted to do about it.'

Maura's mother nodded, her face sympathetic. 'Don't be too hasty,' she said. 'You need to talk to Eamonn and find out what he's got to say about it. There might be a simple explanation.'

Molly couldn't help but think that Maura's mother didn't sound very convincing as she backed out of the room, closing the door gently behind her.

The two girls sat in silence together until Molly eventually stood and said, 'I'll have to see him. Will you come with me?

He'll be down at the field, kicking a ball about with the lads.'

The two girls went down the stairs and through the kitchen where Maura's mother was making pastry. She wiped her floury hands on her apron and put her arm around Molly, pulling her towards her.

'I'm sorry, Molly love,' she said.

Molly rested her head for a moment on Maura's mother's shoulder, then straightened up and shrugged. 'We're just going down to the field to see him.'

As they reached the field they could see Eamonn and two of his pals, Peter and Callum, kicking a ball about and laughing and shouting to each other. She asked Maura to wait for her and taking a deep breath started to cross the field towards Eamonn, who waved at her as she approached.

'Hallo, me darling Molly,' he said smiling but then noticing the expression on her face, he signalled to his friends. 'Whisht! Will you, lads. I need to speak to Molly. I'll catch up with you later.'

'By Jesus, I don't envy him the explaining he's got to do,' said Peter when they were out of earshot.

Molly held her clenched hand out to Eamonn and slowly opened it. Her engagement ring, with the three garnets in a row that they had chosen together in Sligo, rested in the palm of her hand.

'I have no more need of this,' she said.

'Oh, c'mon now, Molly. What's all this about?'

'You know full well what it's about,' Molly said, surprising herself that her voice sounded so calm, when inside her stomach was churning.

He tried to put his arm about her shoulders and she shrugged his arm away violently, the calmness giving way to tears.

'Don't you dare touch me. I trusted you and you've gone and cheated on me with that....that.....whore!'

'I can explain! I was drunk! Sure it doesn't mean anything. Ah! C'mon now, don't be foolish.'

'It means a lot to me, Eamonn McCarthy. So how many

times were you drunk then? According to what I hear you've been seen in her company more than once. Her.... of all people! How could you?' Her face wrinkled in disgust.

He grabbed both her arms and tried to pull her towards him,

'Ah, Molly,' he pleaded. 'I love you. It was just a bit of foolishness.'

'Is it two of us you're going to marry then?' She battered her fists on his chest, tears streaming down her face. 'Just leave me alone. I never want to see you again. Take your bloody ring; you'll be needing it for Rhona by all accounts.'

She thrust the ring into his hand and ran back across the field towards Maura, ignoring Eamonn's calls to come back.

'C'mon, Maura, let's get out of here!'

Molly had told her mother that she didn't want to speak to Eamonn if he called at the house. She didn't elaborate on it. Her mother had noticed that Molly was no longer wearing her ring but said nothing; she thought that it was just a lover's tiff but Molly knew that she couldn't put off telling her mother and father for long, because the news would be all over the village.

When she told her mother, she had put her arms around Molly rocking her backwards and forwards like a baby, but said nothing.

Molly's father, a man who rarely lost his temper, exploded when he heard the news. 'I'll kill the blackguard, so I will.'

With his tape measure still around his neck he started to head for the door. 'I'll sort him out!'

'Daddy, Daddy. Leave it alone,' a tearful Molly pleaded. 'I don't want to see or hear anything about him again. Rhona's welcome to him. I want nothing more to do with him.'

It was only because Molly became so upset that he was prevailed upon to do nothing.

'Ah, love!' he said, tears in his own eyes. 'You're best out of it. You're best off without him, Molly love. Sure it's best you found out what he was like before you married him.'

The days that followed were hard for Molly.

'Why doesn't Eamonn come around any more?' her brothers and sisters had asked and Molly's stock reply had been, 'We've had a row. We're not friends any more.'

Her sisters, Margaret and Josie, were particularly anxious about the development because they were to have been bridesmaids at the wedding, to Maura's matron of honour, and James Patrick had already measured them for their dresses.

It was increasingly painful for her to be around the town where she had thought she was going to have such a happy future. In addition to the pain that she was feeling, she also felt humiliated. She had said to Maura, 'God, I must be the laughing stock of the place. Everyone knowing about her but me!'

After a couple of weeks of watching her daughter's pain, Kathleen, forever practical, said, 'Why don't you take a couple of weeks off work and go and stay with Teresa in Liverpool? It'll take your mind off all this nonsense.'

And Molly had taken a quick decision. She had decided that she would join Teresa, her sister in Liverpool, but not just for a holiday. She would find work in Liverpool and get away from everything associated with Eamonn.

Over the next few weeks she occupied herself with arranging her journey. She gave notice at her workplace and visited the agents in Sligo where she bought her ticket to Liverpool.

Eamonn called at the house a few times but Molly's mother was curt to him. 'On your way, Eamonn. Molly doesn't want to see you. Haven't you caused her enough heartache?'

Molly sighed as she thought about all that had happened and added a few more items to the suitcase. She had not regretted her decision to leave Sligo, apart from missing her family. She felt that it was a long way in the past, despite the pain that she still sometimes felt when she thought about Eamonn. The past few years had been good ones and she had enjoyed the nursing. She smiled once again as she remembered her last morning at home and her mother fussing around her.

Her mother had cooked her breakfast. Bacon, sausage, fried bread, tomato and an egg, its golden centre surrounded by the glistening shiny white. A plate of bread and butter and the compulsory pot of tea. Her mother thought that a full stomach was the solution to all problems.

'You'll need a decent meal to keep your strength up,' her mother had said as she put the plate on the table in front of her.

It was all presented on the best china that had been ceremoniously removed from the mahogany china cabinet in the front room that morning. Fragile, white china, a thin gold border edging the plates and cups and scattered all over with violets.

'I don't think I can eat this, Mammy; my stomach is churning.'

'Sure, you must, Molly love. You never know when you'll get another bite. You'll be glad of it later on.'

Molly had known that she would have to force some of it down. Her mother would fret otherwise. Reluctantly she picked up her knife and fork and cut into a slice of bacon.

'You've plenty of time, love. The car's not ordered for another hour.'

Vincent McGrath's car had been ordered to take Molly to Sligo where she was to catch the bus to Dublin. Her mother and father had insisted on the car instead of the bus and she was glad that they had, because it meant that the goodbyes would be said here at the house and not in the street in Sligo. She knew that her mother would be tearful. She didn't know about her father but at least he would be able to go straight back into the workroom and busy himself. And that was where her father was now, waiting for the door knocker that would signal that Vincent's car had arrived to take Molly away from home.

Molly picked at her breakfast. She could not join in with her mother's nervous small talk. Her own nervousness was making her behave in a totally different way. She felt that she was not functioning at all.

Her mother glanced at her as the knocker sounded and her father came hurrying from the workroom.

'Now just you remember, Molly, if you're not happy there, you come straight back home. There are plenty more fish in the sea who would be glad of the chance of a lovely girl like you,' her father said as he picked up her bag and walked out to the car. He put her bag in the boot, kissed her cheek and hugged her. Her mother said, 'God bless you, Molly love. Now, mind, write as soon as you get there.'

'I will, I will,' said Molly and hurriedly climbed into the car before the tears came.

Kathleen, rubbing at her eyes with a corner of her apron, and James Patrick, his arm around Kathleen's shoulders, stood at the gate and waved as the car moved away. Margaret and Josie and her brothers, Jimmy and poor Kevin who had not been born fully equipped mentally, ran down the road alongside the car waving at Molly until the car had picked up too much speed for them to keep up with it and left them behind, waving furiously.

'And just wouldn't you know,' Kathleen said looking upwards, 'here's the rain again!'

Vincent McGrath dropped Molly in town an hour early. In her worry about missing the bus it had been arranged for him to collect her long before he was needed. The rain had become much heavier. It hit her umbrella, sliding and running in rivulets between the spokes until it ran off and down onto her tweed coat. None of the shops were open so she stood in a shop doorway opposite the bus stop, to shelter until the bus arrived. She could feel the water soaking through her shoes and her feet were beginning to feel cold. She smiled wryly to herself. 'God, if this just doesn't put the tin lid on it all.'

She breathed a sigh of relief when the bus appeared and she was able to climb up the steps and found a seat, putting her bag on the sagging, net luggage racks above her head, her damp clothes steaming as the warmth of the bus, its engine still running, started to dry her wet garments. The final passengers arrived, the doors were closed and Molly was on her way!

She wanted to catch a last glimpse of Sligo and rubbed her gloved hand across the glass in an attempt to clear a patch of the fogged-up surface so that she could see outside but the rain still fell heavily and there was little to be seen outside, so she closed her eyes and leant her head against the back of her seat and tried to sleep.

The bus jolted its way along the rutted roads to Dublin, picking up and dropping off passengers along the way until it eventually pulled into the forecourt of the bus station which was its final stop. Molly saw that there were two cabs waiting and she stopped at one and asked the man in his flat cap to take her to the ferry for Liverpool.

Teresa had met Molly off the boat and they had hugged and kissed each other, making up for the lack of physical contact between them during the last two years.

'It's good to see you, Molly love. My God! Would you just look at yourself. There's not an ounce of flesh on your bones. I'm sorry about Eamonn. I know how much you cared for him but, as Mammy said in her letter, it's as well you found out before you were married. It would have been far worse if you'd found out that he was a philanderer when you were tied hand and foot to him.'

Molly felt tears pricking at her eyes and blinked hurriedly, not allowing herself to cry.

'Ah well! It's all over now. I'm not going to dwell on it. Amn't I here to make a new life for myself?' She smiled and rubbed her hands across her eyes as though wiping away the memories.

'How's everyone at home?' asked Teresa, hurriedly changing the subject.

'They're all well enough. Mammy and Daddy send their

love and Margaret and Josie and the boys send theirs as well.'

They linked arms and walked to the tram stop catching up on all the news as they did so. The tram would take them along the Dock Road to Bootle, where Teresa was lodging. After they stepped down from the tram, Teresa said, 'We'd better share the weight of your bag. I'll take one of the handles. We've a little way to go yet.'

They walked, swapping sides with the bag as the stitched leather straps dug in and numbed their fingers. Molly glanced around her as they walked. Some of the houses appeared to be used for business premises of one sort or another and Molly read some of the names on the gates as she passed.

"N. Heaton. Solicitor."
"Fern Bank. Home For The Elderly."
"McNultys School of Irish Dancing."

Teresa stopped at a pair of wrought-iron gates and swung one half of them open. There was a gravel drive lined on either side by large stones, behind which there was a semblance of a lawn. Behind the lawns were borders filled with glossy, green-leaved shrubs. They climbed the four steps to the green-painted front door and Teresa took her key from her handbag and unlocked the door which led into a vestibule with a half-glazed door, also painted green. The hall was long with pale green walls and dark green painted doors opening onto it. A smell of cabbage cooking hung in the air.

'My God!' said Molly, who couldn't refrain from laughing, 'Even the smell is green.'

'Shush,' said Teresa, laughing as well, 'they'll hear you. It's not such a bad auld place and Mr and Mrs Dooley are good, kind people.'

Teresa and Molly were to share a room. It was painted much the same as the rest of the house.....but another, slightly different shade of green.

'They obviously like green!' said Molly, smiling and shaking her head, but the room looked comfortable enough.

Teresa told Molly that she had organised an interview for her at the Infirmary at Walton where she herself had worked for the two years since she had left Ireland.

'The majority of the nurses are Irish girls. They've a great shortage, so the interview will be just a formality. They just want hard workers and most of the Irish girls who take up nursing here are just that, so there should be no problem about getting the job. The only trouble with the job is that we have to do a stint of nights. Some people don't mind but I find I can't sleep during the day when the rest of the world is awake! I stll haven't got used to it even after this length of time.'

They both sat on one of the beds and exchanged news. Teresa told Molly that one of the advantages about nursing was that there was a good social life.

'Sure, when some of the ships come into dock there are often invitations to go on board ship for a party. I think the men are starved of female company and it's a way that they can be kept happy. God! You should see the carry-on at some of the parties. It would make your hair curl so it would.'

'I notice that you haven't told Mammy about any of the carry-on in any of your letters,' said Molly smiling.

'Ah! Well. I've only been to one or two, but there's some of the girls have got themselves a bit of a reputation, so they have. Anyway, there's more than that. It's just a good laugh being with all the girls. They're a good crowd. Some of them live in the nurses' home and it's often a gas when we all get together. Don't pull faces,' she scolded Molly, 'I know what you're thinking, but there's no men allowed....... although the odd one has slipped in through an open window.' She grinned at Molly.

They chatted well into the night, only stopping while Teresa made them something to eat. Molly had three days before her interview and spent the time, whilst Teresa was working, exploring the area.

Her interview was much as Teresa had predicted, merely a formality and she was offered a job. She was given a uniform but had to buy her own shoes and stockings.

'Get a stout pair with thick soles,' said Teresa. 'You'll be on your feet all day and if you skimp on your shoes you'll end up with your feet and your legs killing you.'

The Sister in charge of the ward where Molly was to start work was a martinet, who had a dislike of the Irish.

'Which is a bit of a pity,' Teresa said, laughing, 'when most of her nurses are Irish.'

But Molly found that, although she was strict and a disciplinarian, she was fair and Molly liked her well enough.

Weeks passed and Teresa and Molly drifted into a routine. As Teresa had said, there was an active social life and Molly soon found that she had a large circle of friends but she did not allow herself to become involved with any of the men she happened to meet. She enjoyed the hospital and nursing and, when she qualified, she couldn't believe how quickly the time had passed.

The only problem for each of them in sharing a room was when their shifts overlapped, as it meant tiptoeing about so as not to disturb the one trying to sleep. They coped as best they could but when Teresa started courting seriously, things began to change and when Teresa and Charlie announced their engagement Molly thought that maybe it was time for her to move on.

At that point, she had been working at the Infirmary for three and a half years and she decided to enrol with a nursing agency. The agency pay was higher than that at the hospital and it had allowed her to rent a large room of her own. It was while she was in the employ of the agency that she was offered the position at Springfield Road.

'It's a terrible shame,' she wrote to her parents about Hannah, 'to see someone so relatively young, in such an awful state, unable to recognise anyone around her. Dear God. When I go, let it be quick.'

She had cared for Hannah at Springfield Road until Hannah's death.

'They've asked me to stay on for a bit,' Molly wrote to her

parents. *'They're all a bit shaken by her death, particularly the youngest boy, David, and there's a bit of sorting out to do. So I've said I will.'*

After a few weeks, when it was felt that Molly had contributed all that she could, she had said her goodbyes and returned to her work at the agency.

'It was a strange coincidence,' she wrote to her parents a few months later, *'when I bumped into Mr Whelan and his son in the grocer's and he asked me back to work there. I'd just finished the job with the agency, the one that I told you about in my last letter, so it didn't take me long to make up my mind.'*

She glanced around her at the room that she had occupied for the time that she had worked at the agency and began to check the cupboards and drawers. She had packed everything. She closed her suitcase and set off for the tram that would take her to Springfield Road.

Chapter 20

Mrs White greeted Molly when she arrived at Springfield Road.

'You can't imagine how relieved I am to know that you've accepted the job. I didn't want to leave them without anyone and I would have felt that I would have had to have stayed until they'd found someone,' she said. 'I'm getting too old to run a big house like this,' she lowered her voice, 'particularly when I've had to cope with that little madam, Oonagh. But you'll find out about her soon enough.'

'Don't be putting me off before I even start,' Molly said, laughing. 'Besides, I can remember what she was like when I was here before.'

'Well, she's not improved in the meantime,' Mrs White said, 'Anyway, let's get your case upstairs. I'm sure that Patrick will take you to collect the rest of your stuff to save you carrying it, when he's finished work.'

Molly was shown to the room that she had occupied when she had previously worked in the house.

'There's Mrs Whelan's room if this isn't big enough but it's not been touched since she died. It would have to be cleared out.'

'I don't think that's such a good idea,' Molly replied. 'The children might object to a stranger occupying their mother's room. After all, it's not that long since she passed away.'

Mrs White looked relieved. 'I'm glad you said that because I think you're right. It might have got you off to a bad start with them, particularly Oonagh if you had wanted the room. I'll leave you to get sorted and when you're ready come down to the kitchen and I'll give you a rough idea of what needs to be done each day.'

Although Molly had been aware of some of the chores that Mrs White was responsible for, the list of tasks that were presented to her made her realise that it was no wonder that Mrs White felt that it was all too much for her. It was a lot for a woman of her age to be coping with.

'I'll be here with you for a month before I leave, so that I can show you the way things are done. Take it easy for today; you'll be in the thick of it soon enough.'

That evening, after Patrick had taken her to collect the rest of her belongings and she had returned her key to her ex-landlady, Molly joined the family and Mrs White for dinner. Prior to Hannah's death she had taken her meals, which had been brought up to her on a tray by Mrs White, in her bedroom so that she could oversee Hannah in the bedroom next door. But now she sat down to eat with the family.

Mikey sat at the head of the table, with Oonagh and Mrs White to his right. David and Molly sat to his left. Molly was aware of Oonagh glaring at her across the table and, remembering Mrs White's words about the "little madam", hoped that there weren't going to be problems.

'I hope that you're settling in OK, Molly?' Mikey said. 'Sure it's not as if it's a strange place you've come to.'

'I'm fine, thank you, Mr Whelan,' Molly responded. 'And Mrs White's been showing me the ropes.'

When the meal was finished, Molly helped Mrs White clear the table and wash the dishes. David went into the sitting room and sat in one of the armchairs reading. Oonagh ran upstairs to her room and came down a few moments later with her coat on. She kissed her father on top of his head and said,

'I'm going out for a couple of hours, Pops.'

'I'll walk you down the road,' Mikey said, standing. 'I'm off to "The Buffs" for a while. Don't lock up, Mrs White; I'll do it when I get in.'

After they had finished clearing up, Mrs White and Molly sat at the kitchen table, each with a cup of tea in front of them.

'I hope he's not starting drinking again,' Mrs White said, referring to Mikey. 'He used to drink an awful lot, but over the last year he's settled down a bit.'

'I didn't know there was a problem. I never noticed any sign of drink on him when I was here before.'

'He eased off the drinking a bit when Mrs Whelan fell ill, so you wouldn't have known about it. I don't want to speak out of turn.' She shook her head. 'I'm probably worrying unnecessarily.'

'Well, you'll be out of it soon enough,' Molly said.

'It's not me I'm worrying about. It's young David. His father used to give him a bad time after he'd had a drink. When his mother was alive she used to protect him, but he's got no one now. Anyway, enough of that, let's talk about tomorrow,' Mrs White said. 'The first thing that has to be done is to rake out the ashes and light the fire before anyone gets up. Barney Gallagher and Patrick always come for breakfast. Barney grew up with Mr Whelan and they're good friends, as you know. Barney is in lodgings and he has his breakfast here every day except Sunday. As for Patrick, well, Carmel is a bit spoilt and now that she has the baby, it gives her even more excuse not to cook breakfast, so Patrick has his breakfast here. So there are four of them for breakfast including Mr Whelan and David and they always have a cooked breakfast: bacon, eggs, fried bread.'

'And what about Oonagh?' Molly asked.

Mrs White sniffed. 'That little madam! She appears as and when she likes, demanding this, that and the other and expecting everything to be dropped so that attention can be paid to her. I tell you, she wouldn't have got away with so much before Mrs Whelan fell ill, but she's got her father twisted around her little finger. She has her breakfast whenever she gets up and that could be any time of the morning.' Mrs White continued, 'Anyway, let's forget about her. Once the men have all left for work, we can sit down and have something to eat ourselves. I usually take David a cup of tea and a piece of cake in the middle of the morning, but he's no bother. He's a lovely lad. Wouldn't want to put you out at all.'

As the evening wore on, Molly began to feel tired. It had been a busy day and she knew that it wouldn't be long before she needed some sleep. David came into the kitchen and said goodnight to them both. Mrs White banked up the fire, put the guard in front of it and she and Molly went up to bed.

The following morning Molly's working week started. Whilst Mrs White began to prepare breakfast, Molly raked out the ashes and lit the fire. Barney arrived and was introduced to Molly. He had met her briefly in the weeks after Hannah's death but had never really spoken to her at any length before.

'No offence to you, Mrs White, but it's great to see a pretty, young face in the kitchen,' he said grinning.

'Away with you, Barney.' Mrs White flicked her cloth at him. 'She's a sensible girl and not likely to be taken in by your blarney.'

David, Patrick and Mikey arrived almost simultaneously. The only time that Molly had met David previously was in the weeks leading up to his mother's death and the weeks immediately afterwards, when he was distraught and uncommunicative. She was pleased to see that he looked a great deal better and that he appeared to have coped with and overcome whatever difficulties he had been experiencing at the time.

Once Mikey, Patrick and Barney had left the house and David had gone to the office, the two women sat for a short while and had their breakfast before starting on the day's chores.

Mrs White's routine was to start at the top of the house and work down. David and Mikey's rooms were the rooms attended to first. Both rooms were fairly bare and without ornamentation but each of the rooms had a photograph of Hannah on display.

'I'm not being nosey, Mrs White, but did Mr and Mrs Whelan not share the same room before she fell ill?' Molly asked, as they made the bed up in Mikey's room.

'I suppose it does no harm to say it now, but in all the time I've worked here, they never slept in the same room. And that,' she indicated the photo of Hannah, 'that only appeared in Mr Whelan's room just before Mrs Whelan died.'

There was a movement outside in the corridor.

'Enough said, I think madam is up and about,' Mrs White said. She went out into the corridor and asked, 'Can we clean your room, now, Oonagh?'

'I'd like my breakfast first,' Oonagh replied.

Mrs White walked back into Mikey's room and raised her eyes to heaven.

'I'll go down and see to madam's breakfast if you want to make a start on her room.'

Molly stood in the doorway and surveyed Oonagh's room. She muttered to herself, 'I might as well start as I mean to go on,' and, picking up all the discarded clothes on the floor, put them in a pile outside the bedroom door. She then busied herself making the bed and hoovering the floor.

By the time the stairs had been hoovered and polished, it was time to begin preparing lunch. Hannah had always kept her menfolk well fed, believing that if they were doing a heavy manual job they needed plenty of good food to fuel them and her legacy continued after her death. The potatoes and vegetables were peeled and the meat put on to cook.

Oonagh had eaten her breakfast and, whilst Mrs White and Molly prepared the midday meal, she had spent most of the morning in her dressing gown, with her legs draped over the arm of a chair in the sitting room, reading.

The back door slammed and Oonagh suddenly rushed from the sitting room and up the stairs. Mikey had arrived home.

Mrs White smiled and gave Molly a knowing look. 'That's got her moving. If he caught her still not dressed at this time in the morning, there'd be all hell let loose.'

But Oonagh was downstairs almost as quickly as she had gone up.

What's the meaning of this?' she demanded, throwing the clothes, which Molly had left outside her bedroom door onto a chair.

Mrs White looked puzzled.

'What's your problem, Oonagh?' Mikey asked.

'I've found all my clothes in a pile outside my bedroom door…on the floor.' Oonagh was furious.

'Oh! I'm sorry, Oonagh,' Molly said sweetly. 'I was cleaning your room and they were all on the floor, so I thought that they were all for washing.'

'If they were for washing, I would have said they were for washing. Why didn't you hang them up?' Oonagh demanded.

By this time, Mikey was watching the exchange with amusement.

Molly was unperturbed.

'I thought that if you had wanted them hung up or put away, then you would have done so yourself.'

'It's your job to put them away. That's what you get paid for.'

'Actually, Oonagh. I haven't been paid for anything yet,' Molly replied.

Mikey decided that it was time to intervene. 'Molly is right, Oonagh. If you wanted your clothes put away, you should have put them away yourself. Molly and Mrs White have plenty to do without fetching and carrying for you. And whilst we're at it,' his voice hardened, 'why are you still in your dressing gown at this time of day?'

Oonagh, determined not to be totally outfaced, picked up the bundle of clothes and threw them at Molly. 'If you thought they were for washing, then wash them and I want them ready by tomorrow.'

'I'll have to see if I have time!' Molly said calmly as Oonagh stormed out of the room.

Mrs White hurriedly began putting the dishes on the table, half expecting Mikey to reprimand Molly, but Mikey was looking at her admiringly.

'Well! What a turn-up for the books,' he said. 'You're quite a little firebrand, aren't you.'

It was, to echo Mikey's phrase, "a turn-up for the books" for Molly as well. She suddenly felt a return of her former confidence, which she had not experienced since before Eamonn had let her down, but she stood beside Mrs White at the cooker now, and said, 'Phew!'

Mrs White looked worried and said quietly, 'She won't let you get away with that.'

The remaining weeks of Mrs White's employment passed quietly enough, as she gradually handed over more and more of the chores to Molly.

When it was time for Mrs White to leave, Patrick was to run her to Lime Street Station where she was to catch a train to Coventry. Mikey handed her an envelope and said gruffly, 'Thanks for all your kindness and help over the years and I wish you well with your sister.'

John and David were there to say their goodbyes, as were Molly and Carmel with the baby, Monica. The only one missing was Oonagh.

'I think that she might have made the effort to be here to say goodbye to you,' Molly said to Mrs White, who replied with a toss of her head, 'It's no great loss. I didn't like her and she didn't like me, so at least she's not being a hypocrite.'

Molly settled swiftly into her role, taking total charge with ease. She had been taught how to cook by her mother and the food that she began producing met with the family's approval. Despite her relative youth she managed the house and family well and everyone, apart from Oonagh, accepted her almost as a member of the family. She felt even more a part of the family when Mikey said to her one evening, 'I think that we can forget the Mr Whelan, Molly. It's about time that you started calling me Mikey.'

Patrick liked Molly, but Carmel was a little wary of her. She was uneasy about Mikey's quick acceptance of Molly, whilst she herself experienced little warmth from him and, in an effort to change the situation, Carmel began to spend more time at Springfield Road. Patrick had still not been given a proper partnership and Carmel thought that if she was around Mikey a little more, with his only grandchild, that it might influence him to do something about it. Patrick suggested that it might be a good idea for Carmel to help Molly with her some of her chores.

'It can't do any harm.' he said. 'You can pick and choose what you do but at least he will see you around and trying to help now that Mammy's gone.'

Mikey's liaisons had largely stopped during the period that Hannah had been ill and had never restarted after Hannah's death, but he still missed the company of women, and particularly a woman in his bed, but he decided that he didn't want any more casual relationships. He wanted someone that he could live with. After Hannah's death he had suddenly realised that he was lonely, for despite her not sharing his bed she had been a companion and a good working partner and he had known that, despite everything that had happened between them, if he had ever had a real problem she would have been there for him.

His thoughts turned to Molly as a replacement for Hannah. She was an attractive young woman, there was no evidence of any man in her life and she appeared to spend what time she had off with her sister. The main problem as far as he could see was her youth and how she would view someone of his age as a partner. A minor problem, in his opinion, was what Oonagh's reaction might be to any relationship with Molly, who was only five years older than Oonagh, but many years older in terms of her maturity. He knew that there were regular confrontations between the two but he had never interfered. He thought that Molly was more than capable of taking care of herself.

Every year, there were still jockeys who visited Springfield Road for the Grand National at Aintree Racecourse and Mikey, planning ahead in his pursuit of Molly and knowing it was her birthday around that time, thought that he would invite her to accompany him to the races on Grand National Day.

He didn't mention it to any of the family but suggested it to Molly one evening as they sat in front of the fire after their evening meal.

'Have you ever been to the races?' he asked Molly.

When Molly replied that she hadn't, Mikey made his suggestion. 'I know it's your birthday soon, Molly. I'll treat you to a day out there. You'll enjoy it. The atmosphere is fantastic.'

'God! I couldn't go to the races. I haven't a thing to wear,' she said. 'And I've seen photos in the Echo of everyone dressed up to the nines.'

'I'm sure you'll look great whatever you wear,' Mikey said. 'I'm not taking "no" for an answer. It's going to be my birthday present to you.'

Molly had one half day off a week, when she normally left food ready prepared for the family and went off after lunch to visit Teresa, her sister, who was now married to Charlie and had a baby daughter, Kathleen. It was agreed that Kathleen would be left with Charlie's mother for the afternoon whilst Teresa went with Molly to Liverpool to choose an outfit.

One of the most prestigious department stores in Liverpool

was The Bon Marche and that was where Teresa and Molly headed for first. They were sidetracked from their mission by a large crowd which had gathered and when they enquired what the all the excitement was about, they heard that Gracie Fields was promoting a particular brand of stocking there.

'God! Gracie Fields,' Teresa said. 'What an opportunity! Let's see if we can see her.'

They struggled through the crowd to try and catch of a glimpse of the young woman who had started life above a chip shop in Rochdale, Lancashire and was now a highly paid film star. Teresa and Molly both bought a pair of silk stockings and Gracie Fields signed the wrappers. The sighting of her was something which featured in both Molly and Teresa's conversations for a long time after the event was buried in many people's memories. The signed wrappers were framed and hung on the wall in Teresa's sitting room and Molly's bedroom.

When they eventually tore themselves away, they began their search for Molly's outfit. A smartly dressed assistant hovered as they looked through racks of clothes.

'I don't know that there's anything here for me,' Molly said. She was disappointed because The Bon Marche was one of the larger department stores and she had thought that if she was to find the appropriate outfit, it was likely to be there.

'Where else can we try?' Molly asked Teresa.

'Can I help you? Are you looking for anything in particular?' The assistant approached them.

'I've been invited to the races to watch the Grand National and I need something to wear. I've not been anywhere like this before and I don't know what sort of thing I should be looking for.'

The assistant looked at Molly, smiled and said, 'I've just the outfit for you. With your colouring it will be just right.'

They followed her to where a mannequin stood, dressed in a burgundy outfit.

'I think this is your size,' she said as she unpinned

the garment from the dummy.

'I don't know,' Molly said, pulling a face, 'I've never worn this colour before.'

But both Molly and Teresa had to agree that the assistant's choice was right when Molly tried on the outfit. She looked stunning.

'You'll surely knock him out when he sees you in that outfit,' Teresa said.

'I'm not trying to knock him out,' Molly replied. 'I just want to make sure that I don't disgrace him.'

The thought occurred to her that it might just have been simpler....and a lot less expensive if she had simply turned down the invitation.

The Grand National took place on a crisp, clear March day and when Molly arrived downstairs to meet Mikey, who was waiting for her in the sitting room, he whistled in appreciation as she walked into the room.

'Well, I told you that you'd look great whatever you wore.'

He escorted her to the Wolseley where Patrick sat in the driving seat.

'We've even got a chauffeur today,' Mikey said as he held the door open for her. 'Patrick's offered to drive us and pick us up afterwards.'

It was an enjoyable day for them both. Before the race, Mikey took Molly to the enclosure to greet the two jockeys who were staying with them at Springfield Road and Molly was pleased that she had bought her new clothes when she saw what many of the other women were wearing.

'Would you just look at some of those outfits,' she said as she glanced around her.

'And don't you look better than any of them,' Mikey replied. He was proud to have Molly on his arm and it reinforced his idea that Molly would be an ideal partner for him.

Chapter 21

Mikey's relationship with David had improved after he had taken over the organisational work in the business but although David worked hard and efficiently and Mikey found him useful, Mikey still felt no love for him. Because of his slight appearance in comparison to his brothers, Mikey thought him a weakling and he had neither time nor respect for what he considered physical weakness.

After an initial decline in his drinking, Mikey started visiting "The Buffs" regularly again, but he was careful to moderate his drinking. He was determined that he would not mar Molly's opinion of him.

Molly had already become aware that Mikey's interest in her was not simply that of an employee and often in the evening when she was sitting sewing or reading, she would glance up to find him watching her. Oonagh too had noticed her father's interest and was annoyed and irritated by it so much so that one evening, in a fit of pique, she had shouted angrily at him, 'Will you stop looking at her with your sheep's eyes? She's just the maid, for God's sake.'

It was the first time that Molly had seen Mikey angry.

'You're forgetting yourself, Oonagh. And you're forgetting your origins. Where do you think you'd be without me and what I've given you. You've done nothing and you'd be nothing. You've become one God Almighty snob and I think that you'd better get out of here before I really lose my temper with you.'

Oonagh left, glancing with venom at Molly but frightened of incurring the further wrath of her father and stinging at what he had said to her.

'I'm sorry about that, Molly,' Mikey said apologetically. 'Oonagh had no right to say what she did but she's just brought this to a head, so I'm not going to beat about the bush. I haven't the time to start courting you and aren't we living under the same roof already, so I'm asking you to marry me. I know that I'm a fair bit older than you but I'm still fit and healthy and you'll always have a roof over your head.'

Although Molly had suspected that Mikey was interested in her, she had not expected a proposal of marriage and asked Mikey if she could have some time to think about it.

That night, in bed, she thought about Mikey's proposition carefully and decided that perhaps accepting his proposal might not be such a bad idea. Although she had been out a few times with friends of Charlie and Teresa, she had not had any sort of emotional involvement with anyone. There had never been anybody that she had felt particularly attracted to since Eamonn.

With Mikey, as far as she was concerned, there was no emotional involvement and she was sure, by the manner of Mikey's proposal, that it was true for him as well. The marriage would provide security for her in the future, she would try to be a good wife and she reassured herself that he wasn't such a bad looking fellow for his age.

'I've just one concern, Mikey, before I agree to anything. I don't think Oonagh will be too happy at the idea of us getting married. And what about the others: Patrick, John and David?' she asked Mikey. 'Have you mentioned anything to them?'

'I'm my own boss and answerable to no one. What I choose to do is my own business,' Mikey replied. 'Patrick, David and Oonagh are all dependent for a living on me anyway, so they'll have to toe the line and John likes you well enough, so there'll be no problem there.'

'In that case,' Molly suggested, 'maybe we ought to get them all together and tell them all at once.'

They decided that the whole family should be invited for lunch the following Sunday and an announcement would be made about the planned marriage. Molly enlisted the help of Carmel to prepare the lunch, without telling her about the wedding, feeling slightly guilty as she did so.

'Mikey wants the whole family over for lunch on Sunday and I could do with a hand. We'll need to put the extra leaves in the table to fit everyone around it,' she said.

The family attended Mass as usual the following Sunday. When they returned home Molly cooked breakfast and after she had cleared away, Carmel arrived to help organise the lunch.

A large leg of pork was put in the oven and the vegetables prepared. The extra leaves were put in the table and a damask tablecloth spread over it. Mikey was to sit at his usual place at the top of the table and he insisted that Molly was to sit at his right-hand side. Molly could immediately see problems.

'I can't sit there, Mikey. That's the place where Oonagh has always sat since her mother died. Look, I don't mind where I sit.'

'Molly, you're going to be my wife. I want you at my side. Anyway, if we put Oonagh at the other end of the table, opposite me, she'll feel well enough there. She'll think she's top dog, so she will.'

Molly shrugged and raised her eyebrows. 'On your own head be it!' But as she said it, she thought that it would not be on Mikey's head but hers that the wrath would fall.

Carmel wondered what was happening when she saw Molly taking champagne glasses out of the cabinet and polishing them. She wished that Patrick was around because a thought had occurred to her which filled her with misapprehension.

She too, had noticed Mikey's attention to Molly. Mikey had proposed to Molly! She was sure of it. She liked Molly well enough, but wondered how this union was likely to affect Patrick and his partnership.

Before everyone arrived, Carmel hurried back home to change her clothes and expressed her concerns to Patrick but Patrick shrugged it off.

'What difference is it likely to make whether he makes me a partner or not if he marries Molly. She's no interest in the business. It takes her all her time to look after the house. Anyway, you don't know that's what it's all about. You're worrying yourself unnecessarily.'

But Carmel was unconvinced.

Molly produced a meal of her normal excellent quality. Oonagh, as Mikey had predicted, had settled happily at the end of the table, assuming that she had been given a position of authority as the main woman in the household. The atmosphere was bright and cheerful and, as they all relaxed afterwards, Mikey produced the champagne. The cork popped and hit the ceiling, which caused much merriment and Mikey began to fill the glasses which Molly had carried in on a silver tray earlier. He passed them around the table.

'I would like you all to raise a glass to Molly, my future wife.'

There was a stunned silence, until John and Violet in unison said, 'To Molly!'

They both stood, raised their glasses and went around the table to kiss her. David, a huge smile on his face, followed and whispered shyly to her, 'If anyone ever replaced Mammy, I would have wanted it to be you.'

Molly grasped his hand and said, 'Thank you, David.'

Patrick followed suit and wished her happiness, as did a slightly subdued Carmel.

But Oonagh sat, unmoving at the table. She stared at her father and said, 'How could you. She's nothing! She's a nobody! How could you allow her to take Mammy's place.'

'That's enough, Oonagh,' Mikey said, his face red with anger. 'I have just about had enough of your bad behaviour. Molly is to be my wife and if you don't like it you can get out, get a job and stand on your own two feet for a change instead of sponging off me.'

Oonagh stood and left the room slamming the door behind her.

Molly stood, her face pale.

'Take no notice of Oonagh,' John said. 'She's had her own way too long. The rest of us are happy for you.'

Although Molly felt that she was more than capable of coping with Oonagh's outburst, it had taken a little of the gloss off the occasion and it wasn't long before John and Violet stood up to leave. Patrick soon followed, taking Monica home whilst Carmel and David helped Molly to clear away.

Molly heaved a sigh of relief when Carmel also left and David settled in the sitting room, as usual, to read his book. She sat in front of the fire in the kitchen with her sewing whilst Mikey dozed in the chair opposite, the champagne and the whiskey that had followed taking their toll. It had been an exhausting day and Molly began to wonder what she had let herself in for.

Mikey had decided that there was no point in delaying the wedding. As he pointed out once again to Molly, 'Aren't we living under the same roof anyway, so what's the point of waiting?'

The tense situation with Oonagh changed. Oonagh had something new to think about. She had met an army captain at a dance and was preoccupied with him, so her attentions were diverted away from what was happening at home. She was scarcely civil to Molly but at least there were no confrontations.

A few weeks prior to the wedding, on Mikey's instructions, Hannah's room had finally been cleared of her clothes and possessions. Mikey had never felt the need to clear the room before as they were not short of space and the door had been kept permanently closed. But eventually he decided that things had to change, as he was now taking a new wife.

'Before your mother's room is cleared, I'd like the four of you to have a look and see if there's anything of hers that you want to keep,' he had told his family.

Oonagh and the boys went into Hannah's bedroom and glanced around. It had been many months since any of them had set foot inside her room.

David shook his head. 'There's nothing I want from here,' he said and left the others to look through Hannah's things.

The only thing that John wanted was a favourite brooch of Hannah's that she had often worn at the neck of her blouse and he soon departed as well.

Patrick and Oonagh had a more thorough search and they both left Hannah's bedroom with some better items of her jewellery.

'There's nothing left worth keeping,' Oonagh said to Molly. 'You can throw the rest of it out.'

Molly looked at Mikey and lowered her eyes. She had no idea what he was feeling. She only remembered how upset he had appeared at the time of Hannah's illness and she was surprised that he did not comment on the casual attitude of Oonagh to her mother's possessions. But then he was well used to her behaviour and perhaps had not expected anything else.

It soon became apparent that Mikey had wanted Hannah's room cleared so that Mikey and Molly could occupy it. It was a large room, but Molly felt uncomfortable with the idea of sleeping in the room in which Mikey's former wife had died.

'It's not the fact that she died in the room,' Molly said. 'I just feel …..I can't really explain it…I just feel that it would be a bit disrespectful.'

And so it was agreed that they would use Molly's room as their bedroom and Hannah's room with the adjoining door as a dressing room which would still give them plenty of space.

It was whilst Molly was sorting through Hannah's wardrobe that she found a worn and battered canvas bag. When she opened it the only thing that it contained was a biscuit tin. It rattled as she lifted it out of the bag, so she realised that it wasn't empty.

'How strange!' she said softly. She tried to force the lid off but it was so rusted that she had difficulty doing so. It was while she attempting to do this that Mikey arrived in the room.

'Good God!' he said in surprise. 'I didn't know that they were still in the house. Hannah must have kept them all these years and I never knew.' He tipped out the contents onto the bed and Molly realised that the tin contained medals all engraved with Mikey's name "Michael Whelan".

'I used to do a bit of running when I was a lad,' Mikey said. 'It was the running that got me here to Liverpool. It was the start of everything for me, got me away from the farm. The children have never seen them. I don't think they even knew about them. I'll put them in my chest of drawers and show them later.'

The wedding was arranged for the eleventh of March. Molly wanted a quiet wedding with only the family. The only exception to the family was Barney.

'Sure, I can't get married without Barney being there,' Mikey had insisted and Molly had no objection to that.

Mikey paid for Molly's family to travel from Sligo for the wedding and, as compensation for the girls, Josie and Margaret, who had missed being bridesmaids at her wedding to Eamonn, they were allowed to be attendants at Molly's wedding to Mikey. Molly had already explained to Mikey, without going into too much detail, about her broken engagement. Molly asked in a letter to her parents,

'Can you tell them that when you get a bit older, as I am now, you don't want the same sort of fuss as you do when you're younger, so their dresses won't be as fancy.'

But the girls were going to have new outfits and carry posies of flowers, so they weren't too disappointed.

The wedding was a simple affair one Saturday in March and everyone went back to Springfield Road after the church ceremony. Molly wore her burgundy outfit and Teresa said, laughing, 'Didn't I tell you that you'd get the wear out of it.'

Oonagh was surprisingly civil and pleasant, her attention focused on her captain, Jeremy Carter. She had persuaded her father that he ought to be at the wedding as well.

'After all,' Oonagh had told her father, 'he might soon be a member of the family anyway.'

Although the wedding itself was a quiet and simple affair the festivities continued, with the arrival of many of Mikey's drinking and gambling friends, until the early hours of the morning.

Molly was nervous on her wedding night. Her new position felt strange and to be sharing a bedroom with Mikey, with some of his family still in the house, felt particularly strange. She was also concerned that she would disappoint Mikey because of her lack of experience but she need not have worried; Mikey had been without a woman in his bed for so long that their union was over almost before she had realised.

Her mother brought them a tray of tea, eggs and toast in bed the following morning.

'Take your time now and enjoy the first day of your marriage,' she said, smiling. 'We'll see to whatever needs to be done.'

The remainder of the day was spent being pampered by her mother and father.

'Sure, it's not every day that you get married,' her mother had said when Molly had protested.

Mikey and Molly had decided that there would be no honeymoon.

'Sure we'll have one when the better weather comes,' Mikey said to Molly. 'That's if you're happy enough to do that.'

'No, I think you're right,' Molly replied. 'We've been living under the same roof for so long that it would be a bit pointless. As you say, let's wait for better weather and we'll have a holiday then.'

So Monday was a standard working day for Molly and Mikey, but Molly had a surprise on Monday morning when she went downstairs. The fire was blazing away in the black-leaded hearth and extra buckets of coal had been filled, normally one of Molly's tasks, and stood ready at the back door.

'It's a bit of a wedding present from me, Molly,' Barney said. 'It'll take a bit of the weight off you.'

'And what a great present as well.' Molly kissed him on his cheek. 'That's saved me a lot of work this morning.'

But Barney had not intended it to be a once only gift. Each morning after that, by the time that Molly arrived downstairs, the fire was lit, the kettle was on and the extra buckets of coal stood waiting at the back door.

David commented to Molly, 'I think that Barney always had a soft spot for Mother, and it looks as if you're taking her place, not just with us but with Barney as well.'

'I don't want to take your mother's place, David,' Molly replied. 'Your mother was obviously a good and special woman and it would be hard for anyone to replace her.'

'Well, I don't think that you're doing too bad a job anyway,' David replied, blushing.

It was soon time for her parents and her brothers and sisters to return home. Her father was tearful.

'It's great to see you settled at last, after all the problems,' he said to Molly, then he turned to Mikey. 'Look after her.'

Molly's parents were impressed with Mikey who, apart from his wedding night when he had drunk too much, had behaved impeccably during their visit. But it wasn't long before things began to slide once again.

David watched with dismay. He had thought it was all too good to be true and realised that his father had been on his best behaviour until he had made Molly his wife. Once again Mikey began visiting "The Buffs" and the visits became more frequent and he began arriving home later and later until, within a few weeks, Molly realised ruefully that she should have taken more notice of Mrs White's comments about Mikey's drinking.

Despite his drinking, Mikey's fertility was certainly not in question and, within a couple of months, Molly found that she was pregnant.

Molly was delighted, for despite Mikey's drinking she felt that her life could have been a lot worse. Mikey didn't appear to have any interest in other women and he was more than generous in terms of anything that she might require financially. In fact he had set up a separate bank account for her into which an allowance was paid monthly. Mikey did not interfere with the way she chose to run the house and he was kind to her.

David and John were pleased when Molly told them the news. They were happy because she was happy but Oonagh rolled her eyes to heaven and said, 'You'd think he'd be past it at his age.'

And Carmel worried about Patrick's position even more, in case it would be affected by the birth of the new baby.

During the pregnancy, Mikey continued going to "The Buffs" and staying out late. In some ways it was a relief to Molly because it meant that he made less demands of her. She was often in bed and asleep before he arrived home and towards the end of the pregnancy he often slept in the dressing room, where a bed had been set up so that Molly's twisting and turning, in an effort to be make herself comfortable, would not disturb his sleep.

Molly's pregnancy also brought with it a new relationship between Molly and Carmel. Carmel often felt lonely and in need of a friend. She knew that Hannah had never really liked nor trusted her, and understood why, and that Oonagh could barely tolerate her. She began to appreciate the friendship that

Molly, who was a similar age and who was unaware that there had ever been any problem between Hannah and Carmel, extended towards her.

Carmel visited the house in Springfield Road regularly and Mikey began to look forward to Monica's presence about the house. She was now a lively child of five years of age and Carmel watched as Mikey played with his granddaughter and thought that perhaps all was not lost; perhaps the partnership might materialise after all.

Molly's pregnancy progressed without problems as did the delivery.

'Good breeding stock,' Molly joked with Mikey.

Molly's baby was also a girl and Mikey and Molly decided to dispense with family names and call the baby Grace. Molly was soon up and functioning normally and it wasn't long before Mikey was back in her bed.

The level of Mikey's drinking still concerned David and he had begun to stay out of Mikey's way anticipating that it wouldn't be too long before Mikey reverted fully to his former habits, but it came as a shock to Molly when she returned one day with Grace in her pram, after visiting her sister Teresa, to find David at his desk, clutching a swollen jaw. There was no sign of Mikey.

'Oh my God!' Molly's concern showed in her face. 'What on earth has happened?'

David turned his face away from her. 'It's nothing.'

Molly, with Grace in her arms, turned David's face towards her. 'You look as if you've been in a fight.'

David shrugged her off. 'If you can call it a fight when your own father hits you in the face.'

Molly was shocked. 'Mikey did this…to you?'

'Well, nobody else did it, that's for sure!' David said angrily.

It appeared that Mikey had gone to "The Jaw Bone", a local public house that he had begun to visit frequently, where he had met up with some of his friends in the early afternoon and had stayed there drinking. He had come home drunk and, as David knew to his cost, whenever Mikey had been drinking heavily David often became the object of his temper. Mikey had begun to find fault with everything that David had done in his absence.

'I wouldn't mind, but I was doing nothing different to what I do every day,' David said. 'But there are days with him,' he emphasised the "him" by jerking his head towards the stairs, 'when whatever I do is wrong. Especially when he's had a few too many.'

David, at first, had remained silent, not wishing to provoke his father, and knowing what the likely outcome would be, but when his father had started shouting at him, 'Answer me! Answer me, you idjit,' he had lost his temper and had told his father for the first time, 'If you don't like what I'm doing, then do it your bloody self.'

Mikey had punched him in the face. There was no way that David could retaliate. Even if he had been physically capable of punching his father in return, which he was not, for his father was bigger and stronger, it was not in his nature to do so. Mikey had then staggered upstairs.

'If you want to know where he is now,' David said, 'he's upstairs snoring his head off.'

Molly put Grace back in her pram and bathed David's face.

'I tell you, Molly. I've had enough of him. He's never going to change.' He left her sitting in the kitchen and went upstairs. Molly sat silently for a while thinking about what had happened. It was her first experience of Mikey's violence.

David did not return to the office that day to continue his work, nor did he join them for the evening meal. Instead, whilst Mikey was asleep, he telephoned John at work and packed a bag and left.

When Mikey eventually arrived downstairs, Molly had fed Grace and put her into her cot. She did not mention what had happened and Mikey made no comment about David's absence at the table when they sat to eat their evening meal.

The meal was eaten in silence.

'Why've you got such a sour puss on you?' Mikey asked her, pushing his empty plate with such force across the table that it shot off the other side and onto the floor.

'Mikey!' Molly said.

'Mikey!' Mikey sneered.

Molly was disturbed at the way Mikey was behaving. He had never before behaved like this with her and she assumed that he was still suffering from the resuts of his drinking session.

'What's wrong with you?'

'What's wrong with you?' Mikey imitated her once again but she was not to be put off.

'I just can't believe that you hit David like that. Surely you could have solved your differences without punching him.'

Mikey glared at her.

'Ah, isn't he the little nancy boy, running to you with his problems!' he said mockingly.

'He didn't run to me about anything, Mikey,' Molly replied. 'I couldn't help but see the state of his face when I came home from Teresa's.'

She shook her head and got up from the table and began clearing away the dishes, whilst Mikey stumbled upstairs once again to bed.

The following morning, Molly felt Mikey's arm around her as she lay in bed. He leant up on his elbow. 'I'm sorry, Molly love,' he said.

Molly turned to face him. 'It's not me you should be saying sorry to,' she said. 'It's David. I think you'd better try and make amends today.'

But David did not arrive for work that morning and Mikey became angry. He had been prepared to make some sort of gesture of apology to David, but now he interpreted David's actions both a challenge and a rebuff. What made the matter worse was that Mikey, in David's absence, had to attempt to work out the schedules for the day whilst the men stood idle awaiting his instructions.

As the morning wore on, Mikey became more and more frustrated and angry and eventually telephoned John's home. When there was no reply he asked Patrick to drive him there. But when they arrived, there was nobody there. Nobody responded to the hammering on the door.

'I told you there was no point,' Patrick told him. 'John and Violet will both be at work and you don't know that this is where David will have come.'

'Where else has he got to go?' Mikey asked him, but he climbed back into the car and they returned to Springfield Road where he went to find Molly.

'You're going to have to give me a hand in sorting this out.'

He took her into the office and showed her the books. 'It'll probably be just for a few days until David cools off.'

But David did not return the next day nor the one following and, although he had stayed with John and Violet initially, John told Mikey that David had moved on to stay with Maisie and Jack, Hannah's parents, and had sent a message to say that he wouldn't be returning to Springfield Road; that his grandfather had found him a job.

Chapter 22

Mikey found it hard to believe that David, his weakling son, had acted so defiantly and, although unable to back down and apologise, for the first time ever he felt a sneaking admiration for him. However, he refused to have any further contact with him, almost as though what had happened was David's fault and was not the result of his own drinking.

Molly kept in touch with David, telephoning to check how he was managing or occasionally popping in to see him at Maisie and Jack's house. But it soon became apparent to Molly that even if Mikey had been willing to attempt to repair the relationship, David on his part had no wish to. He had decided that he had suffered enough, both from his father's lack of love and from his verbal and physical abuse.

He told Molly that he had hoped and believed that things had changed after his mother's death.

'I thought that maybe he had realised that…..' he paused, 'that he had worn her out. But I suppose that he's too set in his ways. Too used to doing what he wants with no concern for anyone but himself. I'm sorry, Molly. You will find this difficult I know, but I'm fed up with not saying anything and protecting him.'

He could still remember when he was a child, how his mother had often stood between his father and himself and accepted the blows meant for him and he worried about Molly and what might happen to her and her children.

'If I ever have children of my own, I hope that I would never behave towards them as he has behaved towards me. I feel sorry for you, Molly. Don't let him do to you what he did to my mother and don't let him do to Grace what he did to me.'

It was a very subdued Molly who returned home that afternoon.

But Molly had married Mikey "for better or for worse". And she had to continue with her life as best she could and so far, he had done no harm to either her or Grace. But David's words about the way that Mikey had treated Hannah would not leave her.

Molly did not take as readily to the office work, which had been assigned to her as a result of David's departure, as either Hannah or David. Unlike Hannah, she had never had to keep accounts nor organise schedules and she struggled with her new tasks but knew that she had little choice as Mikey still had no wish to involve any outsider in the business.

As Molly's office workload increased, Carmel began to take over more of the household duties and Molly insisted that Carmel was paid a proper wage.

'What do I need to do that for?' Mikey protested. 'Haven't I given them a house, for God's sake.'

'And isn't the house in your name?' And Molly couldn't resist adding, remembering that Carmel had told her of one of her fears, on one of the rare occasions that she had confided in her, 'And if you had a bust-up with Patrick, you could turn them all out on the street tomorrow. Anyway, you can't expect her to do it for nothing; she could go off and get a job elsewhere and be paid for it and then where would we be?'

As Molly became more confident with the work, her speed increased and the work became less of a chore. At first the pram was wheeled into the office each morning, then it was later replaced by a playpen, to restrict Grace when she began to crawl. Mikey looked at Molly, with Grace beside her in the office, and remembered the early days of his marriage to Hannah.

Oonagh was spending more and more time away from home and Molly, although personally relieved at Oonagh's absences, felt that if Oonagh had been her daughter, she would have wanted to know a little more about where she was and who she was with.

She realised that she was judging everything based on the relationship that she had with her own parents and thought to herself that this family, of which she was now a member, was a totally different one to any that she had experienced before. Despite having more wealth and financial security there wasn't a great deal of happiness here, as she had discovered. She shrugged and decided that it wasn't her position to question Oonagh. Her relationship with Oonagh had taken a long time to become non-confrontational and she had no intention of disturbing the balance now.

But Mikey was noticeably upset when Oonagh arrived home one weekend with Jeremy, after spending the week away. She had thrown open the door of the office where Molly and Mikey were working and pulling her glove from her left hand she had displayed a gold band.

'I'd like you to meet the new Mrs Carter,' she said, triumphantly.

Molly saw the expression on Mikey's face as he sat down heavily in the chair.

'Well! Aren't you going to congratulate us, Pops?'

'Well, congratulations to you both.' Mikey was angry. 'But I wish you had told us and we could have made the effort to be there. Aren't you my only daughter and I've missed you getting wed?'

'Oh, Daddy, don't go on,' Oonagh replied. 'Aren't you happy for me?'

Molly interpreting the expression on Mikey's face, interrupted quickly. 'What a surprise, Oonagh. It's quite taken our breath away. We had no idea! Where and when? Tell us everything.'

'Oh, we've been thinking about it for a while but Jeremy has just had news that he is being posted to the South of England, so we decided to do the deed so that I could go with him.'

There was a silence as Molly waited for Mikey to speak.

'Do you think some champagne is called for?' Molly nudged Mikey. 'It's not every day that your daughter gets married. I'll go and fetch Patrick and Barney from the yard. They'll be delighted, I'm sure.'

Mikey made no attempt to move until Molly prompted him.

'You're right,' Mikey said, his voice tight. 'I suppose we ought to wish them well. Even if she didn't want her father at her wedding.'

Mikey went down to the cellar and brought out a couple of bottles of champagne and Molly called Barney and Patrick from the yard to join them.

'Well then, Oonagh. You're a bit of a dark horse,' Patrick said. 'You've certainly sprung this one on us.'

'It runs in the family,' Oonagh retorted. 'Perhaps I'm copying you.'

'So a married woman, now!' Barney said, laughing. 'It seems only yesterday when I was wheeling you up and down in your pram and bouncing you on my knee. And when are you off to the South then?'

Oonagh glanced quickly at her father. 'Tonight. So I've come back to pack a few clothes,' she said quickly, then turned to Molly with a glimpse of her former attitude. 'I'll leave you my address and you can pack the rest up and send them on to me.'

When Oonagh went upstairs to pack her clothes Jeremy drew Mikey to one side. 'I'm sorry this is a shock for you, Mr Whelan, but you know what Oonagh's like. I tried to persuade her to wait, that we ought to speak to you first but...' he paused and shrugged, then laughed, shaking his head, 'once she gets an idea into her head.'

Barney turned to Molly and said mischievously, 'I think young Captain Jeremy might have bitten off more than he can chew with that young lady. He might be in for a bit of a rude awakening.'

After they had waved off the newly-weds, Barney and Patrick returned to the yard and Mikey went into the kitchen and sat in the chair.

'That's the last of them to leave. The last of my children.'

Molly sat silently. She was surprised at the hurt she felt at his statement.

'To think that she'd do that to me. To go off and get married without even telling me.'

He felt strangely uneasy. His life was changing too quickly and he felt that he no longer had any control over what was happening.

'You know what she's like, Mikey,' Molly said evenly, despite her pain. 'She won't have thought anything of it. It will have seemed like a good idea and she won't have thought about anyone else. Isn't her head full of cotton wool. And anyway,' Molly paused, 'haven't you still got Patrick here? And Grace!'

Mikey's face brightened slightly. 'You're right,' he said. 'Patrick's a good lad.'

Molly blinked back a tear as she looked at him and realised that he had no idea whatsoever about the effects of his words on her.

That evening, Mikey did not leave the house but sat in his armchair and stared at the fire, only moving to bank it up with coal from time to time. Molly didn't say anything but she realised that Oonagh's secret wedding had obviously upset him a lot more than she would have expected and she was glad that Oonagh hadn't broken the news after Mikey had been drinking. She shuddered at the thought of what might have happened if she had.

The house was very quiet after the departure of David and,

with the departure of Oonagh, despite her spending increasingly less time at home, the house became quieter still and, almost as if he couldn't bear being in the empty house, Mikey also began spending less and less time at home.

During the long winter evenings Molly began to feel very lonely. Once Grace was in bed and she had completed her chores, she would sit alone and listen to the radio doing whatever sewing she had to do. The atmosphere of Springfield Road, with all its hustle and bustle, had changed dramatically since she had first come to live there.

She confided in Teresa her concerns about the level of Mikey's drinking.

'It's not only that it can't be doing him any good,' she said, 'it's that his moods are totally unpredictable. Sometimes after he's had a few drinks, he's all mopey about the baby and other times I daren't speak to him. Sometimes I wonder why on earth he married me, he spends so much time out of the house. I feel so lonely.'

'What if I come around and spend the odd evening with you? Charlie won't mind babysitting,' Teresa laughed, 'but I'll make sure I'm gone before Mikey comes home. I don't want to be on the receiving end of his tongue when he's had a few drinks.'

So Teresa began to visit Molly regularly one night a week, when she knew that Mikey wasn't likely to be there and they sat quietly, the air often thick with cigarette smoke, drinking tea and discussing their children and the rest of the family back home in Ireland.

Molly soon realised that she was pregnant again and she spoke to Teresa about it before telling Mikey.

'I don't know whether I'm pleased or not,' she said. 'He pays little enough attention to Grace as it is. He's not unkind to her but it's as if the only children that ever counted were those that he had with Hannah. It's as if Grace means nothing to him.'

'Well, you never know,' Teresa said, trying to comfort

Molly, 'maybe he'll start spending more time at home once there are two of them.'

When Molly told Mikey that she was pregnant, he was surprisingly pleased at the news and Molly hoped that Teresa was right; that having a second child would make Mikey feel more positively about the fact that he had a second family.

Chapter 23

During the evenings that Molly spent alone she sat, a cigarette never far from her hand, and listened to the radio. She also read newspapers and periodicals to keep herself informed of current events and was aware of Hitler's increasing power in Germany. One evening, after having put Grace to bed, she sat reading sections from The Picture Post to Mikey, who unusually had spent the evening at home.

'It sounds as though that Hitler is a madman. He's forbidden the playing of music composed by Jews and he's even expelled people from Germany who won the Iron Cross in the last war because they're Jews.'

'I can't see how Chamberlain can hold back much longer. The Germans are just grabbing more and more territory, but God knows what will happen if there is a war! The last one was a terrible thing,' Mikey replied.

Germany had suffered greatly as a result of the 1914-18 war. It was a country that had suffered humiliation. Vast areas of land had been taken away and there was mass unemployment and malnutrition.

When in 1933, President Paul von Hindenburg approached Adolf Hitler, an ex-corporal in the German Army and leader of The National Socialist German Workers' Party, and asked him to accept the Chancellorship, it appeared to many that Germany had a saviour.

Europe stood by watching anxiously as a period of increasing legislation was imposed by Hitler which, amongst other things, included the prohibition of sexual intercourse between Jews and Germans. There also followed a period of land reclamation and conscription was reintroduced. The warnings were becoming clearer.

'Well, Chamberlain is back in Germany again. Let's see what happens. Maybe they can talk some sense into the man,' Molly said. 'God knows what sort of a world we're bringing another child into.'

Molly, in her last days of pregnancy, heard the voice of Neville Chamberlain, the Prime Minister, on the radio telling the nation that a peace agreement had been signed with Hitler in Munich and breathed a sigh of relief.

Her son, Joseph, was born on the twelfth of October 1938.

'Another little redhead,' Mikey said with delight as he held his son. 'Baby number six.' He paused, remembering Anthony, and, for a fleeting moment only, the son that he had with Kitty and had chosen not to acknowledge, but quickly dismissed the thought from his mind. That was all in the past. It would do him no good to think about things that had happened long ago.

'How many more are you planning on having, Mikey?' Barney asked, smiling, when he arrived to visit Molly after the birth.

'However many it is, I hope it's not going to be too soon after this one,' Molly said. 'It's hard work looking after little ones.'

By the end of January, Molly's fears about war were once again awakened.

'Would you just listen to this,' she said reading a piece out of the newspaper to Mikey. 'That lunatic Hitler is at again, threatening the Jews in a speech he's just given.'

'He'll not be happy until there's war again,' Mikey said.

'Sure, the man's a megalomaniac.'

And their fears were justified when on September the first 1939, almost one year after Molly had heard Chamberlain's speech on the radio saying 'I believe it is peace for our time', Germany invaded Poland. The previous evening an announcement had been made. Schoolchildren, mothers and babies were to be removed from areas of danger to "safer" places in the countryside. At this stage it was to be a voluntary exercise, but it made Molly and Mikey aware of the seriousness of the situation.

'I don't know how they have the courage to let their children go off like that,' Molly said to Teresa, as she sat with her that evening. She had seen a procession of children being herded onto a bus to Morecambe with labels around their necks or tags around their ankles, carrying their gas masks. Women and grown men were crying as they said their goodbyes. 'I just couldn't do it,' she told Teresa. 'I just couldn't send my children off like that.'

'You would if you had no choice.' Teresa said, 'and we may have to if war is declared.'

At nine o'clock on the morning of the third of September, the British ambassador in Berlin issued an ultimatum to Germany to withdraw troops immediately. The deadline for the withdrawal was eleven o'clock that same morning and at eleven fifteen, three days after Molly had seen the children boarding the buses, Chamberlain broadcast to the nation.

'This morning the British Ambassador in Berlin handed the German Government a final note stating that unless we heard from them by eleven o'clock that they were prepared to withdraw their troops from Poland, a state of war would exist between us. I have to tell you now that no such undertaking has been received, and that consequently this country is at war with Germany.'

Mikey and Molly listened in silence to the remainder of the Prime Minister's speech, Molly's hand across her mouth, her eyes filled with tears. Although it was not unexpected, the announcement was something that Molly had dreaded.

Within the hour, Barney arrived at the house.

'Dear God!' he said. 'I just hope and pray that it doesn't last as long as the last one.'

A short while later Patrick, Carmel and Monica arrived and they sat and discussed the situation, the mood varying from subdued to one of almost hysteria.

Molly now was busier than ever. Earlier in the year leaflets had been distributed warning people about the dangers of light shining from windows in the event of an air raid. Windows had to be shrouded with blackout curtains, which Molly had ready, even though she had never thought that they would be needed. She had already followed instructions and taped the windows in a criss-cross fashion, to avoid flying glass and the three gas masks, one each for Mikey, Molly and Grace hung on hooks inside the front door. A "gas helmet" stood on the table beneath them for baby Joseph.

It became difficult for the lorries to function after dusk in the winter months that followed. The lights on the lorries had to be shrouded and on nights when there was no moon it was impossible to see through the dense blackness, so that it became positively dangerous. It was some help to the drivers when white lines appeared, painted down the middle of roads and along kerb edges to help motorists navigate in the dark. But it made Mikey frustrated to have to paint a broad white line around the body of his new car, a Vauxhall, to conform to regulations to make it more visible in an attempt to reduce casualties on the roads.

One afternoon, Molly had left Teresa's house later than intended. They had been so busy chatting that neither of them had noticed that it was beginning to get dark and, as soon as they did so, Molly had hastily gathered her belongings together and set off for Springfield Road. On her journey home, she had to summon all her common sense to remain calm. She told Mikey afterwards, 'It was eerie. Not a glimmer of light from anywhere. You'd find someone at the side of you and you'd never seen them coming. I was jumping at bits of paper blowing around the ground.' She shuddered. 'I won't be out after dark again in a hurry.'

Initially there were none of the anticipated air raids. There was a feeling of anticlimax and, despite going nowhere without a gas mask and having the constant supervision of the Air Raid Wardens ensuring that, after dark, no lights were visible, Mikey and Molly went about their business almost as usual.

October and November passed without much incident in Springfield Road. Mikey and Molly had adapted to the necessary restrictions without too much difficulty and Molly, despite the war, began to feel more relaxed. The nuisance factor of having to go to "The Buffs" in the dark meant that Mikey was spending more time at home and, as a result, was drinking less.

Molly began to think about Christmas. After a shopping trip to Liverpool she had met up with Teresa.

'It's a shame there's no Christmas lights anywhere and you can't even see what's in the shop windows with all the tape on them.'

'Didn't they say about this war, what they said about the last, that it'll all be over by Christmas. It doesn't look as if that's going to happen what with rationing coming into force next month. I suppose that we should make some effort to cut down but it might be a long time before we'll be able to buy what we like again.'

The family and Barney were all invited for Christmas and there was a full house. Molly cooked a turkey and the whole family sat down for dinner, including Oonagh who had travelled north to be with them. David was the only one absent. Molly had asked him to join them, but he still did not wish for any contact with his father and preferred to spend the time with his grandparents. They danced to music on the gramophone and listened to the radio, joining in the Christmas carols and it was difficult within the confines of the house to know that there was a war in progress. The only evidence was the miniature Red Cross uniform which Molly had bought for Grace, and which she insisted on wearing whilst she ate her Christmas dinner.

Christmas was no sooner over when, on January the eighth, rationing was introduced, with weekly allowances of four ounces of butter, twelve ounces of sugar and four ounces of bacon or ham per person. Molly had registered the family at the butcher's and grocer's and had collected the ration books in October and had also begun to stockpile some items of those foods that were not perishable.

'I wouldn't worry too much,' Mikey told Molly. 'Paddy saw us right last time and I'm sure he'll do the same now.'

But Molly preferred not to rely on Paddy.

Posters could be seen everywhere, encouraging people to "DIG FOR VICTORY" and "KEEP A PIG". The vegetable garden, which Hannah had started many years previously, had been spasmodically tended in the years since her death but Molly now began to grow more vegetables there and she persuaded Mikey to purchase a couple of pigs which he kept in a hastily constructed shed in the yard. It amused Mikey to think about the pig in with the lorries and he remembered the pig that they'd had to sell to provide the money for the rent back in Ireland.

Petrol rationing was introduced for private vehicles and the new Vauxhall spent most of its time parked in the yard, still polished regularly, as the black Wolseley had been, by Patrick.

Oonagh phoned regularly to keep them up to date about Captain Jeremy. With the fall of Belgium, Luxembourg and the Netherlands to the Nazis and France under threat, massive numbers of troops had been sent to defend the territory. Jeremy and his division were some of the many involved. The news was not that of a successful battle and Oonagh was distraught not knowing whether Jeremy was safe or not. A massive withdrawal exercise was undertaken and all the heavy weaponry had to be left behind as Dunkirk was evacuated. The operation to bring back hundreds of thousands of allied troops trapped by the German army lasted only ten days and Winston Churchill, who had replaced Chamberlain as Prime Minister, described it as a "miracle of deliverance". He ended his speech to Parliament with a defiant message.

'We shall defend our island whatever the cost may be. We shall fight on the beaches, we shall fight on the landing grounds, we shall fight in the fields and in the streets, we shall fight in the hills. We shall never surrender.'

Molly listened to the speech on the radio and was moved to tears.

Jeremy had suffered in the onslaught and had been transferred to a military hospital in the South of England with head injuries.

'It's bad, but at least, thank God, he's alive,' Oonagh told them on the phone.

It was also Oonagh who maliciously broke the news to Mikey that David was a conscientious objector.

'I spoke to him on the phone. I couldn't believe it when he just came straight out with it. When Jeremy is risking his life for his country, it sickens me that he's not prepared to do his share,' she told Mikey angrily.

'For Christ's sake,' Mikey said, when he heard. 'Is he a man or a mouse? He's no son of mine,' he said with disgust.

Molly did not point out to him that he had never fought in a war himself, having been exempt from the earlier war because the business was viewed as his contribution to the war effort and he was now exempt again because of his age.

It had not been necessary for David to register as a conscientious objector with the first wave of conscription but he was within the appropriate age group of the second wave.

When Molly next saw David, she informed him that Oonagh had told Mikey about his decision not to fight and how angry Mikey had been.

'Father doesn't need a war as an excuse for fighting,' David replied sarcastically. 'He spends most of his life fighting with somebody or other. And most of the time about nothing. Believe me, abstaining from fighting is not any easy thing to do.' He shook his head. 'Firstly we had to register as conscientious objectors in the same place where people were registering to enlist. There was an enormous great queue of those enlisting and then a few of us at the other counter. It was not a good experience,' David told Molly. 'You should have heard the names they called us.'

Molly realised that David must have felt very strongly about his decision not to fight. He was a gentle person and the verbal assaults that he must have had to suffer as a result of his decision must have been very difficult to cope with. John phoned her a few days later to tell her that David had been put on the military service register as a non-combatant and had been placed in an army-run medical unit.

Patrick was relatively safe from conscription. One of the reserved occupations was that of dockworkers and because most of Mikey's business involved dock-related work, Patrick was not forced to fight and Carmel breathed a sigh of relief.

John was conscripted and joined the Seaforth Highlanders, thankful that he had not been one of those who had experienced Dunkirk.

He and Violet had tried for many years to have a child with no success but, as he said to her, 'I think that I can say that at this moment I am thankful that we didn't succeed.' He echoed Molly's sentiments. 'What a world to bring a child into!'

In August, Liverpool experienced its first air raid and the hideous noise of the sirens filled the air night after night. Because of the large cellar under Springfield Road, there was no need of an air-raid shelter and Patrick, Carmel and Monica moved in with Molly and Mikey at Springfield Road.

'It makes sense,' Molly had persuaded Mikey. 'It will just be one house to keep warm. Patrick has to come here to work anyway and we can all look after each other.' And the two women were glad of each other's company.

When the overhead railway was damaged by the bombing, Mikey told Molly, 'They'll make targets of all main transport centres now. The docks will be the next thing.'

The air raids, which everyone had always thought would be night-time events, began to occur in daylight as well and were largely aimed at the airfields and factories and then came the first air raid on Central London, followed by a retaliatory air raid on Berlin. A few months later Coventry was devastated.

'Dear God! What is the world coming to,' Maisie said on one of Molly's visits. 'When you see the death and destruction all around, I know why David wants no part in it.'

The bombing was indiscriminate and hit everything from churches, to schools, to children's homes and hospitals, not only those areas important for military use. By October, Merseyside had suffered its two hundredth air raid, targeted with such intensity because it was the most important port area outside of London.

By December the twelfth, Merseyside had suffered its three hundredth air raid.

Their second Christmas of the war approached and Molly and Mikey tried to create as much normality as they could for the children. Mikey and Patrick dug up a small tree from the front garden and set it up in the sitting room. Molly and Carmel tested their ingenuity in creating decorations for it from anything that they could find. Bottle tops, which had previously found a use, pressed into the underside of the bar of soap so that there was no waste, now also found a use with holes drilled into them, dangling on bits of string from the branches of the tree. Balls were made out of strips of old newspapers which were mashed up to a paste and then rolled into balls and left to dry, before being dipped in whitewash and hung on the tree. To the children it was of no consequence that the decorations were made from scraps of whatever could be found; they loved it all.

Just before Christmas, the bombing intensified and the two families spent three consecutive nights in the cellar. And then it stopped.

Mikey had butchered a pig a couple of weeks earlier and the carcass had been hung from great meat hooks in the attic. He cut a huge leg joint and Molly put it to roast in the oven. Molly collected some of the potatoes which had also been stored in the attic and the two women prepared Christmas dinner, listening to Christmas carols on the radio once again, whilst the men sat and drank whiskey, which was a present from Paddy. The children sat and played with their toys and when they all sat down to lunch the war and the bombing were, once again, temporarily forgotten.

Chapter 24

After a relatively quiet January and February, as Mikey had predicted, the docks then were heavily targeted, but work continued, with the lorries delivering and collecting from those areas which were still functioning.

Winston Churchill visited Liverpool in April to give his support and express his concern to the people of Liverpool and the onslaught continued. May was the worst month and the family settled night after night in the cellar at Springfield Road whilst the bombs fell all around.

Mikey and Molly amongst many others attended a ceremony when five hundred and fifty "Unknown Warriors of The Battle of Britain" were buried in a common grave at Anfield Cemetery.

'God help us!' Molly shook her head and repeated what she had said so many times before when she had thought about how pointless it all was. 'What's it all about and what is going to be achieved by it all. All the fault of a lunatic, a madman.'

Molly realised when she heard the news on the radio that the Japanese had bombed Pearl Harbour that the war was nowhere near ending and when Britain and the United States declared war on Japan she asked Carmel, shaking her head, 'Is it never going to end?'

And then, when Germany declared war on the United States

three days later, she also expressed her dismay to Carmel. 'It's frightening! And I suppose the more countries that are involved, the longer it's going to go on and more and more people are going to die.'

It was a surprise to Molly that with all this going on, there was a decrease in the bombing in Liverpool.

Soon, American soldiers began to be drafted to England and a series of camps were set up to accommodate them. Molly and Mikey had no quarrel with the Americans, although there were many people unhappy with the situation, who saw the Americans, after claiming neutrality early in the war, now entering the war when a lot of the hard work had been done and when a lot of lives had already been lost. With their pockets full of silk stockings and chocolate, they appeared affluent to those who had been forced to survive on rationed goods, which inspired feelings of animosity and resentment.

In the spring of 1943, Molly realised that she was pregnant again.

'It seems strange,' she told Carmel. 'In one way I feel as if this war has been going on forever, and then I look at Grace and Joseph and realise that they are still only babies and then it doesn't seem so long after all. But God help us there's been enough killed.'

She was glad to have Carmel around. She had found her a good friend and companion in the war years and they worked together as a team in the running of the house and the three children, Monica, Grace and Joseph, played together happily.

Oonagh was in regular contact with Mikey and Molly. She had an active social life with the other army wives and had surprised both Molly and Mikey by volunteering to drive an ambulance as her contribution to the war effort. Captain Jeremy, although still involved with the fighting, had escaped so far with no further injury.

Molly's third baby was born on Christmas Eve and was

presented to Grace and Joseph as "the best Christmas present ever". He was called Nicholas. The children were delighted with their new baby brother.

It was another relatively frugal Christmas but a happy one, shared with Barney who arrived, as usual, one of the first to see the new baby.

'He'll soon lose count if he keeps on like this,' he joked about Mikey.

Barney, who was from a large family himself, was glad of the opportunity to share in the festivities with Mikey and his family. He always enjoyed the times that he spent with them and was soon lying on the floor playing with the children who called him "Uncle Barney".

Although Barney had been very fond of Hannah, he had even more affection for Molly and on one occasion when Molly had asked him why he had never married, he had looked at her and said, 'I didn't meet the right girl until too late. She was already spoken for.'

Molly had blushed. Given her conversation with David many years earlier, she wasn't sure whether Barney meant herself or Hannah, but she felt that the way that Barney had looked at her indicated that, even if Hannah had been the original target of his affections, she had now replaced Hannah.

Oonagh joined them for Christmas. Captain Jeremy was still away as were John and David, but the family had begun to mean more to Oonagh as the war years had continued. She made more effort to keep in touch and to visit.

With John still away, Violet had joined her own family as she had done on previous Christmas Days.

There had been no further children for Carmel. She had experienced a series of miscarriages and had resigned herself to having only one child and sometimes wondered if this was her punishment for having deceived Patrick in the beginning. But Patrick loved his little daughter and Carmel thanked God that she, unlike Violet, had at least been able to have one child.

Oonagh, on the other hand, had no wish for children. As far

as she was concerned, she had a good life and didn't want it disrupted by "little brats".

But they all agreed that Christmas would not be the same without children and their enjoyment of it.

By coincidence, John and David arrived home on leave at the same time a few months later and the two brothers met up with Patrick at their grandparents' house, where David still stayed when he was home on leave, and they talked at length about their experiences. The rift between Maisie and Jack and Mikey, firstly as a result of his treatment of Hannah, but then reinforced by his treatment of their grandson, had never healed. Mikey never visited their house and neither Maisie, Jack nor David visited Springfield Road. But Molly, unknown to Mikey, still continued to visit David at Jack and Maisie's house.

As soon as Maisie told Molly that David was home, Molly paid them a visit.

'You're looking thin,' Molly said as she put her arms around him and kissed him. 'How are you? How are they treating you?'

Molly had heard tales of how so many of the men who had refused to fight had been subjected to abuse, both verbal and physical.

'I'm fine,' David replied.

Molly tilted her head and gave him a questioning look.

'Don't look at me like that, Molly. I'm fine. There's nothing that I can't handle. Anyway, I've a bit of news for you.'

Maisie looked at Molly over David's head and smiled.

'She's a nurse and her name is Sarah. When this mess is all over, we're going to get married. You and Grandma'll like her.'

Maisie told Molly later, after David had returned to duty, 'It did my heart good to know that he's met someone. He needs someone to give him love and he's got so much love in him waiting to be given.'

She looked at Molly with a look that did not falter. And Molly knew that she was speaking not only of David, but of Hannah also, when she said, 'Mikey has a lot to answer for.'

On May the seventh, 1945, the German forces surrendered unconditionally to the Allies and on May the eighth, Mikey, Molly, Carmel, Patrick and all the children joined the celebrations in the street. Union Jacks hung from windows and bunting was hung from side to side across the street. There were processions with people marching arm in arm and singing so many of the songs that had become familiar on the radio over the war years. "The White Cliffs of Dover", "Run, Rabbit, Run" and "We're Gonna Hang Out The Washing on the Siegfried Line" amongst many others filled the air that day and Mikey produced another couple of bottles of champagne from the cellar which he had been keeping "for when it's all over".

Oonagh phoned, in tears. 'Isn't it wonderful,' she said. 'At long last! And soon Jeremy will be home for good.'

All the servicemen did not return home immediately. Many had been imprisoned in prisoner of war camps by the Germans and they were the more fortunate; Japan had not surrendered and there were many British servicemen still fighting or in the hands of the Japanese.

At the beginning of August and within a few days of each other, atomic bombs were dropped on Hiroshima and Nagasaki with horrific consequences and on September the seventh, the Japanese surrendered.

There was a great deal of criticism of these two events but the general consensus was that, as the Japanese had surrendered, the end justified the means.

'I don't think David would agree with that view,' Molly told Teresa, ' and I have to say that nor do I.'

'Well! I don't know,' Teresa countered. 'Isn't it better that it has all been brought to an end and everyone can return home to their families, rather than drag on for any more years. It's been long enough.'

'I think that if we were involved in another war,' Molly said, 'I would be joining David as a conscientious objector. I think that you and I had just better agree to differ on this one. But just remember that, this time, we've been lucky. None of ours have been killed. You might think differently if they had been.'

Gradually things began to return to normal. Food and clothing were still rationed and Molly continued to be accompanied by her ration book whenever she went shopping. The business began to thrive again and David and John returned home, John to Violet and David to his grandparents until his wedding was to take place.

Oonagh, John and Patrick had all been invited to the wedding but there was no invitation for Mikey, although David had said that he would like Molly to be there.

'I can't do that, David,' Molly had replied. 'I would love to attend but I can't come without your father. Won't you think again and ask him?'

'I'm sorry, Molly, but I don't want him there. It is to be a happy day for me and having my father there would only spoil it. We'd probably end up fighting and anyway I think that even if I asked him, he wouldn't come. There'll be plenty there without him.'

Mikey was still unaware that she had maintained regular contact with David over the years because she knew that he would have objected and tried to stop her. She decided not to mention the wedding to him, thinking that he would find out soon enough from the others. She also didn't tell him that David had been accepted at medical school to train as a surgeon, something that he had realised that he wanted to do during the war years when he had been caring for injured servicemen and women.

'The less that he knows, the less there'll be to trouble him,' she told Teresa. 'He still gets angry at the very mention of

David's name. He has never forgiven him for defying him.'

It was a supposedly chance remark from Oonagh that made Mikey aware of the wedding but Molly, in retrospect, wondered if it was a chance remark or whether the way it was presented to Mikey was more mischief-making on Oonagh's part. But whether mischief was intended or not, mischief was created.

Oonagh had telephoned her father and told him that she and Jeremy would be coming up north for David's wedding which was to take place in Harrogate. When Mikey expressed surprise, Oonagh said, 'Well, I thought you'd be sure to know about it. Molly's known about it for months. The girl's name is Sarah and he met her in the hospital where he was working. She's a nurse. In that case, I don't suppose she's told you either that David is to start training as a doctor. He's going to medical college in London. Isn't it amazing! All as a result of his being a conscientious objector.'

Molly was surprised when Mikey came off the telephone after speaking to Oonagh and, without saying anything, left the house, slamming the door behind him.

She waited up until after midnight and when he was still not home she went to bed.

Mikey stayed out all night. Where he was, who he was with, or what he was doing, Molly never found out but when he returned home drunk, at five o'clock in the morning, he dragged her out of her bed and hit her again and again, calling her a cunning, lying, deceitful bitch. Then he had once more left the house, leaving her lying on the floor.

She struggled to her feet and bathed her face and as soon as she considered that she was not disturbing her too early, she telephoned Carmel.

'Can you come a bit early, Carmel. I need you to look after the children.'

'Is something wrong?' Carmel asked. 'You sound strange.'

'I'll tell you about it when you come,' Molly replied.

Carmel and Patrick had arrived together and were dismayed

and shocked when they saw Molly's condition.

'We'd better call the doctor,' Carmel said as soon as she saw her.

'There's nothing broken,' Molly had said through swollen lips. 'Nothing that won't heal. I don't want a fuss. Just leave it be. The fewer people who know about it the better.'

'What in hell's name was it all about?' Patrick asked her.

'He just kept calling me a cunning, deceitful bitch, hiding things from him. He'd come off the phone after speaking to Oonagh and I don't know what she'd said to him but he went storming out of the house. He was out all night…and when he came back he was drunk, out of his head and he did…. this. She must have told him about David's wedding, I suppose.'

'There must be more to it than that. She must have told him that you knew about it. Otherwise he wouldn't have got in such a state. Had he been drinking?' Patrick asked.

'Not before he went out, he hadn't. But he'd had more than enough when he arrived back home.'

Barney arrived in the kitchen at that moment and when he saw Molly he was aghast. 'For heaven's sake, Molly. What in God's name has happened to you?'

Molly shook her head and said, 'I'm OK. I'll be alright.'

'You don't look alright to me.'

Barney sat in the chair beside her and held her hand. There were tears in his eyes. 'I always knew that one day he'd go too far. What's wrong with the man? Why is he so full of anger?'

Carmel went off to attend to the children whilst Patrick stood helplessly by.

'I don't know what to say, Molly. He's always had a temper but he's never done anything like this before.' But then remembering Mikey's outburst at some of the men in the yard, he qualified his statement, 'At least not to any of the family.'

'And have you forgotten David?' Molly asked quietly.

After Carmel had attended to the children, she cooked breakfast for Patrick and Barney. There was no sign of Mikey and if anybody was bothered by that fact, nobody showed it.

Chapter 25

They brought him in from the yard. Albert had found him in the cab of one of the lorries, slumped over the steering wheel, where he had gone after leaving Molly. They carried him upstairs with difficulty because of his size and weight and laid him on the bed.

Molly, despite her damaged face and attracting glances of sympathy from the two men who had helped Barney and Patrick carry Mikey up to his bed, called the doctor and then attempted to undress him. Carmel took the children back with her to her house and Molly called Teresa and asked her to help.

Teresa arrived, looked at Molly, asked no questions and did as she was requested to do. It was afterwards, when Mikey was settled and the doctor had departed, that Barney told her what had happened and she shook her head in disbelief.

At the age of sixty-four, Mikey had suffered a stroke, which robbed him of his independence. From being strong and dominant, in control of his family and business, he became totally dependent on others. He now lay incapable of managing any part of his life.

In the days that followed Molly mused to herself about the strange familiarity of the situation. Here she was nursing Mikey as the result of a stroke when only a few years earlier, in the same situation, she had nursed Hannah.

Molly took great care of him, helped by Carmel. They turned him regularly to prevent bedsores, heaving his great body, rolling him over from his back, where he lay with his mouth open, spittle forming at the junction of his lips, his eyes half open but staring blankly. If he was aware of anything happening around him, they didn't know, because he was totally unable to communicate with them.

'It's a good job that he doesn't know what's going on,' Molly said sadly to Carmel, surprising her with her compassion after what had happened to her. 'He would hate people seeing him in this state.'

The work was never ending. They had to bed-bath him, soaping and washing his body, change his sheets and spoon the liquid food into his dribbling mouth.

An easy chair was carried upstairs and placed at the side of the fireplace in the bedroom. A single bed, in which Molly now slept, was moved into the dressing room, where Mikey had slept in the latter months of Molly's first pregnancy, the door left open through the night so that Molly could hear him if there were problems, as she had done for Hannah.

As it became apparent that Mikey's recovery was not going to be immediate, if at all, further pieces of furniture and other items of convenience appeared. Another comfortable chair, a small oblong table, carefully positioned, complete with the essential kettle, tea, sugar and a small fridge, which housed the milk.

In the evenings, this room slowly became the hub of the house.

Teresa visited regularly. At first, she couldn't understand Molly's devotion after what Mikey had done to her, but Molly simply said, 'No matter what he's done, he's still my husband.'

They would sit beside the ever-blazing fire with their cups of tea and their cigarettes and talk in quiet voices, about the events of the day, their respective children and ….Mikey.

Occasionally, one of them would go downstairs to the back door to bring up yet another bucket of coal, left ready for them by Barney, to feed the greedy fire.

Molly insisted that the children came for a short while each evening, before their bedtime and sit with her and Mikey. They chatted to their mother, glancing at their father with little interest, bringing their toys and sitting or sprawling on the spark-damaged rag rug in front of the blazing fire before they were washed and put to bed.

This was the evening routine. The daytime routine was different. Carmel was now an essential person in Molly's life. She was always up early and arrived with Patrick and Monica to attend to the other three children. Barney took Grace and Monica to school, having already carried out the task of filling the coal buckets, the wedding present which still survived, and Carmel stayed to watch the two younger children and to help Molly with her care of Mikey.

Patrick had taken over Mikey's role in the yard and surprisingly, after his bad start many years earlier, managed the men as well as Mikey had done. He did not allow shirking but was a far more gentle taskmaster than Mikey and Molly thought sadly that it was a pity that Mikey couldn't have seen the changes in Patrick. He would have been proud of him.

Barney was becoming increasingly less able to manage the heavier tasks in the yard that he had carried out in his younger days but he had begun to help Molly more with the tasks in the office and Molly found his help and his friendship invaluable.

Molly spent six months going up and down the dark polished staircase, tending to Mikey. Initially her journey up the stairs had been brisk and efficient but, as the weeks dragged on with no improvement in Mikey's condition, her steps became slower until eventually she began to dread reaching the top step because then she had to cross the landing and enter the bedroom to attend to her husband. It had not been a task of love but one of duty and Molly was not one to shirk her duties.

And then……at last, it was all over.

Molly, with the help of Carmel moved the coat stand. It had stood at the bottom of the stairs ever since Molly had come to live in the house many years earlier and had probably been in the same position for as many years before. They had cleared the coat stand of the coats and hats and walking sticks and had moved it from the bottom of the stairs, across the hallway, to position it under the painting of the racehorse Lough Conn. If the painting were to be moved it would no doubt also leave evidence behind to show that it too had been in the same position for as many years.

The men had to negotiate nineteen steps…. as Molly well knew. She had counted them often enough.

Three of the men had taken off their jackets and rolled up the sleeves of their shirts. They had only just started their task and already dark wet patches were appearing under their arms and down their backs. Above their heads, shafts of light streamed in from the skylight and fell, making a chequerboard of the coffin lid.

Molly stood, silent and still, her back against the wall. Her eyes, scratched raw from lack of sleep, were closed. She felt that, if she fully relaxed, her legs would cave in beneath her. Strands of hair had escaped from the front of her hairband, pulled on in haste that morning and even now she had a cigarette in her hand, the spiral of silvery ash slowly bending and about to fall on the terracotta tiles below.

Patrick and Barney had been called from the yard as soon as Molly had seen that the men from the funeral parlour were struggling. It had taken four of them to lift Mikey from his bed into the coffin and then six of them to carry the coffin across the landing to the top of the stairs where it now rested precariously between two chairs.

Molly was still at the bottom of the stairs, her eyes now open. Her cigarette end had joined the blackened, squashed assembly on the chipped saucer, which was sitting on the bottom step of the stairs. She waited for the men to start again.

'One, two, three.'

In unison, they lifted the coffin. Patrick and Barney at the front, walking carefully backwards, sliding each foot carefully down until it reached the tread below, grunting and panting with the exertion. Two of the four men from the undertaker's supported the middle of the coffin and two were at the head end, trying to ensure that the weight of the body sliding forward in the coffin did not unbalance Patrick and Barney at the front.

Now, without the coat stand, there was room for the coffin to be turned at the bottom of the stairs on its way to the sitting room, where the purple draped trestles stood waiting.

Despite it only being midday the room was in semi-darkness, lit only by a single lamp in the corner. The heavy maroon, velvet curtains were drawn and the mirrors covered with dark cloths. Two large, creamy candles in tall brass candleholders stood ready, waiting to be placed like sentinels, one each side of the coffin.

The men reached the bottom of the stairs and Molly stood aside to allow them to pass. She followed them into the room, collecting a bundle from the coat stand as she passed.

'These belong with him,' she said softly, handing the men a worn and grubby canvas bag, a battered biscuit tin and a fistful of medals.

'Call me if you need anything,' she said and with the stub-filled saucer in her hand, she left them and walked away down the hall.

Printed in the United Kingdom
by Lightning Source UK Ltd.
131115UK00001B/52-66/P